DATE DUE		

A Journey to Here

Margaret
Johnson-Hodge

A Journey to Here

Dafina
Books

KENSINGTON PUBLISHING CORP.
http://www.kensingtonbooks.com

Library of Congress Card Catalogue Number: 2003103719
ISBN 1-57566-918-8

First Printing: October 2003
10 9 8 7 6 5 4 3 2 1

Printed in the United States of America

In Loving Memory of

Edward "Parker" Rhoden
Rafael Diaz
Carl and Shirley Johnson
Emily Duprey Lawrence
Lillie Farrior
Jessie Wilson
Lucy Bellinger
Josh Floyd

Chapter 1

In no way is it large, assuming or worthy of a prize, but it is my backyard, this place I cultivated full of sweet-smelling blooms. To my left and right are my roses, my pansies and the marigolds I planted to replace the daffodils that did not bloom this year. Bright, pretty, vibrant, my flowers are everywhere, surrounding me like perpetual ladies-in-waiting.

It is my garden, my Eden. My own bit of heaven. A secular place I've carved for myself. This is where I come in the warmer months, cultivating, tilling, nurturing my flowers as I do my soul.

I look upon my life and can't complain. I have a husband of nineteen years who can still make me laugh and two daughters, twelve and fifteen, who have resisted the temptations of the streets. I look at this life I have and know it is better than most.

Blessed, something whispers, as Stevie Wonder sings from my portable CD player and I join in on the second chorus, my voice soft and light. Together Stevie and I lament about a superwoman as my oldest daughter, Aaron, appears.

"Someone's here to see you."

"Who is it?"

"I dunno."

I move around the side of the house and come in through the side door. Going through the kitchen, I come into the living room; the front door is closed, no one about. "Where are they?"

"Outside."

"You didn't let them in?"

"Nope."

"You don't know who it is?"

"No, I don't."

"Man or woman?"

"Man."

I move to the door, open it slowly. My mouth opens. "Philip?" Refuses to close. I strain my neck, look beyond him. "Where's Dorothy?"

"Georgia."

"Come in."

"I can't stay long," he tells me as he takes a seat. "Just passing through, visiting my folks."

"This is a surprise." I feel Aaron's eyes on us. My hand sweeps the air. "You remember my daughter Aaron? Aaron, this is Philip Butler." I take note that though she has met him before, she doesn't remember. Her eye shifts between mine and his. She will not leave unless I send her. "Did you finish your chores?"

"Almost."

"Well, let's get to it."

She gives Philip one last look. Moves slow as molasses out of the room. I watch Philip follow her with his eyes. Know he will say something about the child I have raised.

"She looking more and more like you."

I shake my head, laugh a little. "Nope, that Emory's child. But thanks for the compliment."

His eyes sweep the room. Come full circle, finds mine. "How is your husband?"

"Just fine. How's Dorothy?"

"Dorothy's Dorothy."

I nod my head, let his words drift. Try to assemble all the pieces that have scattered in his arrival. Silence comes as I scramble for words to say. I go for the simple. Ask about his folks.

"Doing okay." He does not ask about mine. I find myself glad about it. The past cannot be altered. "Haven't changed one bit," he decides with too soft a smile.

"Yes, I have," I say quickly, and what was once forgivable, no longer is.

Chapter 2

Nineteen seventy-two was neither a grand year nor a specific one. The War in Vietnam was drawing to a close and Nixon was headed for disgrace, but neither of those occurrences had happened yet.

Still for some, it was a year that would forever be engraved in their memory. For Sylvia Morrow, Nineteen seventy-two marked the sweetest beginning and the most bitter of ends.

When Philip Butler arrived at Jamaica High and the black girls had lined up like dominoes, no one, not even Sylvia herself, had thought she was in the running.

Dana, the cocaptain on the cheerleader squad, had given him her number. Sheila, a second-skin jeans-wearing junior, had invited him over more times than he could count. Juliet had offered to trade the large silver bracelet he wore for three smaller ones on her wrist while Phyllis Bartow insisted that the fact they had the same first and last initials meant they were meant to be.

There had been Bernadette, Mora and Kathy. April, Darlene and Dawn. All of them after him, vying for his attention, Philip turning them away, kind but direct.

He hadn't been looking for popular or hip. He wasn't in need of someone who had been around the block or eager to take the trip again. Philip wasn't interested in loud or brassy. In search of a gentle beauty, he found it in Sylvia, the quiet, somewhat timid sophomore who didn't even know she was in the running.

He took the metal steps two at a time because he knew she would be coming up from shop class. Philip made the descent fast because he was coming from the second floor and he had to get to the basement.

Out of the door before the first bell faded, Philip had moved like a linebacker through the crowded halls, jostling his way down the stairway, uttering "sorry, excuse me" the whole way. By the time he reached the first floor, the way was clear and his feet took flight.

For over a month he had been trying to find some way to share a minute with her. But being a junior and she a sophomore, they shared no classes and only passed each other once a day going in opposite directions.

For over a month he had managed to catch her eye, but it never went further than that. That day Philip raised the stakes, entering her world like he never had before as he rounded the last set of stairs, took his first breath at the sight of her, head down, finger out, coming up the stairs.

She couldn't stop looking at it.

Sylvia could not stop staring at the half inch of sterling wrapped around her finger of her left hand. That she'd made it herself in the basement of Jamaica High, down in the dusty dingy metal shop made it all the more wondrous.

Sylvia had never crafted anything out of metal before. Had had little faith in the final product for all the weeks that she marked out a pattern and used a hacksaw to cut into the square of sterling with the sawtooth blade.

High school had given her few joys. She wasn't a part of the in-crowd, had no physical talents to make the cheering squad, and though she possessed the intelligence, she didn't join the debate team because being smart made her seem nerdy enough. In an uneventful sophomore year, the ring became an unexpected joy. She couldn't stop looking at it.

Didn't see Philip coming either.

She had no idea that he was making his way down toward her, no knowledge that he was about to enter her world. She wasn't aware of his presence, his soft footfalls on the stairs until his voice filled the air. "You did the ring thing?"

She looked up, startled. Flustered. Philip, closer then he had ever been.

She saw the long full legs, sleek muscled arms, the big brown eyes beneath the Afro sitting six inches from his scalp. She knew he was tall, but he felt even taller as he paused on the third step from the bottom, brown eyes dazzling her way.

"Ring?" was all she could manage.

"Yeah"—he pointed to her hand—"you made it, right? In shop?"

"Right, yeah . . . I did." She searched his face for a reason for him being there. She wanted to ask him, but her heart had stopped and her mouth forgot how to open.

"Can I see?"

"See?"

"Your ring, can I?" Her hand lifted. Four fingers slid softly under her palm. "Real silver?"

She took a first breath, dizzy. "I paid extra for it."

He let her hand go, lifted his own. "I made mine out of silver, too." There, on his finger, the same exact ring.

"You had Mr. Icharia?"

"No. I did it at my other school."

"That's right, you transferred or something."

"Or something . . . . Where are you headed?"

"Spanish, fourth floor."

Philip whistled. "I'm headed to the second." His eyes found her. "After school, can I walk you?"

Her head nodded once, twice, three times.

Before the start of fourth period, Sylvia was just another black girl in a sophomore class of over four hundred, invisible as the wind, as incidental as the sky. Before the start of fourth period, few knew her name and even fewer considered her a part of anything important.

Sylvia didn't hang out with the CDD kids, black students involved with a program to make them college ready, or the black students' organization. She didn't play an instrument and had no vocal talents. She had been in the leaders' program for a hot minute, but it cut into her study time and she dropped out.

A nobody, she had grown comfortable with that status, never being in the mix of things and staying below radar. But when she stepped outside the huge colonial-style building, the mid-fall day filled with a periwinkle sky, and Philip called out to her, things changed.

People who didn't even know her name turned, giving uncertain smiles, stunned blinking eyes and nodding smirks. The ultra-cool CDD girls were suddenly giving her the once and twice-over, gathering in fast little clusters and agitated whispers.

Guys who had never really glanced her, found themselves doing just that, trying to find what they had missed in the last year they had seen her in the halls, deciding in an instant, it was the way her corduroys were hugging her butt; that the slew of acne across her forehead didn't detract from her, but somehow added.

They decided that though her Afro wasn't big and fluffy, it did look cute pushed back behind the headband, and the pinkness of her lips was a natural color. Late with their discovery, Philip had known it first look.

The whole of Sylvia presented an innocence he was searching for and as she hesitantly walked up to him, murmured "hi" and took the hand he extended, he knew that his search was over.

History was being made.

Philip didn't know it, but it was all Sylvia could think about as they made their way down the long downward slope of 168th Street.

It was the first time she ever felt so many eyes on her, the first time a thousand words became locked in her throat and stayed there. It was the first time the most popular, finest boy in school had walked her anywhere, and she kept on blinking to make sure it wasn't a dream.

"Right?" he asked, warm hand grasping hers lightly.

"Yeah," she answered, not knowing the question. Sylvia was in a fog.

She could feel the ground beneath the soles of her Fred Braun leather shoes. She could feel the sensation of corduroy meeting corduroy where her thighs touched at the top. She could feel her heart beating hard in her chest, the tingles that had taken permanent residence inside of her.

Sylvia was aware of the light easy way Philip was holding her hand, the occasional bump of his leg against her hip. She could feel the fall sunshine pouring down upon them and the noisy voices of hundreds of students off in just as many directions.

But what she wasn't aware of was if he really liked her. She could not decide if Philip *the fine*, the Philip *the most wanted*, really wanted her. He was the junior who made girls *snap, crackle* and *pop* whenever he walked by and she was just Sylvia, barely fifteen, a sophomore and not popular by anybody's count.

By the time they reached the dim dusty cloister of the bus terminal on Archer Avenue and New York Boulevard, her mind still wasn't made up. But when he asked for her phone number, she found herself closer to a determination.

Pink wasn't a very strong color or very mature. Innocent, Sylvia decided, tossing her books on one twin bed, flopping down on the other.

Nine hours ago her bedroom had suited her just fine. She had liked the soft pink of the walls, the even fainter pink of her bedspreads. But that was before Philip had found her down in the stairwell. Before he had asked about her ring and walked her to her bus.

That was before he had held her hand and moved close enough for their bodies to brush, before he had asked for her number.

Would he understand the colors of her walls? The innocence of her heart? The boundaries she'd set for herself? Or would he expect more, more than her fifteen-year-old sensibilities would allow?

He was older.

Older and tall. Older and handsome. Older and *fine*, no doubt engaging in things she wasn't ready for. No doubt experienced in ways she wasn't. She had yet to really kiss a boy, virgin, her middle name.

She moved to her dresser. Stared at her reflection in the large mirror. The first thing she saw was the slew of acne that lined the slope of her forehead. Second, the four-inch Afro pushed back in a headband. She saw her eyes, simple brown and slim at the sides, the nose that had been accused of being pixie.

Sylvia took in the medium gold hoops in her ears and the swell of her slightly pink lips. She took in the caramel brown of her skin and wanted, just for a second, to climb in behind Philip's eyes. She wanted to see what he saw and she didn't. She wanted to know what it was about her that had made her visible to him.

Lastly, she wanted to run down the street and tell her best friend, Dorothy, the news but didn't.

Philip had asked for her number. Not even a house fire would make her leave.

Dorothy knew before she walked through the front door what she'd find. The television would be playing in the living room and the radio would be blasting from upstairs. Her little brother, Dean, would be in front of the TV and her sister, DeAnna, up in their room dancing like she was auditioning for *Soul Train.*

Knowing this changed little for her, Dorothy finding herself falling into routine as she closed the front door and stuck her head into the living room. "You do your homework?"

Without turning his head, Dean uttered "Yeah."

Dorothy looked toward the stairs. Opened her mouth and shouted, "DeAnna!" When she heard no reply, she shouted again. "De-An—Na!"

Two skinny legs appeared at the top of the step. "What?"

"You do your homework?"

"Ain't got none."

Dorothy looked at the face of her thirteen-year-old sister with intensity. "What you mean you ain't got none? Since when?"

"Since now."

Dorothy felt the weight of the world on her. Beyond the ton of things she would have to do, only one thing really stuck. Only one thing really mattered.

Philip had picked Sylvia.

Phyllis Bartow had told her at lunch, coming to her, giddy and angry in the same breath. Bewilderment mixed up with awe as she shoved her way through the food line till she was wedged against Dorothy. *"You hear?"* she'd begun, reaching for a hero sandwich.

"Hear what?" Dorothy had asked, the hunger in her belly deep.

"About Philip and your friend?"

"What friend?"

"You Ace Coon Boon."

And though Phyllis had said it like Dorothy would know exactly who she was talking about, it didn't come together for her. She frowned. "Who?"

"Who's your girl?"

What didn't come together managed itself into a complete picture and the hero Dorothy had been reaching for was forgotten. "Suvie?"

"The one and only. Sheila saw them. Down in the basement stairs."

"You lying."

"If I'm lying, I'm flying and I ain't sprout no wings . . . damn. Why her?"

Dorothy couldn't find an answer and one wasn't needed as Phyllis moved her tray toward the juices containers, then on to the cashier.

It had been Dorothy's intention to get the full story at the end of the school day. She had planned on meeting up with Sylvia at the flagpole, but when she got there, she saw it for herself—Sylvia and Philip, heading down the long set of marble stairs. She saw them walking close, just as Phyllis said and suddenly she couldn't approach her friend. Could not find the strength to walk faster, catch up to them. Dorothy just slowed her footsteps until they were half a block away, walking slower still until the distance between them measured a block.

At the bottom of the hill, Dorothy ducked into the candy store and looked over magazines until she was certain they were too far away to be seen, too far away to see her and witness the hurt in her face.

It took everything she owned not to go to Sylvia's house after she got off of the bus; now that she was home, it was all she wanted to do. But her sister was talking about not having homework and her brother was insisting he had already done his. Responsibility was responsibility.

With a sigh, she headed up the stairs and found her sister, a looseleaf paper in her hand. "What's that?"

"Nutten."

"Let me see it."

"Why?"

"Cause I said. Give it here." She made a grab for it, but DeAnna held on tight. The paper ripped, one half in each other's hand. "You better give that piece or I'm getting the belt."

The belt.

Some days it was Dorothy's only ally in the war to raise the siblings. She didn't like to beat them, she herself having more encounters than she liked, but it was a handy problem-solver and like it or not she used it.

"I mean it," she said, eyes fiery and hard.

DeAnna handed it over. Dorothy put the pages together, all the homework her sister "didn't" have, before her. *Math: pages 208-211, Social Studies: read chapter 7 and do the end of the chapter test. Science project due Monday.*

She looked at her sister. "What's the science project?"

Her sister shrugged. "I dunno."

Dorothy went to get the belt.

The attached two-story house on Clinksdale Avenue wasn't a big one, but the kitchen was large enough to eat in and this was where Dorothy's brother and sister sat, sniffling and red eyed as they worked figures and read chapters.

"Let me see a tear drop here, and I will beat your asses again."

Four-thirty had arrived faster than Dorothy could think and with her parents due home in less than an hour, she had dinner to make.

Her friends didn't understand why so much had been put on Dorothy's shoulders. Dorothy didn't understand it herself. But it was a decision that had come down at the age of ten, and since that time Dorothy had taken care of the homefront while her parents worked.

She cooked; she cleaned. Did the laundry and changed all the linens. She washed and pressed her sister's hair, took her little brother to the barbershop and food-shopped at the local A&P.

"We're working hard for you and your brother's and sister's future, so we need you to take up the slack," her father told her often. But she wasn't interested in college, just wanted to live a teenage life. Visit friends, go to parties, not be tied down to children she hadn't birthed.

Now as she readied dinner, she realized that she didn't have any milk. She couldn't make cornbread without it. "I got to go get some milk. Don't let me come back here and not find you two sitting there or I swear I'll beat your asses again."

Dorothy left, walked down the walkway and out the gate. Instinct drew her eyes to Sylvia's house, envy dancing at the sight.

It was the same attached-style house she had just left, but it was hard telling from looking at it. There was new aluminum siding that Dorothy's own lacked. The slice of front yard, though tiny, offered an oasis of grass that was lush as green velvet. The black lamppost worked with a timer, coming on at dusk like magic and the shutters around the window had been recently repainted a glossy black.

Inside were the same three bedrooms, one bathroom and finished basement just like her own. But whereas every bedroom was claimed by somebody in Dorothy's house, in Sylvia's there was just her and her parents.

Dorothy had always envied Sylvia. It seemed Sylvia always got the best. When the World's Fair came to New York in '64, Sylvia and her parents had been there opening day. When Easy Bake Ovens had come out that Christmas of '63, Sylvia had been the first to own one. A week at Disneyland and getting her hair hot-curled were more firsts she had garnered. The only things Dorothy could claim were the need for a training bra and the onslaught of her menses.

And now Sylvia had gotten Philip. Milk, cornbread and dinner were forgotten as Dorothy headed to Sylvia's house. She didn't stay

long, but in the three minutes Dorothy took out of her busy afternoon, she left having no doubt.

Everyone may have wanted Philip, but Philip only wanted Sylvia.

The car doors' slamming on the sixty-nine Buick was the first
sign that her parents had arrived home. The sound of the key
turning in the front lock, the second. Dorothy glanced around the
kitchen making sure everything was in place.

The table was set, ice tea awaited pouring and ice half filled the
metal-colored tumblers. Employees of the New York Telephone
Company, her mother was a switchboard operator and her father,
a janitor. They took the commute to work together, but that was as
far as that together seemed to extend.

When Dorothy had gotten up the nerve to ask her father, ask if
he and her mother ever had any good times, his answer had been
wounding.

"Good times? We had a bunch, then you and your brother and
sister arrived. Took something out of us, something important.
Things haven't been the same since." There had never been a
name to all Dorothy felt inside her house, but in that moment she
realized it—the misery of two people bonded only by children. At
the ripe age of twelve, Dorothy decided marriage yes, kids no.

Her mother came through the living room, slipping off her low
black heels, heading for the kitchen. "Dinner ready?" she wanted
to know as she went to the refrigerator and took out the glass jar of
ice water.

"All done," Dorothy answered as she got a clean cup from the
cabinet. Handing it over, she heard her father's butt squawk against
the plastic on the living-room sofa.

"Doe," he called, "Come turn on Channel Five for me. I want to
catch the scores."

She was on her way to do just that when her mother asked about
salad. "Feel like some cucumbers and onions. Can you cut some
up for me?"

"Sure." Dorothy went to the living room and turned on the television. She had just found Channel Four when her father asked
about the mail. Dorothy had forgotten to check the box when she
came in.

"I'll go look." She went out the front door and lifted the little tin box affixed to the front of their house. It was empty. Instinct took over. She headed up the stairs. Peeped her head into her brother's room.

His eyes were still full of the whipping she'd given him. Just be a good boy, that's all I ask, she was thinking when she asked if he took the mail.

"Un-uh."

She turned, left out, headed for her bedroom. She was nearly there when her mother began calling for her. "Come on, Doe, come make this salad. I'm ready to eat now."

"Daddy wants the mail," she yelled back.

"He got two feet. Let him get it himself. I want to eat."

"Coming." But she wasn't. Not yet. She opened her bedroom door and fixed her sister with a mean eye. "You better get that mail to Daddy and quick, or I'm going to tell him how you lied about the homework." Turning, Dorothy headed back down the stairs, onions and cucumbers, the next order of business.

They were seated at the kitchen table, piles of food on their plates, everyone silent, waiting for Dorothy's father. No one was allowed to eat until he came to the table and today like always, he seemed in no great hurry.

"Daddy?" Dorothy found herself calling, hungry, tired, homework heavy on her mind. "You coming?"

He appeared at the doorway, an envelope in his hand, his New York Telephone Company uniform still on his back. He was not a big man, but there was power in his posture. He worked hard and ruled hard; that was his way. "Where the letter?" he asked, his eyes fixed on Dorothy.

"What letter, Daddy?"

"The one from the school. Envelope here, but there's nothing inside. Where is it?"

"I don't know. DeAnna got the mail today." Dorothy defended.

"Where the letter, Dee?"

"What letter, Daddy?" she said thickly.

"Not going to ask you again."

"I tore it up."

He nodded. "Come on."

The whole room grew silent. Dorothy's mother's face grew pinched. "Can we eat first, Darnell? Come sit and eat first," she asked part pleading, part annoyed.

"No, we eat after I get finished tearing her behind."

"What about the rest of us? We hungry, sitting up here waiting for you."

"You can eat. Dean, too. But Dee can't and neither can Doe. She supposed to be in charge. She slack off; she get beat, too."

Ten houses down on the same side of the block, a telephone rang.

The jangle of the bell from the rotary phone was no different than how it had sounded the first day it had been installed, but that day it played music just for Sylvia.

"I got it," she yelled, bounding out of her bedroom and flying down the stairs. She grabbed the black plastic receiver and with a deep breath, brought it to her ear. "Hello?"

"Can I speak to Sylvia?"

"This is her."

"It's me, Philip."

"Hi."

"Are you busy?"

"No. I was just watching TV." But the open page of her science book waiting for her to answer questions seven through twelve made her a liar.

"Just got finished with dinner."

"Yeah?"

"Yeah?"

"What did you have?"

"Meatloaf, mash potatoes, green beans."

"Sounds good."

Silence came into the line, a pause that expanded the universe. Then Philip spoke, a different timbre in his voice. "I'm surprised you even talked to me."

"What do you mean?"

"You always acted like I had two heads or something."

"When?"

"All the time. I'd see you in the hall and smile and wave and you'd get this look like you were petrified or something."

"Not petrified."

"Then what was it?"

"Scared."

"Of me?"

"Yeah."

"Why?"

"No reason."

"No. It has to be some reason."

Because you're tall and fine and smart. Because my heart just jumped to you the moment I saw you and there's nothing special about me and I don't understand any of it. "No reason," she uttered again.

She glanced at the clock. Saw they had been on the phone less than a minute. Wondered how long the conversation would last and if he'd ever call her back again.

As if he had read her mind, felt all her thoughts and knew all her doubts, Philip spoke the words she thought she'd never hear. "So, are you going with anybody?"

It took a few seconds to remove the lump from her throat. A few seconds to utter no, his next question coming in less time than it took for her heart to reach the next beat.

Dungarees covered the welts on her legs; her long shirt, the ones on her arms. But there was no missing the angry welt across her face. Dorothy didn't even try.

"You got beat?" Sylvia asked, her voice a near whisper as she sat on one twin bed, Dorothy on the other.

"Yeah. Something my sister did," Dorothy answered, taking in the Talking Book album nailed to Sylvia's wall. Colorful blowups of Jermaine Jackson of the Jackson Five filled the others.

"Aren't you kind of old?"

Dorothy shrugged, leaned back. Opened the bag of Wise Barbecue Potato Chips she had bought. "Just the way it goes . . ." Her eyes rolled up to Sylvia's carefully. "He call?"

Sylvia had been dying to tell it since it happened. She had wanted to run down the street to Dorothy's the moment she'd hung up, but visiting was hard. Dorothy always seemed to be in motion: cooking, cleaning, washing, yelling at her brother and sister. The only place they could have a decent conversation was at Sylvia's house.

"Yeah . . . he asked me," Sylvia gushed.

"*Asked* you, asked you."

"Yeah."

"What did you say?" A simple prayer, Dorothy knew the request to God that jumped her soul held no possibility. But she thought it anyway.

"Yeah . . . oh God, Dorothy, can you believe it?"

Dorothy couldn't. Wouldn't.

Chapter 3

By fourth period the next day, Sylvia's neck hurt.
From the moment she had arrived at school, people she never thought even knew her name were waving and saying hi, the black student body discovering her like a new find.

There were other actions, not so kind, loudly uttered untruths that invaded her joy. Things like: "I heard she . . ." and, "They were down in the basement doing . . ." topped off with eye rolls and teeth sucking.

Sylvia knew why.

It wasn't the cherry body oil she had doused her soul with early that morning. It wasn't because of the dollop of Vaseline she had put on her lips to make them shiny. It wasn't the tight knit sweater with the large strip that perfectly matched the burgundy of her corduroy jeans.

It was Philip.

By her last class she felt overwhelmed by it all, unused to the scrutiny, unsettled in her new status. But when she came through the heavy metal doors of Jamaica High and saw Philip waiting, all that mattered was him.

* * *

The second walk was different. The second walk loosened Sylvia up, allowing her to share a little bit of her heart and her concerns.

"You got a lot people upset," she told him.

"Who?"

"About half the girls at school."

"Why?"

"Why do you think?"

"They need to get a life."

"Yeah and they want one—with you." It was more than words Sylvia was speaking. She was in search of a truth. She needed to know if he was serious about her.

"You worried?"

"Yeah, I am."

"Shouldn't be. Besides, girls can be so stupid."

"Not all of them," she answered quickly.

Philip caught it. Understood what she was feeling, the silent question she was asking. "No, not all of them. But the way I see it, it's not about who wants me, it's about who I want."

"Which is?"

"Who am I walking beside right now?"

"Me."

"Then that says it all, don't you think?" They passed the public library, crossed over toward the dance studio on the other side. "I don't have much homework and we don't live too far away. You think I could come over?"

"My house?"

"Yeah, if that's okay with your folks."

Okay with her folks. Sylvia had no idea. The only boy who had ever come to her house had been Rodger, a childhood friend, who, for a hot minute, had dated her. Even then her parents had been home, sitting in the kitchen while they listened to music in the living room.

Sylvia doubted Philip coming over would be okay. Doubted that they would take kindly to a junior a year and some months older holed up in their house with their only child while they weren't home.

But something in how he was holding her hand, something in

how he seemed to be holding his breath as he awaited her answer snared her and without thought she told him okay.

A thousand eyes seemed to be on her as she turned the corner of her block. Sylvia felt as if every single curtained window were shifting, as if the whole block were watching as she moved down her walkway, key in her hand, Philip a pace behind her.

She was certain that Mr. Ellis who was retired and had set up a one-man block watch was right that minute calling her father at work to tell him that Sylvia was "taking some boy into the house."

She was certain alarms would start to ring the moment Philip stepped inside. That the voice of the robot from *Lost in Space* would start bellowing, *Warning! Warning!* the moment his foot touched the carpet runner. But the only sound she heard as she closed the door behind them was the *thrum* of her own heartbeat.

"Come on in," she told him, heading to the living room and putting her books on the coffee table. Then she was out of things to do, eyes everywhere but on him, unsure of what to do next.

"Can I see it?"

Sylvia swallowed. "See what?"

"Your house?"

She knew there was only one room he really wanted to see—her bedroom. What she had to decide was once they were inside of it, would they stay.

She spread her arms. "This, of course, is the living room." Then her feet were moving and Philip was following, every step taking her toward uncertainty.

She showed him the dining room, the kitchen, opened the basement door but didn't go down the steps. Sylvia took him to the back kitchen window where they looked out the backyard that was barely green with the onslaught of fall and the empty rose trellises awaiting the faraway bloom of spring.

She showed him the pantry, the powder room, and then she was out of safe things to show. Only upstairs remained. Upstairs where the bedrooms were, hers included. She hesitated for a second and then started up the stairs.

She swung open the first door. "This is the bathroom." Moved out of the way for him to have a look. "And the study," she said, opening another, revealing a room lined with bookshelves, a small black-and-white television and an easy chair.

She pointed down the short hall. "Down there is my parents' room." Then she took four paces and paused. It seemed forever before her hand found the knob. Forever before she could give it a twist. The door glided back smooth and easy. "My room."

Philip stepped inside, his eyes taking in everything, before they stopped on the twin beds. "You share a room?"

"No. I'm an only child."

He nodded as if that idea pleased him and went and sat on a bed. Hers. That he had chosen the one she rested her body in every night, the one that she had had dreams of him in—some innocent, some not—surprised her. But nothing about the moment was familiar.

He patted the space beside him and she made her feet move, each step feeling like a lifetime. She sat three feet away, not trusting the moment, his closeness. Sylvia sat, looked off, the silence thick, her mind in a whirl. She sensed his hand reaching out to her more so than she saw it, and blinked when it found hers.

"It's okay."

But it was a certainty she didn't have as she debated to let him hold her hand or pull it away. Maybe by allowing it to stay, she was giving a silent signal that she was a willing participant to whatever he wanted.

In a heartbeat she was on her feet, moving to her portable record player. "Want to hear something?"

"Yeah, that would be great." There was a smile in his voice, an easy, unencumbered melody to his pitch and Sylvia realized being in a girl's room with her parents gone was a simple and uncomplicated thing for him. But it wasn't for her.

She turned quickly, facing him, truths burning on her tongue. "I've never done this before, Philip. I've never had a boy in my room, or anything. I don't even know if it's cool with my parents, and I'm sure it's not." Her head shook, fear moving into something else—resolve. "And you shouldn't be up here like this."

He didn't blink, didn't look away or change his expression.

"Then we won't be. We can go back downstairs, or I can leave. I'm not going to pressure you about anything, Sylvia."

"Anything?"

"Not anything." He stood. "You want to go back downstairs?"

No, she didn't. Suddenly all she wanted was to be in her bedroom with him. She smiled, a tiny laugh leaving her. "I guess we can hang out here for a little while." Gil Scot Heron was replaced with Stevie Wonder, and a few seconds later, music filled the air as Sylvia experienced her first real kiss.

It took her awhile to catch the rhythm Philip was making with his mouth, a few minutes to understand that she was opening her mouth too wide, then not wide enough. That her tongue was moving too quick and erratic; that kissing wasn't a race, but a journey.

What didn't take long was for her body to respond, a wetness coming between her thighs, parts of her wanting to be touched all over. It didn't take long for her hands to embark on their own voyage, marveling over the muscles of Philip's back, his shoulders, the taut waist.

Sitting became awkward. Lying down seemed a much better accommodation. Lying on her side, Philip following suit, her heart opening like a new spring flower, her soul touched with a new heat. It was easy to press against him, allow his hands to slip up under her sweater because every inch of her wanted to be touched.

Stevie Wonder's voice became the perfect soundtrack to the music they were making. And when the end of the album came, the needle scratching over finished grooves, it was hard to leave it all. Hard to leave the wonder that was Philip.

She didn't want to leave his lips, his hands, the hard full flesh that was trying to bury itself into the hollow of her belly. She could have gone on forever, ignoring the *swish swish* of the stylus had he not pulled away and uttered, "Record's over."

Her heart was open for the first time. Opened in a way it would never be again, filled with brushes of first love, a sweetness she'd never anticipated.

"The record," he said again, nudging her gently.

Sylvia got up, pulled down her sweater and made her way to the turntable. She started to flip the album, but loved side A best.

Realigning the stylus, Philip invited her back to the bed with open arms and a smile that melted what remained of her heart.

His hands slipped along the edge of her corduroys, gliding back and forward as if they were reading braille. She knew where his fingers wanted to go and debated if she would let them.

She did, kissing him deeper, pressing herself into him more fully, her signal that it was okay. Soon his hands were inside the snug fit of her pants, touching the flesh of her behind, making her quiver. Fingers drifted over the round of her hips, teased the edges of her pubic hair, moved toward her center.

Her thighs shifted, parted, as a single finger slid downward. Pulses shot through her as her first touch by someone other than herself arrived. Her thighs clamped; her pelvis began moving, the feel of Philip's finger, nirvana. Her breath caught and a moan she couldn't hold back left her as she came against his hand with an intensity that was blinding.

New ground, new territory, within a whole new space, it seemed natural that he wanted to be touched, too. Natural that he took her hand and guided them into his jeans, her first touch of a man, shocking. Sylvia pulled her hand back as if burned, unprepared for the feel of bristly pubic hair against her palm, surprised that he had hair down there, too.

"What's wrong?" he whispered.

She blinked. "I didn't know."

"Know what?"

"That boys had hair down there, too."

Philip laughed, reached for her, brought her close, pleased with the knowledge that he was indeed her first. "Oh, yeah. A whole bunch." He eased away, shifted onto his back, unsnapped his jeans, pulled down his zipper, eased back his jockeys. "Look."

Sylvia did, the curious part of her not the least bit embarrassed. His bush was thicker than hers. "Wow."

He laughed again. "Okay, that's enough." Releasing his underwear, the elastic band popping against his skin.

"No. I want to see."

"See what?"

"All of it."

He shrugged, shifted back his jockeys, reached in and lifted his penis out. It was a shade darker than the rest of him, as wide as her wrist and long. The tip had a glistening eye and it leaned to the left. A thick vein ran up the back. Her mouth opened. Closed.

"You've never seen one before, have you?"

She shook her head no.

"So what do you think?"

She inhaled. Let her breath go. "It's huge." Her answer pleased him. He smiled and a question found her. "How many times?"

"How many times what?"

"Have you done it?" Because there was something about him that said he had. Something confident and at ease with his showing himself to her like that.

Philip shrugged.

"You don't know?"

"I never counted."

It wasn't a surprise that he wasn't a virgin, a part of her glad he wasn't because it took the pressure off of her. But the idea he had done it so much he couldn't remember bothered her. It was a bit of rain in their otherwise sunny world. "How could you not know?"

"Does it matter, Sylvia? I'm here with you. I want to be with you."

"But I won't be with you like that. Not now anyway."

"But later, right? I mean, sometime down the road, right?"

She remembered his words, his promise not to pressure her. She thought about his willingness to leave if she wanted him to go. Understood that he did have feelings for her, real ones. "Down the road, yes. But no time soon."

"Then I'll wait." He looked at his watch. Whistled. "I better be going."

"What time is it?"

"Four-thirty."

She thought about her parents getting home in under an hour. The homework she had to do. She thought about the sogginess of her underwear, the strange funk that now filled her room.

Sylvia sat up. Philip sat up, too. Sitting on the edge of her now-messy bed, they looked at each other and shared goofy grins. "You're something special, do you know that?" he confessed.

"Am I?"

"Why else would I be here?"

She looked away. "For a lot of reasons."

A finger touched her cheek, guided her eyes back to his. "Only one reason," he said softly, kissing her, his mouth slipping over her bottom lip, sucking so gently she just knew she'd died and gone to heaven.

She had changed her underwear, remade her bed and aired out her room. Sylvia began her homework, her mother coming through the door twenty minutes after she cracked open her books.

She hadn't told her parents about the junior who had walked her to the bus stop and asked for her phone number. Nor had she told them that he asked her to go with him and that she said yes.

She had wanted to be certain it was a real thing before she introduced Philip. Now that she had the certainty, she knew the time had come. Problem was she wasn't certain if her folks would see it as something wonderful or detrimental.

Her father was the easy egg to crack, her mother hard-boiled. If she could get past her mother, the rest would be gravy.

Sylvia came running down the stairs the moment her mother stepped inside the house. Different approaches were called for, depending on the situation, and Sylvia decided to go with excitement. After a long day at work, she knew her mother would be more interested in resting her feet than any news her daughter had. So Sylvia tried the ambush route.

"Guess what?"

Virginia Morrow looked up at her only child, standing breathless and excited before her and couldn't begin to guess. "I have no idea, Sylvia."

"No, Mom, guess."

"You got another *A?*"

"No, Mom, guess."

"Honey, I had such a long day, can you just tell me?"

"Philip Butler asked me to go with him."

"Who?"

"Philip Butler. He's only like the finest, smartest boy in the whole school."

The word *finest* shrugged off the weariness Sylvia's mother had. She had been young once and knew "finest" meant "popular." Popular meant other things. "How old is he?"

That her mother honed in on the issue without it even being mentioned didn't really surprise Sylvia, but it did disappoint her. "Sixteen."

"Sixteen?"

"Yeah."

"What grade?"

"Eleventh."

"What's his name again?'

"Philip. Philip Butler."

"Where does he live?"

"South Ozone Park."

Her mother nodded to herself. Studied her daughter carefully. "Is he a good boy?"

"Yeah. A student and everything."

Sylvia's answer knocked back some of her mother's concern. Allowed a small smile to come into her face. "And I guess there's no need to ask you how much you like him." Sylvia blushed. "So when do we get to meet him?"

"Saturday?"

"Saturday, it is. You want me to tell your father, or do you want to?"

"You can tell him," Sylvia decided.

All parents have nightmares about the first girl or boy their child brings home. Sylvia's parents were no different. They knew Philip's first and last name, that he was older and gorgeous, according to their daughter's account and he lived a bus ride away. But that was all they knew.

When the tall, handsome, mannerly young man stepped through their door, extending his hand and taking theirs, addressing Mr. Morrow as "Sir," good proper English came from his lips as he talked about his future plans of going to college and having only the deepest respect for their only child, they breathed a huge sigh of relief.

They didn't hang around the kitchen but retreated upstairs, leaving Philip and Sylvia alone in the living room.

"They must really like you," Sylvia said, happy and relieved.

"How can you tell?"

"They left us alone."

"They're right upstairs."

"For my parents, that's leaving us alone."

By the fourth visit, Philip had her parent's full trust. By the eighth visit, she was allowed to keep company in her room as long as the door remained open. After a while, it stopped mattering if her door was opened or closed.

As far as they were concerned, Sylvia was a good girl and Philip was a good boy. Nothing illicit was going to happen behind that door. Her parents were absolutely right.

Chapter 4

There was a lot going on at Dorothy's house when Sylvia arrived. Mr. Alexander was fussing; Mrs. Alexander was blasting the radio to drown him out; and DeAnna and Dean were rushing around the kitchen, quickly putting away the freshly washed dishes from dinner.

Dorothy had been wiping off the countertops when Sylvia rang the doorbell, but her mother wanted another pack of Tarrytowns and her father, a beer. Dorothy would be going to the store when she finished up and Sylvia could take the walk with her.

"Almost done," she said as she rinsed the dishcloth under the running water. "Then I have to go to the store."

Sylvia nodded, hovering in the doorway, out of the way of Dorothy's fast-moving siblings, Mr. Alexander's voice to her back. ". . . asking for much. Not asking for a whole lot. Knuckleheads, the all of them."

But hearing him complain was as old and familiar as the cat clock hung on the wall. It had always been there, as much a part of the Alexander household as air.

"Done," Dorothy said, carefully laying the wet cloth over the sink spigot. She reached into her blue jeans, making sure she had the money and took her keys off the countertop. "Let's go."

They moved through the dining room, into the living room where Mr. Alexander had lowered his rage to a mutter. "Going to get your beer, Daddy. I'll be back." His eyes swept his oldest child, nodded and turned his attention to the television as Dorothy and Sylvia left out the front door.

It had been days since she had had a real moment with her friend and Dorothy was eager for the updates. She needed to know everything Philip did and didn't do, because she was waiting.

She was waiting for the virginal Sylvia to tell the manly Philip no one time too many. Dorothy was waiting for Philip's patience to grow thin, then vanish. She was waiting for Philip to drop Sylvia like a hot potato because no boy would wait that long.

Since the age of five, Dorothy had known Sylvia. She knew what Sylvia didn't do and just when she planned to do it. It would be years down the road; a couple of dozen months away and it had become obvious that not even Philip could make her change her mind.

But Philip wasn't a fifteen-year-old virgin. He was a sixteen-year-old boy who had no doubt traversed the road Sylvia wouldn't. Philip would grow tired of her, would grow weary of a girl who wouldn't put out. It was just a matter of time.

Dorothy knew about boys. Knew about them in a way Sylvia never would. With all the limitations put on her life, she still got around. She was kind of seeing Burt, who was okay, but he wasn't a Philip kind of guy.

He wasn't cute and fine and smart. He wasn't the type who would go to a good college, get a great job and make a woman truly happy. He didn't have the potential to be someone and take her far away from her meager South Jamaica neighborhood. He would not be able to buy her a big, wide sun-drenched house, with rolling lawns, and a backyard big enough to put in an in-ground pool, like the kind she'd seen in magazines.

Burt would graduate high school and get some low-paying city job. Marry and live in a tiny apartment until one child too many arrived and then be forced to find a house somewhere on the wrong side of town. Burt was the type who would never dream of bigger and brighter things but would spend a lifetime wanting them. He would work hard everyday and be displeased about everything, including his wife.

Burt was Dorothy's father in the making.

But Philip? He was a dream come true, and Sylvia didn't seem to know that or care.

A seed had been planted that first day she had seen them together, a seed that had long nestled in her soul. Its name was envy and every time Sylvia talked about Philip, it blossomed a little more.

The envy took giant leaps at Christmastime when Philip gave Sylvia an ankle bracelet with their initials inscribed on the two delicate gold hearts. The envy became nearly uncontainable when he brought her chocolates and a teddy bear on Valentine's Day.

It threatened to consume her when Sylvia began wearing his high school ring around her neck, there every time Dorothy looked her way, like now as they moved slowly up the block, the size eleven ring laying softly against Sylvia's chest.

"You do it yet?" Dorothy's question.

"No girl," Sylvia said with a nudge. "Why you always ask me that?"

Dorothy shrugged. "Just curious."

"As long as you've known me, you know I'm not till I'm ready."

"And that won't be for a while, right?"

"Dag on skippy," Sylvia proclaimed, proud.

Dorothy looked off, seeing newer brighter horizons. For seven months she had waited for Sylvia to understand and appreciate what she had. For seven months she had waited for her friend to realize all that Philip had to offer. She had given Sylvia a fair chance and Sylvia was blowing it.

Friendship or not, the wait was over.

Philip stood in the second-floor hallway of Jamaica High hushed with the absence of students, the final bell come and gone.

He stood taking in Dorothy, Sylvia's best friend, who was batting her lashes his way and close enough for their thighs to touch.

That Sylvia's best friend had been waiting for him outside his class wasn't any big surprise. In the passing weeks, Dorothy always seemed to run into him. And though he had been fighting off her advances for all those weeks, what had just come from her mouth—silken promises full of betrayal, raised the stakes.

"Isn't Sylvia like your best friend?"

Dorothy sucked her teeth, rolled her eyes. "Who's talking about her? I'm talking 'bout me and you."

"What me and you? I go with Sylvia."

"Yeah, but she ain't giving you what you want, now, is she?"

There was not a drop of anger in her words, her tone or the round hip jutted his way. Her smile remained cunning and seductive, unruffled. Knowing.

"You are something else, you know that."

"Am I?" A moist tongue moved over glossy pink lips. "Want to find out just how much?"

"No, I don't."

"Yes, you do, because if you really didn't, you wouldn't be here with me when you should be outside meeting Sylvia by the flagpole."

Sylvia.

Philip blinked. Blinked again. Muttered, "Damn." He took one last look at Dorothy and hurried down the hall. Slipping into the stairwell, he took the metal painted steps two at a time. Bursting through the heavy glass-paned exit doors, his sneakers skidded against the hard-shined marble foyer floor.

Through another set of doors, he moved, breath heaving. He took the inner marble steps two at a time and exploded into the early May sunshine. He saw Sylvia leaning against the flagpole, the Stars and Stripes at the top flapping violently in a fast wind.

She squinted in his direction, concern on her face. "Where have you been? I've been waiting forever."

"I was talking to a teacher. Sorry I was so late." He slipped his arm around her waist. Giving her a fast squeeze, they began the journey to her bus stop.

Philip knew a few things as they stepped inside Sylvia's house. He knew her parents wouldn't be home for two hours, that her bedroom of pink and white would be where they would spend their time.

He knew that she would play Stevie Wonder and the Main Ingredients—their make-out music, and that her skin would be caramel velvet in his hands. Philip knew she'd touch him with all the passion and want her virginal sensibilities would allow. That at the end of their time together, parts if him would be tender and aching.

What he didn't know was if she would consider taking things to the next level, if seven months allowed for the possibility.

They lay on her bed, side by side, locked up tight, her lips tasting of Juicy Fruit. With one hand he tested the hardness of her nipple, while the other was drenched in her wetness and her heat. She was touching him, too, and they would go on that way until he was forced to pull away. It was that predicament that was bothering him.

He moved from her, taking his hands with him. Staring at the ceiling, a forearm fell over his forehead. He lay there waiting for her questions, in need of it to be spoken. She didn't disappoint.

Up on an elbow, face peering down into his, the ridge of her brow furrowed. "What's wrong?"

Philip knew the answer. It had been there from the moment he had left Dorothy in the second-floor hallway. But it was hard to say. So he sighed instead.

"What's the matter?"

He took his time finding her eyes, wanting her to feel the weight that was lying heavy on his heart. He needed her to know that it was more than hormones and lust. That in this moment he needed her as he had never needed her before.

His voice came low, near-defeated. "Tired of waiting."

"Since when?" Sylvia's reply because he had promised he would wait and he had kept that promise for over half a year.

"Since forever," he said carefully.

Sylvia looked into the face of her first real boyfriend, the first taste of love she had known. Shook her head. "When I'm ready," she said and got up off her bed.

He didn't stay long and Sylvia was glad to see him go.

He had just raised the stakes and she needed to talk about it with her best friend. Calling on the phone, she asked Dorothy if she could come down. "Got something I need to talk about" was how she ended the conversation.

In the middle of washing her sister's hair, Dorothy told her she'd be down in a few. But there was no need to hear Sylvia speak it. Dorothy knew exactly what it was about.

She arrived carrying a paper bag full of potato chips, Now and Laters and a Blow Pop because Sylvia loved them. They went to her room, Sylvia sitting on one twin, Dorothy on the other. Reaching into the bag, she retrieved the sweet and handed it over. "Figure you'd need it."

The smile Sylvia attempted failed. "Thanks."

"So, what gives?"

"He's tired."

"Tired of what?"

"Waiting."

"To have sex?"

"Yeah. We were kissing and stuff and the next thing I know, he pulling away and sighing and I asked him what was wrong and he said he was tired of waiting."

"What did you do?"

Sylvia rolled her eyes. "I told him not until I'm ready."

"What did he say?"

"Nothing."

"You sure?"

"Sure what?'

"Sure you didn't let him."

The question was ludicrous to Sylvia. "No, girl."

Dorothy looked away, looked back at her friend. "You're right to tell Philip no. If he really loves you, he'll wait."

"That's right. If he really loves me."

Philip did.

It was in his heart that ached when she wasn't around, the very same that filled whenever their eyes met. It had been his heart that gave the promise to wait. But something was emerging, shifting, stirring. Something was rearing up inside him.

Philip wasn't a virgin before he got together with Sylvia. He had had more than a few encounters. There had been a couple of girls who gave it willingly without asking a thing, but he had been in search of a deeper connection and he had found it in Sylvia. She had claimed his heart like no one else had before.

When she told him that she wasn't ready, he had no problems respecting that and was certain he could handle it. He loved her and so he put that part of him on the back burner, willing to go the distance. But like nature itself, the arrival of spring had put a new fire in him and Dorothy had just turned up the flame.

It was a flame he was ducking, a flame he was running from even as thoughts filled his head. He needed Sylvia to save him, to keep them together. Needed Sylvia to do the one thing she would not.

Worst of all, he had made her angry. She didn't come to the phone when he called later that evening and had barely looked at him the next day in school. He reminded himself that she was just fifteen, still young, still innocent, the very reason he had been drawn to her.

Philip decided to stick by his word, that at the end of the school day he would tell her just that. Tell her that he would never force the issue again. But when the end of class bell rang and he dashed out of his seat and into the hallway, he ran smack-dab into Dorothy, her books flying from her arms.

He was about to apologize, continue on his way, when she bent over, gathering up her fallen books, a vision of pink silk panties cupping round firm cheeks before him, the short denim skirt hiding nothing.

Righting herself, she smiled, waggling a finger. "You need to be watching where you going." Turning, she walked away.

Two seconds passed before he remembered his hurry, his need to find Sylvia. Two seconds coming before he could remember his promise, the image of pink silk, tight and taut, branding.

Sylvia was fast-walking.

She was fast-walking because she didn't want to see Philip. Fast-walking because she wanted him to know exactly how pissed off she was at him. The fact that he would even open his mouth to tell

her he was tired of waiting since "forever" meant he had lied when
he had made his promise. That they had just been words to get her
trust and that hurt.

She was half a block from school when she risked a look behind
her, hope and anger riding her bones. She expected to see Philip
running after her, but she didn't see him anywhere and it slowed
her pace.

It wasn't supposed to go this far. Her payback didn't include taking the long walk to the bus stop by herself, with him nowhere in
sight. Philip was supposed to be making a mad dash her way,
yelling her name, insisting that she stop.

He was supposed to trail her, begging and pleading to forgive
him, insisting that he would never even think about pressuring
her, as she headed to the bus terminal. She was supposed to make
him suffer before she gave in, the two of them making up by the
time she stood on the bus line. But as she entered the diesel-
smelling building, bus pass in hand, she knew she had figured
wrong.

Philip was nowhere in sight.

Philip stood in the quad of Jamaica High school searching the
perimeter. He saw hundreds of students moving about but could
not find Sylvia anywhere. Tucking his books tight under one arm,
he began running. Did not stop until the red light caught him.

He hurried down the four long blocks to Archer Avenue, made
a sharp right, his destination two blocks away. He skidded around
pedestrians, ignored the calls of those who knew him and wanted
to know where he was off to.

He was off to his heart, off to his whole world. He was off to find
Sylvia, make her listen, make her understand that he loved her
and if ever there was a time, it was now.

Philip ran and thought, ran and pondered, emotions and hormones moving through him hard. His mind flip-flopped between
what he wanted and what he needed, desperate for some middle
ground.

Sweaty, near-exhausted by the time he entered the dim dirty bus
terminal, he scanned the line for the Q-6 and saw Sylvia about to

board. Muscling his way, jumping the line, he fumbled for his pass, the nickel that would give him boarding, ignoring the grumbles erupting around him.

Sylvia didn't know he was there until he plopped musky and damp beside her. She wasn't certain if she should be mad or glad. Decided for somewhere in between. "I wasn't waiting," she told him. "I wasn't," something hard and nebulous filling her soul.

They were in her room, each of them on a twin bed, separate from each other. There was no music, no making out. It was talk time.

"I need to know when, Sylvia."

It was not what she expected him to say. She considered such talk over and done with, but there he was, resurrecting it. Sylvia had anticipated an apology, a heartfelt promise that it was her decision and hers alone. She would let him know when she was ready, with words or perhaps deeds, but the time for asking was over.

"We're back to that?" she asked hotly.

"I need some idea."

"How can I tell you what I don't know?" Or feel, because in that moment she was so far from sleeping with Philip it wasn't even funny.

"I was thinking next month."

Next month. June. Her birthday. She would be sixteen. But seventeen had been the real number that played in her head, like reaching eighteen and being able to vote. But now that he was pushing her, she couldn't even consider it. "What is up with you?" she asked, leery and disappointed. "Why are you pressuring me?"

He looked away, looked back at her. "I'm not pressuring you. I just want to,"

"Want to what? Sleep with me? You didn't before."

But he had, every time he shared her space. He had wanted to discover the sweet secrets, feel her love to the fullest. But he knew to speak that would make it worse. He was at an impasse, Dorothy stirring up a lust he had been forcing down for almost a year.

He did love Sylvia; he did want to wait. But he was finding it harder and harder, especially when he found himself thinking about the things Dorothy promised to do to him from the moment he opened his eyes in the morning till he drifted off to sleep at night.

He left the bed, closing the space between them. He dropped down to a knee, his eyes leveled her. "I love you, Sylvia. I never loved anyone like I love you. Don't you know that?"

"Get up from there," she said disgusted with his neediness, the new un-cool boy he had become.

"Sylvia, please . . ."

She may have been an innocent, but she knew a little something, like how boys would do that. They would beg and plead and act as if they were going to die if you didn't let them. She had heard the stories. Just never thought Philip would allow her to witness it.

She grabbed his shoulders, the bulk awkward in her hands. "Get up."

"I really do love you," his final plea.

But Sylvia wasn't feeling it. She wasn't in any mood to try. She was mad, angry, and disappointed, pissed off that he was trying to run the game on her. Every fiber in her body said so.

Philip got up, something gone from him. Picking up his books, he left.

Same script, different day Dorothy was thinking as she let herself into the house, the television blaring from the living room, the radio from upstairs. But unlike the day before and the days before that she didn't care. She didn't ask her brother a thing as she climbed the stairs, didn't let go one word as she entered the room she and her sister shared.

She had made a decision and was sticking with the plan. She was only going to be responsible for Dorothy from now on. She took off her shoes, put them in the closet. Headed back out the door.

"Ain't you gonna ask me?"

"Ask you what?"

"What you always ask me, if I did my homework?"

"DeAnna, I don't care if you do or you don't."

"Daddy'll beat you if I don't."

Yes, he would, but the day was coming when she'd be gone from the belt, the intense tight voice, the rage she sensed from the day she'd been born. "Won't be the first time and it won't be the last."

Eleven minutes later as Dorothy was doing the second math problem, the sound of books landing on the kitchen table drew her attention. She looked up and saw her sister DeAnna, near fuming. "You still a stink heifer, but I don't want you to get beat," last words before she sat down in the chair.

Her brother had joined them by the time Dorothy had finished. She made dinner, thought about the thing she had begun. Realized she was Muhammad and Philip the mountain. Understood she had to take the journey.

"Be back," all she told her brother and sister, snatching up her keys. If she had been old enough to watch them at the age of ten, then DeAnna was certainly capable of doing the same at thirteen.

She had only been there once with Sylvia, but she knew the house by heart. A ten-minute bus ride, Dorothy felt near faint by the time she got off Q-40 bus.

I'll just ring the bell and ask for him. If he's not home, I'll turn around. Take the beating Daddy's gonna give me and try again another day . . . Sylvia has to understand. Understand that she smart and can get out and away, but me, I need help. I need somebody who can do it for me. Someone who can take me from my house of misery. Someone I could love and cherish, give me the fine things in life.

Fine things.

It was right before her eyes, the single-family detached two-story home in salmon-colored stone with three-foot-high stone lions guarding the gateway and black wrought iron over the door, evidence.

Up the flagstone steps she walked. Rang the bell and waited. The door swung open. Philip looked out at her through the glass of the storm door, Dorothy returning the favor. It was awhile before she could smile, work her mouth enough to say, "Hi."

He peered past her, looking for Sylvia. Was slightly dismayed that Dorothy was standing there all alone. Then the image of those silky pink panties cupping the roundness of her behind flashed through him. Swallowing, Philip said hi back.

* * *

They were down in the basement, locked up, sweaty, naked. He had never seen a girl fully unclothed before and he could not hide the pleasure of his discovery. Sex had always been a quick affair, unzip, pull it out, stick it in, hump a few seconds, come, pull out, wipe, stuff, zip and be gone.

But here Dorothy was. His parents upstairs and she buck naked against the old sofa, he on top, trying to get to her honey pot. "Stop rushing," she said with a giggle, sliding her hand down, stroking him like a champ.

Her hand felt good, but the image of that pink tongue behind those watermelon icy-colored lips seemed better. It was what she had promised just a few days ago in the second-floor hallway of Jamaica High. *Blow you into tomorrow,* she had whispered to him, starting a fever that obliterated his world.

Hesitant before, he was now in the middle of it. He had passed the gate of no return the moment he had opened the door to Dorothy. All Philip knew was need. Not love, not promises, not the sweet innocence he had been drawn to. Just need.

As if reading his mind, Dorothy slipped from beneath him, the firm round soft-brown ass moving past his startled face, the briny perfume of her loins, filling his nose.

Slender ankles slid past his shoulders, hard points of nipple nestling the hollow of his stomach. Her bush, thick and onyx, arched around dappled lips swollen and glistening fuscia. He wanted to press his whole face against it.

He watched in fascination as her head disappeared past her shoulders. Nearly came when her breath whisked across his pubic hair. Then those lips—warm, wet and luscious—were sliding onto him, making him buck and shiver so hard he knocked her whole body off him

She landed on her behind with a thump. Sat there, stunned, rubbing one buttock. "Damn, Philip."

He couldn't apologize, could only reach for her, wanting nothing more than to have her back there, back to where heaven met earth and he lay in its blissful center.

Burt had taught her.

He had taught Dorothy the art of taking a man into her mouth and giving up that pleasure. It had been an eye-opening moment.

Dorothy had had no idea that with just her lips, she could turn a man into putty in her hands. By the second time she had Burt begging and pleading, understanding full well the power she could wield.

It was a power she was testing, her ultimate weapon in her war to win Philip. She knew she was succeeding as Philip moaned and grimaced and bucked.

She sucked him till he was dry and then went on to suck him again just for good measure. She swallowed with a smile, though his semen was bitter in her mouth. Then she was getting dressed and he knew she was leaving, his heart yearning in a way it never had before.

"Where you going?"

"Home."

"No, not yet," he decided, reaching for her. He began kissing as if she were magic. As if there were no Sylvia and never would be again.

Dorothy's father was waiting for her when she got home. She had expected that much. She had expected the belt to be flying the moment she stepped through the door. But what could he accuse her of? Trying to live her life?

"Next time you leave out of here, you tell somebody where you going," all he said, looking her over closely before going up the steps.

Dorothy stood there dumbstruck. She was standing there with her mouth wide open, looking up toward the father who hadn't beat her but offered common sense, when her mother came out of the kitchen, a sad smile on her face.

"Sixteen . . . you need to be going places. Not cooped up here all the time. But like your Daddy said, next time you tell somebody where you off to."

Dorothy nodded, headed up the stairs. Went to the bathroom and brushed her teeth. The whole ride home the taste of Philip had been bitter in her mouth. Toothpaste did the trick, but there was no scrubbing away the unexpected sorrow that had found her heart. Dorothy pushed it away. Nearly to the finish line, she couldn't turn back now.

Yes, she had gone after her best friend's boyfriend. Yes, she had gone to his house and got buck naked, doing things with his penis and her mouth. It wasn't like she hadn't given Sylvia the chance to keep him. Besides, Philip had held and kissed her for a long time after that. So how true could his love for Sylvia have been?

Chapter 5

At sixteen, a boy's body was nearly fully developed, but the mind still had years to go and all Philip could think about was the feel of Dorothy's mouth on his dick. He couldn't think about Sylvia, school, teachers, nothing. Just what Dorothy had done and how he'd give his life to have it again.

Philip found himself waiting for that final bell, unable to get out of the classroom fast enough. He wasn't sure if Sylvia was waiting or not, but didn't care. He had already decided to stake out an alternate route home.

He couldn't think about Sylvia, school, right, wrong or anything. Philip could only think about Dorothy and the chance to get what he had gotten just yesterday. But his heart sunk to the bottom of his size thirteen sneakers when he left the class and Dorothy was nowhere to be found.

Life was full of lessons and at almost sixteen Sylvia had begun the journey of learning them. She learned that sometimes it was better to forgive first chance then try to drag it out. She learned that Philip had a will, too, and the fact that he didn't call her last night was proving it.

Sylvia hoped Philip knew she was waiting by the flagpole and that he would meet her there. Hoped he understood that she still loved him and they could work their problems out. But as the stream of students moved to a trickle, doubt took hold.

She waited an extra five minutes for good measure before abandoning her wait. Heading down the hill, she couldn't help but wonder where he was and if he was thinking of her.

Dorothy was finishing up her science homework when her brother came into the kitchen. "Dere's some boy out there want to see you."

Dorothy knew before she moved a muscle. Knew before she rounded the small foyer. Knew it was Philip at her door in broad daylight with Sylvia living just ten doors away.

She opened the door, grabbed Philip by his shirt and pulled him inside. "What are you doing here?"

His brows drew up, soft agony in his voice. "You weren't there, after class."

"You weren't there after class," her brother mimicked.

"Shut. Up!" Dorothy said, giving her brother an evil look. Taking Philip by the hand, she led him into the basement.

"Where were you?" Philip wanted to know, a need deep and plaintive in his eyes.

It was crazy, yes, the whole thing was nuts, but she wanted Philip, always had. That he had come to her house with Sylvia just a few doors away said he wanted her, too. But Dorothy knew she had to be careful, had to be sure. Would not play second fiddle to nobody. Had to be first.

She fixed her face with a puzzling look. "Was I supposed to wait for you or something?"

He looked away.

"Because last time I checked, you were going with Sylvia. Has something changed?"

His eyes found hers, riddled with guilt, harbored with longing. "You know it has."

"What's changed?" She said, folding her arms, leaning back away from him. "How you feel about Sylvia or the fact that I gave you a blow job?"

"Both," he said so softly that she knew he was torn right down the middle.

But she would not allow herself to pity him. Forced him to make the hard choice. "Well, if you think I'm going to see you behind my friend's back, you wrong."

Conflict. It was all in his eyes. She had performed magic, but it had not been as strong as she thought. She reared her head, determined. "My parents will be home soon and you can't be here."

"I—"

"What? Love her? Then fine, go on down the street and you two dry-hump yourselves into tomorrow. Go on down the street and never have again what I gave you yesterday. Go on."

His head lowered. She had gotten him where he lived at sixteen—below the belt. "Okay."

She put a hand to her ear. "What? I can't hear you?"

"I said okay. I'll go tell her."

Dorothy's voice grew soft, careful. More than performance, the words came straight from her heart. Because despite it all, she didn't want Sylvia to hurt any more than she had to. Despite it all, she still cared. "Don't tell her about the other day, okay? She's going to be hurt enough."

Philip looked in the eyes of a girl who had stolen his soul, changed his whole world in a single sweep. He wasn't certain if he really knew her, even liked her. All he knew in that moment was he needed her like he had never needed anything in his young life.

"Philip?"

She had not expected him but was so glad to see him, she could not help but throw her arms around him. It took a while before she realized he was not holding her back, that his eyes would not hold hers. That they danced away from her and stayed.

"We got to talk."

They headed toward her bedroom.

He did not sit by her. Took the other bed. Swallowed, his voice choked with pain. "I asked you, Sylvia. Begged you, pleaded with you, but you wouldn't even consider it."

"I'm not ready, Philip. Can't you see that, I'm just not."

He nodded, aggrieved. "Yeah, I know . . . you said if I love you I can wait." His eyes found hers. "I do love you, Sylvia, more than I love anybody, more than I probably ever will love anybody, but I can't wait. I'm letting you go."

She couldn't speak. Couldn't blink. Could hardly breathe for a second. His words, Letting you go, not registering. How do you send away somebody you love? "But I thought you loved me?"

"I do. But I guess you didn't believe me, or it wasn't enough." He shook his head, in turmoil.

She had always had a fast mind. Moments coming when she could calculate swiftly. This was such a moment. "Oh, so you found somebody who would, right?" It hurt to say those words, hurt even harder to think them.

"Yeah."

"Who?" Because there were a couple of dozen girls from which he could choose, Philip turning heads from the moment he entered her high school.

"Don't matter, does it?"

"Yes, it does." She was so angry she could pummel him.

She's going to be hurt enough. But in that moment Philip found that he hurt more. Because before him was the only one he loved. The truth left him softly. "Dorothy."

The room spun. Sylvia choked on her own breath, saliva slipping down the wrong pipe. She choked, coughed, struggled for air, for reason. Sylvia struggled for calm. For sense. For the end of the pain of that hard-hitting reality.

"Dorothy!? My best friend, Dorothy?" Her body trembled. Not Dorothy. Not her best friend in the whole live world.

"Yeah."

She was standing, her hands in tiny balls, ready to rain down on his lowered head. But he grabbed her wrist. Stood. Steadied her with his eyes, the facts. "You wouldn't, but she did."

Not could, not would. But did. Did as in done. Did as in the past. Hadn't she and Dorothy walked to school this morning? Judas under her nose and she didn't even know.

Sylvia tore her wrist away from him. Hurried out of the room. It wasn't until the sound of the front door's opening reached him that Philip realized where she was going. He jumped up and hightailed after her, catching her just as she reached Dorothy's gate. His arms, the same ones that could hold her like the world was most perfect, now restraining her as she raged against him.

He had her hands, but she had full use of her mouth. She howled her friend's name until people appeared at front doors, taking in the wild scene of the scorned ex-girlfriend baying at the girl who had taken her love away.

Neighbors, people she had known since she was a child, came to their front doors, stoops and windows, watching her spit in the wind. Hidden behind the curtains, Dorothy looked on, her heart breaking at the sight.

And when Sylvia got tired, had no fight in her, was nearly sinking against Philip's tight hold, she twisted and looked into the face she had loved with all her heart, asking, "You love her too?" pulling away and heading home before he could answer.

The parents found out. Sylvia's parents and Dorothy's parents. While they did not know all the details, they knew a few facts. Number one was that Sylvia and Dorothy had been best friends forever, and number two, a boy had disrupted their lives, so much so the normally quiet, mild-mannered Sylvia Morrow had become a wild thing on the street, a sight that would take some time to live down.

When Dorothy told her parents it had happened because Sylvia's boyfriend broke up with Sylvia to go with her, Dorothy's parents demanded to know how Dorothy could even consider doing such a thing.

When Sylvia told her parents that Philip had left her to go with Dorothy, her parents had wondered how could Dorothy do such a thing, thus the weight all fell on Dorothy.

"You go down there and you apologize to Sylvia right this minute," her father told her. He was ushering her through the front door when the phone rang. Dorothy's mother picked up. It was Sylvia's parents demanding that Dorothy come and apologize. "She's on her way now."

Dorothy did not want to go. Sylvia didn't want her to come. But it was the early seventies and children were still doing what they were told.

* * *

"Wasn't me, Sylvia," the first words out of Dorothy's mouth as she stood at the edge of the bedroom that had become a shrine of sadness. It was evident in the blinds drawn against the sunlight and the lost love record that poured from the portable record player.

It was there in the stuffed animals and letters gathered in the middle of Sylvia's floor as if awaiting a torching. But mostly it was in the red wounded eyes of Sylvia who looked as if she had been crying a lifetime.

Dorothy hovered at the doorway, feeling the pressure of Sylvia's parents behind her and the brunt of sorrow before her. She stepped into the room, but knew better than to get too close.

"It was Philip. He came to me," Dorothy implored. "And I asked him, you know? Asked him if you and him were over and he told me yeah. It's not how I wanted it to be, but he came to me. And he is fine, and everybody wants him. I just couldn't say no."

Sylvia had been looking down until then. Her head shot up and her eyes latched onto Dorothy like a ray gun. "After you fucked him right?" There was so much emphasis on the foul four-letter word, both her parents gasped. Her mother wanted to go in, but her father restrained her.

"I ain't fucked him."

"You lie, you lie, you lie. Telling me 'That's right, Sylvia, make him wait,' and all the time . . ." she couldn't finish. Couldn't look at Dorothy anymore, hating her like she'd never hated. Hating her because she had done what Sylvia wouldn't. Did it and took her heart away.

"I swear, Sylvia, I didn't."

Sylvia jumped up, knowing in her heart she did. Knowing that it was the only thing that could take Philip from her. The one thing she hadn't been ready to give. Sylvia was up, inches from Dorothy's face, fist tight, ready to strike. "Yes, you did, you stank ho. Nothing but a stinking nasty little ho and I never want to see you again." She shoved Dorothy hard, sending her tripping backward. "Get out of my house!"

Dorothy went.

The next day Sylvia waited at a different bus stop for school, turned her head when Dorothy boarded. By the end of the day the whole school was abuzz with the news, rumors flying fast, picking up stories like a snowball down a long snowy hill.

"Yeah, she busted them. They were doing the do and Sylvia caught them."

"I heard she sucked his dick in the boys' bathroom."

"No, it was under the bleachers."

By the end of that school day, Sylvia discovered more friends than she ever knew she had and Dorothy lost all of hers but she had her man.

Philip, on the other hand wasn't certain what he had gained, only what he no longer had.

"Sylvia."

She jumped, startled, nearly missing the step in the stairwell. She turned, saw Philip hovering by the entry door, eyes wounded, full of pain.

"Go away, Philip." She hurried down the school stairs, not surprised that he was running after her.

He caught her on the midlanding, his arm tight on her wrist. "Hear me out, please."

There were tears in his eyes and seeing them broke her heart all over again. But the world did not possess enough sorrys to forgive him. "You fucked my best friend, right?"

She wrenched her arm away and hurried down the next flight of stairs, swinging the entry door open so hard and fast it banged against the wall. Rounding the hall, she leaned against the wall, trembling, too on fire to cry, so consumed with anger she had to stop herself from screaming.

She was still there, the late bell pealing, when he found her. Philip stood before her, the empty hallway hushed. "It's you I love, not her." She twisted her eyes from his. "I know you don't believe it. But it's true."

Her eyes found his, wet yet feral. "You wanted Dorothy, you got her. I'm through." Peeling herself off of the wall, Sylvia hurried off to class.

* * *

"I always knew that family was no damn good," her father said as they sat around the kitchen table the next day. "And I guess Philip isn't much better."

"You can't cry over spilled milk, Sylvia," her mother said watching the tears that refused to stop. "It's not like you can scoop it back up and put it in the glass."

Her father joined in. "Your mother's right. You're sitting up here and all you can see is a big bowl of lemons. Life is just soured now. But you take those same lemons, add a little water, a little sugar and you got lemonade. It's the same thing with life. You can take your troubles and just let them sour everything, or add a little something and make it better." He lowered his head, catching her eyes. "You want to know the best revenge against someone who has wronged you?"

Sylvia sniffled. "What?"

"A good successful life. And there's only one way to get that, you have to want it. You have to say yesterday is just that and tomorrow anything is possible. Now I know how much you liked Philip."

"I loved him, Daddy."

Her father nodded. "Yes, of course you did. But he's gone now, Suvie, and I'm certain he is not home crying tears over his dinner like you are. I don't know what he's doing, but I know he's not all weepy. It's going to take time, but you will get over it. There's somebody better for you. But you have to be ready for them when they come."

Bossy. Selfish. Demanding.

This was the real Dorothy behind the talent. This was the Dorothy Philip found himself connected to, her claws so deep inside of him he was certain he would never be freed. It was just the type of girl his parents warned him not to get involved with, but Sylvia wouldn't even look his way anymore.

He had tried to talk to her since that fateful day, his heart telling him the mistake he had made, his head just wanting to fix it. But when he called her house, her parents refused to call her to the phone. There had been no response to the notes passed to her through a myriad of student hands or the five he had written in the late night, stamped and mailed through the local post office.

He didn't love Dorothy, and it didn't take a long time to figure that out. He was all set to break things off, when she took them to the next level. She let him go all the way. They went on the summer, having sex as often as they could, but even that pleasure began to wane.

In October when he had had his fill and told her he didn't want to see her, Dorothy had threatened to kill herself. "I mean it, Philip. I gave up so much to be with you, don't think I won't."

Philip decided to hold on until next June when he graduated. He would take her to the senior prom and then be off to a faraway college. He would be a free man then, and maybe just maybe he could convince Sylvia to forgive him.

Sylvia had her share of troubles that following year. The easygoing teenager who had everything going for her became withdrawn and depressed. Her grades began to slip; she spent all her free time in her room, listening to music and not much else.

She kept the letters from Philip but did not read them. If, whatever he wrote, had any merit, then he would break up with Dorothy, but they seemed to be going strong. So the letters became more lies.

Her refusal to care about much didn't bother her until her guidance counselor called her into his office to discuss her poor marks. "You were an A student; now you're headed for a C. You do want to go to college, don't you?"

It was a transforming moment. Her father said the best revenge was good living, and she couldn't get that by flunking out of school. She began paying attention to herself and the world around her. When Kenneth Peterson asked her out, she told him yes. She liked him enough, but it didn't touch anywhere near what she felt for Philip.

On that late afternoon in June when the white limo pulled up to Dorothy's door and neighbors gathered on their front stoops to see the supposedly "happy" couple on the way to Philip's senior prom, Sylvia wasn't one of them. She was at Kenneth Peterson's house, giving him what she had denied Philip.

Those few times she ran into Dorothy, or Dorothy and Philip,

Sylvia simply turned her head, making them invisible in her world, but there wasn't much she could do to make them invisible in her heart.

Philip, who would be off to college soon, decided he was leaving Dorothy and if she wanted to kill herself, then let her, but he was going to live his life. He was getting up the courage to break things off with her when she told him the heart-stopping news.

"I'm pregnant."

On August 7, 1973, Dorothy and Philip said I do. On August 8, 1973, Philip left to start Morehouse College. On September 2, 1973 Dorothy "lost" the baby. And though Philip still longed for freedom from Dorothy, it never came. Philip was Catholic. Divorce did not exist in his vocabulary.

The only married senior in high school, with no friends and her husband six hundred miles away, Dorothy found herself reflecting. She found herself missing. She found herself thinking about Sylvia as much as she did Philip. Dorothy tried to mend the broken bridge, but Sylvia wasn't having it.

When Dorothy graduated high school the following June, she was invited to none of the senior parties. Packing her bags, Dorothy caught a Greyhound to Atlanta, Georgia, to join her husband who would be going into his second year at Morehouse.

Hitting the ground running, Dorothy got off the bus, flagged a cab to the campus and laid eyes on her husband for the first time in months. Philip didn't even try to pretend he was happy to see her, just said he'd show her the place he found, a tiny studio half a mile from campus.

That first year of living together as man and wife, Dorothy and Philip's life was blatantly absent of the newly married blues. There were no arguments about leaving the toilet seat up, the toothpaste uncapped or the garbage that needed to be taken out. There were no dissertations about who got to watch what on TV or him spending too much time with the boys.

They went about life like hospitable roommates trying not to get in each other's way. Philip slept on the couch. Dorothy got the bed. There was little discussion about anything beyond what bills were due and who was going to pay them. And though their apartment was small enough to spit from one end to the other, they managed not to collide too often.

Yet while they were in different places emotionally, there was no doubt where they were headed: forward. Dorothy made sure of it.

She took the first job she could find—waitressing—at the local Hotcake House and attended secretarial classes at night. Within a year she had a full-time clerical job and a part-time one at Macy's. Saving up her money, she moved them from the dismal studio apartment on the wrong side of town to a two-bedroom with a balcony and working fireplace in College Park.

When Philip graduated from Morehouse, she coached him on how to land his first job. With a better income, Dorothy found a ranch-house for them to rent. By the time Philip got his first promotion, Dorothy had set her sights on a new subdivision going up near I-85.

Four years after she had arrived in Atlanta, Georgia, Dorothy's plan was in full swing, while Philip, beat down by her determination, settled into the life Dorothy carved for him.

At twenty-four, sorrow still had Sylvia. She said good-bye to Kenneth Peterson in her junior year of college, because she didn't love him and never would. After getting her degree, Sylvia got a job with the state and a place of her own, but emotionally she was stunted.

She made friends with a coworker named Lisa who went on to become her best friend. Lisa spotted Sylvia's depression at first glance and made it her lifelong mission to pull Sylvia out of it.

At least once a week she was dragging Sylvia somewhere. Sometimes Sylvia had a good time, but most times she didn't. One particular night Sylvia found herself at a local disco, drink in her hand and all alone at the bar. She sat there a good twenty minutes waiting for Lisa's return. When the wait grew too long, she left the stool and wandered about the club.

Men looked at her and looked away. Sylvia who had never had

the ability to hide her emotions on her face was certain that her sorrow draped her like gossamer. She felt invisible, out of her league, depressed and ready to go home.

Bitter, she was just about to search out Lisa to tell her she was leaving when a man came up to her, asked her to dance.

She did not trust either his offer or the way he looked at her. Sylvia found herself checking him over for defects but didn't find any. He was neither ugly, short nor out of shape. He wasn't the finest man she'd ever seen, but he looked good enough so she went with him to the dance floor.

He danced well, spoke good English and asked her questions while they hustled. He introduced himself as Emory. By the time the fourth fast record started, her feet were throbbing and she knew she couldn't dance another step.

Pulling out of his arms, she thanked him, turned and walked away. *A seat,* she was thinking when she felt his hand on hers. "Can I buy you a drink?" Thus began the start of their relationship that ended in marriage two years later. A marriage that was good and strong as far as Sylvia was concerned, but getting there took some work.

As a couple, their life centered on getting together once or twice a week. Marriage meant that they were in each other's face twenty-four/seven. Those long soulful good-byes they had shared while dating became quick afterthought pecks on their cheeks.

The passion they'd shared while they were just a couple drifted into new waters as they learned to maneuver around each other's idiosyncrasies.

Sylvia found herself making a new acquaintance with the kitchen because dinner demanded more than a bowl of cereal or a grilled cheese sandwich. Having a husband meant three-course meals on a nightly basis.

Sylvia had to learn the hard way that it was best to make sure the toilet seat was down before she sat and Emory had to get used to sanitary products up under the bathroom sink. Socks on the floor and dirty dishes in the sink were enough to cause a nuclear melt-down their first year, but by their fourth, they'd found a rhythm to their lives.

It was during that fourth year that a letter from Dorothy arrived for Sylvia at her parents' house. It had been full of "I'm sorry" and "Please forgive me," with a good dose of "I never meant to hurt you."

The words didn't impact Sylvia as much as she thought they would. Her marriage to Emory made it less important. He offered her the happiness she had been looking for, a happiness that gave her the strength to move on. So much so that the first time Dorothy and Philip showed up at her house, she didn't close the door on them.

Sylvia loved her husband. There was no need to search her soul for that truth. Like living and breathing, it was automatic, not overwhelming, but constant and there. So she opened her home to the two who had betrayed her most as if it had never happened, and called out to Emory to "come and meet my old friends."

The love between her and Emory allowed her to play the hostess, Emory firing up the grill. The four of them sat in the backyard, eating hot dogs and hamburgers, three careful with their talk.

When that long-ago afternoon turned to evening, they parted with the promise to keep in touch. Since that time Dorothy and Philip had made a few more visits, but neither one had ever come alone.

Chapter 6

But Philip has. He sits on my sofa sans Dorothy, stirring up memories, a hornet's nest of hurt. My body trembles and I cannot stop the rage I had put aside so long ago.

"You changed me. Dorothy changed me," I want to shout, but can only whisper, "What you two did to me . . ." I can't finish, cannot reveal any more how deep the pain still moves.

There is the sound of a key being pushed into a lock. Tumblers fight before they slide back. I look up and feel unspent tears in my eyes. I wipe at them quickly and blink. Getting up, I am unprepared for my husband's arrival, unprepared for the stranger sitting on my sofa, the angst in my own heart.

I know I've just betrayed something, something special and real. I know I have just betrayed the facade of a happy life I've lived with Emory and Philip has witnessed the revelation. I blink some more, whisk away the last bit of wetness, sniffle, get composure as the front door swings open.

I reach for my husband, my body pressing his hard. He urges me back, my eyes full of a fake smile. "Hey," I say, turning him toward Philip. "You remember Philip." My hand glides along Emory's spine, shifting the surprise that stiffens his shoulders.

But the look in Emory's face says he doesn't. That he can't place the face. He does not remember the man who laughed too hard and too loud in our backyard a while back.

I feel currents running from Philip to me, wonder if Emory can sense them, too. The room is charged with bitterness and regret. My mouth forms words against the silence. "Dorothy's husband, remember? They live in Georgia? Visit us sometimes."

It takes awhile, but Emory does, recognition moving into the surprise. He smiles a little, still caught off-guard and closes the space between them.

Emory stretches out his hand; Philip rises to meet it. Two hands join, giving each other a hard shake. "Nice to see you again."

"Same here," Philip manages. He is looking at Emory, but I know my outbreak still has a fast hold.

Emory and Philip are standing side by side, and I can't help but experience their differences. I see that Emory is shorter, Philip, more built. My heart lies somewhere in the middle.

"I have to be going." Philip says moreso to my husband than to me. "It was great seeing you again."

"Same here," Emory confesses, but there is uncertainty in his proclamation.

My husband works hard and this day is no different. I know what he wants when he comes in from work, and company in his house is not it. He longs to slip off his leather loafers and undo the knot in his tie. He longs to relieve his wrist of the Casio watch, take the gabardine slacks and dress shirt off his body.

He wants to sit in front of the television while I fix him a plate. Hear my voice calling him to the table; be his witness as he shares his day. But Philip has prevented this downtime, the letting go of being a benefits analyst. There is a streak of impatience as Emory waits for Philip to depart.

Philip moves toward me and I am going to explode, shatter into a thousand unrepairable pieces the moment he hugs me good-bye. Like flint against stone, something sparks as he does. I pull away quickly, my eyes along the floor.

"Safe trip," Emory calls as he gathers up the mail.

"Thanks," Philip says as he reaches for the door. There is a slight pause, a hesitation not even a half second long, but in that space I feel it. Philip is still within me, and I, within him.

* * *

I am up in my workspace, the attic-come-office I've turned into my personal haven. Here is where I work, smoke, listen to music no one else wants to hear.

Here is where I find money for organizations, writing up proposals that will get them funding. Here is where I do my nine to five, never having to ask for a day off, or stand out in the rain to appease my nicotine addiction. Here is where I shuffle around in my pajamas, teeth unbrushed sometimes.

Here is where I've taken my schooling and a love for English and math and turned it into a profession that adds between ten and twenty thousand dollars a year to our household. It's not a lot of money and there are times when months go by and I don't make a dime, but I can do it at home and you can't beat that.

But I retreat here now because Philip has sent my thoughts in a thousand directions and I need to evaluate all that I have and the struggles to get here.

My husband is a typical forty-something middle-class black man with a college education and a nice private sector job. Yet while people look at him and marvel at his mild success, I look at him and see all the struggles.

He makes over $86,000 a year now, but I will never forget when he first started working for his company decades ago and brought home a whole lot less. He takes me out to dinner at this little Italian restaurant in SoHo, but I can still remember dates that were simply a drive-through at Wendy's.

He drives a late-model Lexus, but his '73 Mustang holds a special place in my heart. That car saw us through our dating years and the birth of our first child. And by the time it landed at the scrap heap, it had only one side-view mirror, ripped upholstery and empty oyster shells from too many trips to Coney Island.

For over a year we lived in a tiny studio apartment with a newborn until we had enough to move to a two-bedroom. I will never forget the sadness in his eyes when I worked the third shift at a packing plant so that we could save for our house. He would always get a look in his eyes like I wouldn't make it back in the morning, my hour commute on the late-night roads causing him deep concern.

I love my husband and he loves me, but in truth, it has never felt like a Philip kind of love, just a bountiful concession that I am grateful for and at peace with.

Maybe it was the innocence. Maybe it's because Philip was the first boy who spoke to my heart. Maybe it's because of the way we ended, the betrayal of best friend and first love. I'm not certain, only that suddenly a fifteen-year-old's heart has taken up residence inside this forty-six-year-old body and all I want to know now is why Philip came to my house, alone.

The phone rings. Before I can think to pick up the cordless on my desk, the shrill stops. I wait three seconds to hear *"Mom, the phone"* but it does not come. Once upon a time most of the calls to my house had been for me, but those days have vanished with my daughter Aaron not only discovering herself, but being *discovered*.

She has reached the point where both girlfriends and boys search her out like a heat-seeking missile. She has reached a stage where her presence in their life is a mandate. So often is the phone for her, so many times I've had to insist she get off so that I can get on, I've considered getting her her own line.

But I resist that notion. It would give up a power I struggle to maintain on her on a daily basis. Still a part of me wishes my good friend Lisa were calling. I need to share what has occurred in my home not twenty minutes ago. I need to let go of the new fears that bitter the inside of my mouth like new pennies.

I need to flesh out all the whys that I try not to consider as the feel of Philip pressed against me remains.

Sunset is but a few minutes away.

Dinner has been eaten, my daughters are in the midst of their chores and I take my glass of after-dinner ice tea and head for my backyard. A warm early evening, the humidity is low and the sky is streaked in royal colors.

I gaze up at the sky, feel the coming darkness creeping closer and light a Salem. I hear the side door bang close, turn my head and in a few seconds, see it's Emory.

He swats an arm before he reaches me, pats his neck as he sits down. "They're not biting you?" he asks nonplused.

"Off!" I say, lifting the plastic bottle from besides my chair. I hand it over. Watch as he steps away from me, sprays himself from neck to sandaled feet. He sits next to me, smelling of sweet insect spray. I take another drag on my cigarette.

"Chelsea wants to know when we are coming up."

Chelsea is his sister. She lives in Westchester County. Every summer for the past six, we've spent a week up there. What had once been pleasure now feels like drudgery. "I don't know." I feel his stare.

"You want to go?"

I look at him. "Do you?" His answer comes through his eyes. "We always go though."

"Yeah, I know, but the lake's been condemned and she's gotten rid of the horses. What else is there?"

That his sister lives in a place that has a lake in its backyard and once held a stable of six horses doesn't surprise me. Chelsea had always been driven that way. She married into money and when the man behind the pockets left her, she kept the house.

"She is expecting us," I say, comforted in knowing Emory doesn't want to make the trip either.

"I know."

"And it's not like Kent is still there." I look off, new emotions touching me. "She's in that big old house, all by herself."

"Nobody told her to move all the way up there in no-man's land." He considers me. "Besides, you don't want to go anyway."

I chuckle, at ease revealing my heart. "You're right. There's no relaxing. All those rooms off limits, all those things you're not supposed to touch."

Emory joins in my laughter. "Couldn't even bring myself to take a crap in her bathroom. I'm always constipated by the time we got back. What kind of thing is that? Afraid to take a dump in your own sister's bathroom?"

"Well, Chelsea is different."

Emory looks off, nods his head. Reaches for my hand and I allow him to take it, my thoughts everywhere but with him.

Aaron is sweeping the floor as we come in through the kitchen. We step over the minute mound of kitchen droppings and make our way into the slight hall. Emory heads for the living room, I for my attic. I feel a need to unwind and decide on a few games of computer solitaire.

I click on lights, turn on my compact stereo, listen as music fills my workspace. I light another cigarette and have just requested a new game when Aaron appears.

"I'm going to run over to Keisha's."

I look at the clock. See it is nearly nine-thirty. "You have to be back by ten. It's nine-thirty now."

"I know, I just got to tell her something."

"Ten, Aaron, not a minute later."

A smile lights her face like sunshine and then she is heading back down the steps. I hear the front door bang shut, wondering what news she wishes to share that cannot be told over the phone.

Aaron and I have never been close. She has a deeper connection to her father. Monet is my child, the one who still looks to me for comfort. Just twelve, Monet is still in many ways a child. As I take my mouse and click a black jack onto a red queen, I wonder if becoming a teenager will change Monet. If moving into the next step of her life will take her away from mine.

Morning comes as it often does this time of the year, hot, bright and sunny. I hear Emory moving around our bedroom and I nestle deeper into the bed. I do not have to look at the clock to know it's just a little after seven. I find myself grateful that the commute my husband makes everyday is no longer mine.

I have a proposal I need to finish, but I have the luxury of making my own time. A kiss lands on my forehead. I open my eyes, see Emory hovering. "Have a good day," I say as he heads out of the bedroom, and I stretch my legs wide across the queen-size mattress. In no time sleep claims me. When I awake, it is past ten.

I know what I have to do but can't seem to get it done. Like riding a bike, I know the motion, the balance, what amount of energy I need to exert, but I just can't seem to get myself started.

I am up in my office. My Gateway computer sits before me silent and efficient and I've clicked off the game of solitaire five minutes ago but that's as far as I've gotten and I need to get started on the proposal for Leaders, Inc.

I know I can do this and have done this, but today I'm distracted and not up to the challenge. A day has passed since Philip's surprise visit and like a stray cat in need of sustenance, I keep shooing away the thought of him. My deadline is two days away and I'm not even halfway finished. I must get into my superwoman mode, but today the costume is a poor fit.

The phone rings once, twice and then there is silence. *For Aaron,* I think as I pick up my cup of cold coffee, take a quick sip. I glance at my ashtray and see it's overflowing. There is a slight gnawing at my temple and I know head pain is on its way.

I sit back and take a reading, debating whether to pop an Advil or go for the superdrug Imitrex. I suffer from both headaches and migraines, though a bad headache is a bad headache no matter what it's called. Advil does nothing for a migraine, and Imitrex does nothing for a headache. I have to figure out which one is coming.

I rise from my desk, click off the light and descend the stairs. The bathroom door is closed and I rap on it slightly. Hear "Justa men-net" and know Monet is in there. I hear the toilet flush, the hiss of air freshener and seconds later Monet is before me with wide eyes. I have her by a good two inches and I think of her as I always have—my little girl. I probe her face and her gaze shifts away, full of secrets. I just hope it's not a bad one I think as I enter, look around and see nothing out of place.

I catch my own reflection in the mirror. See the dark brown hair, the sensible eyes. I turn sideways trying to catch my profile. I am trying to see myself as I must have appeared as a teenager and wonder if I had known myself then as I do now, how would my life have been?

Different is the only answer I can find.

"Mom, can I go to the mall?"

I look upon my oldest daughter, see her father's thin build and my grandmother's eyes. I see the edgy desperation that cuts her cheeks into sharp edges and the slight twitch of her fingers.

"The mall." It is not a question.

Her face screws, braids rustle. "Yeah, Mom, the *mall.*"

My next question is as automatic as breathing. "Who's going?"

"Me, Paula, Keisha, Monifa and J'Qaun and dem."

J'Qaun and dem is what draws her. J'Qaun and dem are the boys who circle my daughter and her friends like wolves around a fresh kill. J'Qaun and dem are the wannabe roughnecks who have dictated my daughter's life since the summer started. A hard rock of a boy, he fills me with mistrust.

"The mall," I say again, giving Aaron a chance to tell me the truth. My eyes are steady on her. She squirms under the gaze.

"Yeah, well, you know," she says.

"No, I don't," I insist. "So where are you really going, Aaron?" I have played this hand a dozen times with her. At fifteen she is still too young to know how to win.

"To the mall, Mom, I swear."

"And *after?*"

"We was gonna hang out at the park."

My eyes narrow, my lips purse. I feel as I'm certain my mother did when I tried to tell a half-truth, insulted. "Let me get this straight. You and your friends are going to go all the way to the mall to hang out at the park?" She hears the absurdity; her excitement vanishes. She knows she is caught. "No, you can't go to the mall because you're lying and I know it." Guilt rushes her cheeks, and I thank God it does. "So you get on the phone and you call Keisha and Monifa and Paula and J'Qaun *an' dem* and tell them you won't be wherever the hell you thought you were going today. And while you're at it, tell them that you got caught in a lie and for the next two weeks you are grounded. No calls, no visits, nothing, you understand me?"

She looks at me stunned. Cannot believe I have decided this. I look away. Resuming my typing, the clicking of my keys punctuating the air as she vanishes down the attic steps.

A door slams. Voices youthful and excited drift up to my attic window. I hear Monet, Charlette and Ayesha exchanging their views, the latest rap heartthrob, the hub of their conversation.

As much as things change some things remain the same like preteen crushes on people who sing. Jermaine Jackson had been my pinup boy. While Dorothy was gushing over Jackie and even Michael, Jermaine was the Jackson Five I adored.

I bought every single *Tiger Beat* and *Black Beat* magazine that came out, pasting Jermaine's picture on my bedroom walls. I wrote long heartfelt letters in care of Motown praying he would find mine out of the pile and write back. And even when Philip came into my life, I quietly held tight to my Jermaine Jackson fantasy, re-evoking it when Philip left me. To me, in 1972, Jermaine Jackson had been the epitome of fine.

The phone rings. I pick up quickly. It's Keisha. I deliver the bad news. "Aaron can't have phone calls or visits or anything for two weeks. Tell J'Qaun *and dem.*"

Two weeks of punishment in the heart of summer when you're fifteen is the equivalent of being in a box with no air. You just know you're going to die. But Aaron has attempted to lie to me and I will not tolerate it. A bed she has made, she must lie in.

My husband, Emory, is in the backyard, his T-shirt is plastered to his sweaty back and the muscles in his arms strain as he grabs a stubborn weed with both hands. I look out my bedroom window and watch my husband work the yard.

We all come with things, certain gifts, talents, personal joys. Yard work is not one of my husband's simple pleasures, but every now and then he will go out there and tend to those spots I've missed.

Down the hall Ja-Rule slips noisily from behind my daughter's closed door. Despite my reservations about rap music, I am glad to hear Aaron play something other than Alicia Keyes, which had been going nonstop for over an hour.

I used to know Aaron, but in a blink of an eye she is becoming someone else. Never an out-there child, she always preferred the edges of things instead of being in the mix. But this year I've seen the changes.

The tennis she excelled at, the karate she's mastered no longer holds any interest for her. She wants to be a cheerleader and plans to try out when school starts. It is a goal I can see for her, but Emory can't. He sees cheerleading as a girly-girl sport that re-quires no brain and excessive enthusiasm. He's wrong on both fronts.

The cheerleaders I knew in high school were far from airheads.

They were in the top eighty-fifth percentile and went on to receive college degrees. Socially they were invited to the best parties and the short skirts were an instant status maker.

But the very notion clashes with who Emory expected Aaron to become—the next Serena Williams. Without sons to nurture that NBA dream, having a daughter as a Tennis Pro is his next best thing.

We argued about it in the way we always do. I talked, he half-listened; then he talked and I didn't listen at all. I tossed on my silent mode and he gave in, which was the way most of our disagreements went. Still moments come when Emory's foot is firmly planted and his decision becomes law.

I take one last look at my husband, in need of a reconnection. For two days, Philip has ran rapid through my heart and I find myself in need of cleansing. I go to the kitchen and retrieve a plastic tumbler from the cabinet. Into the freezer I go, dropping ice cubes into the cup. I let the tap run for a good thirty seconds and then fill it to the brim. Sipping off the top, I go through the side door and along the house. Emory looks up as I approach, his smile easy as he reaches for the glass. "Must be psychic," he tells me.

The sun is hot. My husband is before me and I relinquish the specter that appeared at my door. Emory downs the water in one long gulp, the bob of his Adam's apple moving. He hands me back the tumbler and my eyes dance.

In one quick motion he takes the work gloves off and his hands circle my waist. I fall into him easy, breathe deeply on his sweat. Without words we head toward the side-door, our bodies thrumming with its own melody, a sonata in the making.

We are in the basement whispering and giddy as children. Above us the sound of Ja-Rule comes muffled through the floor and the blaring of the living room TV drifts down the stairs. We are in the storage room next to the boiler room. An old mattress on the floor is our bed.

We'd discovered this place in need of a refuge away from children. It is where we venture from time to time. Hot, sweaty and on fire, we are deep in our groove when I hear my name being called.

"Mommy?" It is faint, faraway but rings with persistence. I pause, listen, knowing I must find my daughter before she finds me.

I leave the confines of Emory's embrace and fumble into my shorts. No time for a bra, I slip the big T-shirt over my head. My face is flush, my hair, wild. I run fingers through it, use the T-shirt to wipe my brow.

Up the stairs I go, calling out, "Yeah?"

"Telephone." Monet hands me the cordless. Studies me, knowing something is amiss. Her eyes linger another second as I bring the receiver to my ear. Walks away as I say hello.

"Suvie?"

I know the voice even though it has been awhile since I heard it. Despite the civilities we shared at our last meeting, the call takes me by surprise. "Dorothy?"

"Yeah, I know . . . long time."

I nod, look around for my cigarettes and realize I left them in the attic. I will need them for this talk and up the stairs I go. I am on my way when I run into Emory. "Dorothy," I say; then I am gone.

"This may seem like a strange question and believe me, the last thing I want to do is ask it, but have you seen Philip lately?"

"Philip?"

"Yeah, you know. My husband?" Her tone tries to be light, but it fails. It is riddled with fear and hurt. I struggle hard not to connect the dots, but my mind is not that sterile. It is a fertile ground that is fueling thoughts I have no business thinking.

"He did drop by to say hello to me and Em." I add my husband's name as a counterbalance.

"When?"

"What?" I pause as if I don't know the date, the time, what he wore, how he smiled. "Two days ago?"

Her voice is an old dishrag tossed into the sink, flat, near useless. "Well, at least I know he's still living."

"Everything okay?" I don't want to ask the question but it has left me before I could reel it in.

"Just great . . . take care, alright?"

I nod, glad Dorothy has hung up.

* * *

Chapter 7

It is neither early nor late, but the forty-six-year-old woman sits on the edge of her bed, weary to the bone.

She stares at the phone wondering if she has it in her to make another long-distance call, feeling the hurt from the one she's just made. Never in a thousand years did she ever think she'd have to call Sylvia in search of her husband, but Dorothy Butler has.

A little after nine, Dorothy is not ready to climb into the 350-thread-count comfort of her sheets, is not ready to draw the damask comforter over her against the room that is chilled with central air.

Dorothy does not want to retreat to the family room of her three-bedroom ranch in the subdivision thirty miles outside of Atlanta and watch TV. Dorothy Butler wants to hop a plane.

She wants to take a week from work and go to New York and track down her husband. She wants him to call her, full of apology and professing a love she knows he's never felt. She wants to hold fast to the myths of which she's carved her life. Wants to believe it will sustain a future.

But it's been four days since she's talked to her husband, seven since he announced he was going to New York. His reason for going—*Because I have to*—feels as vague as when he first said it but in his absence, Dorothy knows.

Her mind conjures up moments her soul cannot bear. Fear grabs her every time she goes to the mailbox, afraid to confront end-of-the-line papers, handwritten or legally drawn.

Philip, the stout Catholic at eighteen has grown into a lapsed one at forty-seven. Divorce does exists in his vocabulary. Dorothy knows because he has uttered it too many times.

Yet for all the times Philip talked of leaving her, he never did. Until now.

Gone for days; calls to his parents house go unanswered. Still Dorothy knows he is there. Back to what he physically left behind but could not leave emotionally. Back to Sylvia.

Those many years back when Dorothy schemed, planned and deceived, she knew where Philip's heart lay. When she put her mouth on him that first time, when they lay in the illicit darkness of his basement, when she lied about being pregnant and lied again about having lost the child, she knew.

Dorothy had known when she had traveled all those miles on the Greyhound from New York to Atlanta after her high school graduation and there had been no joy in his eyes at first look. Knew when they settled into a routine of being married, working hard together, struggling to reach the pinnacle of middle-class dreams, she knew.

Knew and had hope. Knew and dared to dream that one day Philip would love her.

For thirty years she has been waiting but as four days of no contact heads slowly into five, she has no faith that arrival will ever come.

Chapter 8

My proposal for Leaders, Inc., is finished. I've called Dehlila the director and let her know I'm dropping it off and to make sure my check is ready. Freed up for the next two months, I can kick back, have some real leisure time and enjoy the rest of the summer.

I head down the stairs, decide on a shower when I hear retching coming from behind the bathroom door. I knock hard. "Aaron?"

"No."

"Monet?"

It is a while before she answers. "Yeah."

"You okay?"

Her voice is whiny. Scared. "Yeah."

"Are you sick?"

"No."

"Why are you throwing up?" I hear spitting, the sound of the toilet flushing. Soon after water is running and there is the hiss of air spray. I wait for the door to open to stare into my twelve-year-old's face.

It seems a hundred years before she's appearing, her eyes full of secrets, the rims red as if she's been crying. But I know it is the strain of vomiting that has tinted them. We stare at each other and in the silence an unnamed guilt finds me. I don't know what I am guilty of, but it is something dire. I reach out my hand, feel her forehead. It's warm but not hot. "Is your stomach upset?"

"No."

"Well, what is it?"

She looks at me like she has never looked at me before. Her eyes are dancing with anger and outrage before she looks away. "It's nothing, Mom."

But I know in my gut it's something.

My life goes from the slow lazy day I had planned to a fast for-wardness of loading up both of my daughters into my car, racing over to Leaders, Inc., dropping off the grant proposal and picking up my fee.

Then it's off to the bank where I wait on the long line to deposit my four thousand-dollar check, Aaron and Monet sullen and quiet on the red Naugahyde bench. Soon after I am at the medical cen-ter waiting an hour to see Doctor Medici, the children's pediatri-cian. I am not allowed in the examination room, and it is only when Monet is dressed and sent to the waiting room, am I allowed in.

I sit before her doctor, gut twisting, thinking horrible thoughts. Doctor Medici smiles at me, moves a slip of shiny black hair be-hind one ear. "Not pregnant."

I find my breath.

"Hymen still intact."

I want to weep. I want to throw my arms around Doctor Medici, but my calm starts to slip as she takes a breath. "But she's bulimic."

Someone has hit me in the head with a sledgehammer.

"A check of her throat shows that she has been engaging in this for sometime. I'd say at least since May."

It is July.

Bulimic. That was for young white girls with Barbie doll com-plexes. My daughter is black and never even had a Barbie. I shake my head not wanting to believe it.

"You didn't notice anything different about her?"

I shake my head again.

"Well, from the last time she was here, she's dropped ten pounds."

That much I knew. Was glad for her. Monet's a bit roly-poly.

"She's conscious of her weight. Feels like that's why boys don't like her."

My brow raises. I am furious. "She's only twelve."

"And girls are getting boyfriends and having sex by age ten. It's different, Mrs. Allen. It's not like when you and I were young." I nod absently. "So what I want to do is to get her a referral for a specialist. Someone she can talk to, share things with."

Someone not like me, I think as the day slips away and disappears into a void.

In my head is a list. I am trying to remember all the do's and don'ts as we sit at the kitchen table. Both daughters and my husband looked at me like I was crazy when I told them this was where we'd be eating all our meals—at the table and together. We are not a table-gathering family. We normally get our plates and drift off to wherever a free TV is available. The girls eat in their room, Emory in the kitchen and sometimes I take meals in the living room. The only time we gather as a family is when company comes.

I have told no one what Doctor Medici told me. Not Emory, not Aaron and certainly not Monet. I say that something did not agree with her stomach and that's why she threw up. I am grateful Monet allows me this lie.

I will tell Emory later when the children are asleep. I will have to take him to our secret place to do so. I know his reaction. He will not want to believe. Will want to storm off to Monet's messy room and confront her, which isn't the way to go.

She did not ask for this illness and doesn't even know why she has it. As much as I want to shake her, scream at her, beat her into oblivion at this moment as she wolfs down her food faster than anyone ever would, I can't.

In a blink of an eye she's finished, her plate empty of the tiniest food. She is halfway through the doorway when I call her back. She turns, chipmunk cheeks full, mouth in fast motion.

"You didn't ask permission to leave, number one, and number two, the new rule is that no one leaves the table until the last person is finished." I am making this up as I go. I myself cannot see sitting here, staring at my empty plate while Aaron leisurely finishes her meal. She is always the last one, the wise one I am thinking as Monet comes back to the table, color draining from her face.

"Since when?" Emory wants to know, his own helping nearly gone. I give him a look, part begging, part threat. It is the secret code between parents, but often Emory misses the signal, like now as he stares at me without a clue.

"Since now," I insist returning to my last forkful of Kraft Macaroni and Cheese and pot roast. The collards have long ago vanished and I know I could go for seconds. But I don't want to show greed so I put the last of my food in my mouth eyeing the slowness with which Aaron eats.

We all stare at her, my newest rule leaving us anxious for her to finish. Aaron looks up. Stops chewing. "What?" We look away. I sip the rest of my Kool-Aid. Emory picks meat out of his teeth and Monet sits eyeing the doorway as if it were her last friend in the world.

Rule number two: Do not try to intervene until she has begun therapy.

As much as I want to knock on the door as the sound of my daughter's retching drifts through, I know I can't. I hear the same ritual spitting, the flushing, the spraying. I hear it in a way I've never heard it before.

Since May, the doctor has told me, but somehow I never noticed. Somehow I paid no attention to how much Monet always went to the bathroom right after she ate. I certainly never heard her throwing up.

But it is no longer a secret and perhaps she no longer feels the need to do it quietly because I know now. I'm not sure, only that I hear water run. I turn and hurry down the hall to my room, easing the door shut.

Emory looks up from his baseball game, his eyes full of concern. "What's going on?"

As much as I want to tell him, shift the burden to stronger shoulders, I have to wait. My eyes dance with lies. "A family that eats together stays together," I say.

He dismisses my rhetoric. Goes back to the game. *My nutty wife,* he thinks. I'm in no position to disagree.

* * *

Monet is a night owl. It seems forever before she finally falls off to sleep. I stand in her doorway watching for movement. See none. I leave her and go check on Aaron. She sleeps flat on her back, thighs and arms spread. Her nightshirt has risen to her hips. I stare at the body that her sister never owned. At fifteen Aaron is still coltish and lean. Little hips, high derriere, "perky" breasts. Though I too once had "perky" breasts, I was never as lithe as Aaron is.

Monet has genes from my father's side of the family. At twelve, her chest is somewhat flat but her hips are fleshy and round and her behind is a wide rumpled affair.

While Aaron runs around in booty-cutter shorts and tight knit tops that show her belly button, Monet prefers the loose baggy look. I wonder if having a sister so trim could force her into throwing up. Or is it simply what the doctor suggested, she thinks she's too fat for boys?

Videos don't help.

Not Ashanti or Shakira, slim-waisted vixens with enough sex appeal to heat the world. Where does my daughter fit into such pictures?

We tried to get Monet active. We enrolled her with her sister into tennis and karate, but Monet never got into the swing or the joy of it and stopped. But I know we have to find something for her. Something fun and athletic, a thought I hold onto as I shake Emory from his sound sleep.

Emory is staring at Monet. It is Saturday, four days from Monet's appointment with the eating disorder specialist. Emory believes in family and when things go wrong all he wants to do is fix it and fast. Unfortunately, this is one problem that could take years, if then.

In my heart I believe Monet can come through this, but that's just a mother's love talking. I'm supposed to believe in miracles and the impossible when it comes to my children. I am supposed to be their number-one cheerleader, fighting back the naysayers who don't have the faith.

But my faith fades as Monet forces Frosted Flakes and milk into her gullet, then brings the bowl to her lips to drink the remainder. Aaron rolls her eyes, but that is nothing new. Eye rolling seems to be a permanent station in my daughter's life.

Emory's mouth opens and he stares at Monet like she is a stranger. She starts out of her chair, stops. Her eyes find mine. "Can I be excused?" I nod, hold my breath as she dumps her bowl in the sink and leaves. The slam of the bathroom door rings down the hall.

Emory rises; I place my hand on his wrist. Shake my head. Aaron watches us, deciphering things. After a few seconds, she shakes her head and goes back to her cereal, a *Vibe* magazine at her side.

I have relayed the list, the rules, the do's and the don'ts, but Emory is ignoring most of them. We are at the track at the junior high school. I am sitting on the bench and Emory is beside me. Our eyes are on Monet as she walks. Emory is embittered with her and no matter how much I tell him to whisper, his angry voice slices the air.

"She's not fat," he is insisting.

"I never said she was. She feels she is and that's the problem."

"I mean she ain't no string bean like Aaron, but she is not obese."

I agree. From where we sit, Monet just looks a little pudgy. I figure fifteen pounds would do her good. Twenty-five would have her in her sister's clothes, but I would take her just as she is if she would stop purging.

We have been here for forty-five minutes, although Emory promised no more than thirty. He told Monet that as a family we were going to get fit, but he might as well have shouted that he knew she was throwing up everything she ate because the expression on her face had been the same—terror.

Her eyes had danced to mine as if I had told (which I had) and that *I hate you* look seared my soul. When Monet told her father she didn't want to, he slapped her.

Pop! Just like that, his hand against her soft brown cheek. Monet was stunned. Tears moved down her face at an incredible rate. My mouth hung open as I stared at the man who rarely strikes out. Moments came when he didn't hesitate, still this morning caught him off-guard, and he fumbled for words, drawing back a pace but not enough to change his mind.

"I'm sorry, Monie . . . didn't mean to hit you . . . but we're still going." It was the quietest walk we ever took. Me walking fast, Monet struggling to keep up and Emory somewhere behind us. I hated him in that moment. Hated Mr. Fix-It. Hated him for betraying my daughter and my trust, for his ignorance in thinking he could cure what her own mother could not.

I wanted to scream at him that this trip to the track was just a waste of time, that he had not made anything better just worse. I wanted to shout that if walking was all it took, we'd be out here five hours a day, that he was an asshole, but instead I walked fast.

I refused to join them as he put Monet through her paces. Jumped off the bench a couple of times as Monet implored me with her eyes to come and save her. I felt a rush of relief when Emory broke off and sat. But my ease was short-lived as Monet, mouth open and sweat pouring, kept on walking.

I was ready to snatch my child, take her home and lock my husband out of the house. I was so angry at Emory I moved to another bench. She had been at lap three when I decided that was enough.

I shouted to her to call it a day, but she shook her head at me, mouthed the word *no* and kept on walking. Her pace increased some and she no longer looked ready for a stroke. That's when Emory came over, placed his hand on mine and softly said, "Let her be, Suvie."

That had been two laps ago. And despite my anger, my reservation and my fears, Monet seems to be holding her own. There is a seriousness to her face, a raw determination that says she's going to do this, which fills me with both fear and admiration.

She quits on her seventh and I resist the urge to hold her as she comes up to us, face flushed and sweaty, a single question in her eye. *Did I do good, Daddy?* Emory smiles, opens his arms to her, giving her all the answer she needs.

I extend the bottle of water, but she ignores it for the embrace of her father.

"Ready?" I say, breaking the silence, their sweet joy.

* * *

Back home I shower and change into a denim jumper. I tell Emory I will be back later and kiss him good-bye. Into my Eclipse I go and head toward Lisa's house. I blast my music, roll down my windows and let the hot summer day in.

I navigate down the street, urging my car ahead of a bus and switch lanes. I turn onto the boulevard, under an overpass and make a right. At the corner I make a left and ease to a stop. Lisa's son, Kelvin, is in the yard cutting the grass. He is tall and lean like his father, but that's where the similarities end.

I open the gate and he pauses from his yard work. He is shirtless and I see muscles where baby fat used to live. He and Aaron are the same age and where I see a fine young man, Aaron says he's not her type. Too bad, I think as he speaks to me, proper and full of good English.

"Hello, Aunt Suvie."

"Hey, Kelvin, how you doing?"

His smile is infectious. "I'm doing okay."

"Mommy home?"

He nods. "Yeah, she's inside."

I make my way up the stone pebble steps. Rap on the dusty screen door and peer inside. The smell of cooking food drifts toward me.

"Lee-sah," I call out, stepping into the living room. "Where you at?"

A head appears. It is the same pecan face, the same tiny features that I have known for all these years. "Suvie, come on in. I was just getting out of the shower."

I take a seat on her couch, pick up the photo album, ecru with age. It is her wedding album and I flip through the book, Lisa's joy filling the pages. I come across my own face, the floor-length mint green chiffon gown a hoot. Back then it had been the fashion; now it seems dated and frou-frou.

I sense motion to my left, turn my head and see Mack. "How you doing, Suvie?"

My eyes peel away. "Doing okay, Mack." We never liked each other.

With a towel around his waist and nothing else on, he has just told me business I don't even want to know about. I look out the front window and see Kelvin hard at work with the mower, hear Lisa say she'll be out in just a sec.

We are in the backyard. While the season has been dry, the wasps and bees seem to be thriving. I have jumped screaming from my chair four times already since I sat down. "They ain't studying you," Lisa insists, a hickey the size of a quarter on her neck. Once such a thing was cause célèbres; now it seems juvenile and outdated.

We sit, the expanse of a hundred-year old oak providing us deep shade. I look at Lisa's life and see a thousand faults, but her child is an honor student who, despite an irresponsible dad, is growing up right. Whereas my child, my baby, is suffering from an illness that you only hear about on TV or in some article.

Still the need to share presses me into a corner and while hope did live for a little while when Monet clocked off seven laps around the track, after lunch she was right back in the bathroom throwing up.

It comes out of me in a rush. "Monet's bulimic."

"Ba what?"

"Lee-mick," I offer.

"Is that the thing white girls do where they throw up what they eat?"

I nod, add, "Not just white girls."

She is stunned like I am. Babies stopped happening for Lisa after Kelvin. She always had an affection for Monet. "Why?"

I look away. I've got a half-baked theory, but I don't want to put it out there unless I get the information certified. "She thinks she's fat."

Lisa pulls back in disgust. "She ain't fat. A little chubby, yes, but she's just twelve." How many times have I said that? Just twelve. Some magic number that's supposed to keep bad things and serious situations away. But twelve is no different than ten and not too far from fourteen nowadays. Anything can happen to a twelve-year-old and does. "How did you find out?"

"Heard her throwing up and took her to the doctor. Doctor says she's been doing it since May."

"May? That's a long time." I see it in Lisa's eyes. The same thing that showed in Doctor Medici's and my own husband's: Where have you been? What has been going on in your life that you didn't even notice your own daughter running off to the bathroom every time she eats? I can not dispute their judgment. I may have been an at-home mother, but up in my attic I might as well have been commuting to and from Manhattan.

"I knew she had lost some weight, but I figured it was because she was heading toward teenhood. I didn't know it was because she was sticking her finger down her throat. Now it's all I know," My eyes drift in memory. "As soon as the last morsel is in her mouth, she's off throwing up."

"Still?"

"It's not like I can stop her. I mean, until we see the doctor on Wednesday I just have to let her be."

"Like hell, Suvie. That's *your* daughter. You run the roost." Lisa shakes her head, her face is full of disgust. "I'd beat her ass till she wouldn't even think about throwing up it if she were my child."

"You can't beat an illness out of nobody," I implore.

"Illness? Illness is getting a cold or having a ruptured spleen. Throwing up ain't no disease."

I'm stunned. I look at Lisa with hurt eyes. It takes a second or two for her to look away. She will not apologize and it's all I want. I want her to take back what she said about my daughter, about her "Monie," but the endless silence says she is not budging.

I stand. "Better be on my way."

"I'll walk you to the door."

I stop her. "No, it's alright." I make my way through the kitchen. I bypass Mack still in the towel reading the paper in his easy chair. I force myself to say good-bye.

I move down the front door steps and watch Kelvin rake grass clippings. Our eyes lock; mine's full of pity.

His dark eyes drink it in as I smile. I want to hug him, take him away from here. I want to be the parent his own seem incapable of being. But he is perfect and my own children are not. The thought is midnight blue around me.

Chapter 9

I have not allowed my thoughts to consume me. I have been forcibly pushing them away. But this morning they gather like the pelts of rain hitting the kitchen window. They collide and mix, making slick trails of wetness against my mind.

It has been six days since Philip. Four since Dorothy called. I can't help but wonder if she had found him yet. Cannot help but wonder about his ability not to let his wife know his whereabouts.

I sit at my kitchen table chastising myself for thinking about anything but Monet. My child is where every single thought I possess should lay. My daughter struck with a severe illness should be the only thought roaming my brain. But it isn't.

A wind is riding shotgun with the rain, shaking the trees and moving plastic garbage cans up and down the street. I turn the page of the *New York Newsday* and try to find my own bit of quiet in a house that is already hushed. It is the absence of noise that disturbs me. No TV, no radio, no voices, just the hiss of the wind-driven rain.

I remember such days from my youth, early September, late April, rainy mornings when I didn't want to leave my bed even though there were places I had to be. I remember promising myself that when I became an adult I would live a life so I wouldn't have to. I'd be rich or so self-supporting that leaving a warm bed on such a drowsy morning would be an option, not the rule.

I have the luxury now but hardly sleep past seven. I find myself always up doing something, into some niche that needs my presence whether it's the cleaning of a cluttered basement or simply sitting and filling my empty belly with caffeine.

Today is the type of day I want to be by myself, to disappear from the world and just be. I read the paper, smoke cigarettes and finish my coffee. I come across the movie section and see ads for four movies that make me want to drive out into the rain.

I look out into the world gone gray and think back to who I was going to be—a New York University graduate living in the East Village driving a '74 orange Volkswagen Beetle and making my life as a graphic artist. I was going to become one of those artsy folk, wearing long Indian cotton skirts, peasant blouses and tons of Aztec jewelry. I was going to become a white girl within my own black skin.

That dream died when my life with Philip did, broken under failing grades that obliterated my New York University dream. By the time I graduated, my A average had taken a real pounding and though I managed an eighty-six, there were far too many students that year who did better.

Regrets. I have no use for them. I check the movie timetable, my fallout with Lisa in me. Who will forgive whom I wonder as I look up at the clock and shout to my daughters that we are going to the movies later.

Aaron doesn't want to go, but I ignore her protests. There is no way I am going to leave her in the house alone for three hours when she has not seen her friends or J'Qaun *an dem* in days.

"Twenty-six fifty."

I hand over two twenties, look down at the counter filled with two buttered popcorns, a box of Raisinettes, one Malt Balls, three Cokes, a hot dog and an order of nachos with cheese. Monet grabs the Malt Balls and stuffs them into her pocket book. Aaron picks up a soda and a popcorn. I ask for a tray and put the rest of the snacks inside the flimsy cardboard holder.

I have just handed over the tickets when Aaron squeals, delighted and surprised. I see Keisha running our way. Watch as she and Aaron embrace. Her eyes find mine, but my answer is ready.

"No."

The whine. "But, Mom."

My voice drops to a hiss. "You are still on punishment and the answer is no." I move toward the theater, Monet at my side, Aaron somewhere behind us. I pause when I get to the door and wait. She is talking in solemn whispers with Keisha. I count to ten in my head and then call out to her. "Come on, Aaron, let's go."

They hug again, reluctant to part. They have been best friends since grade school. It will be ten more days before they will see each other. Keisha puts her thumb toward her ear, her pinky toward her mouth. Aaron nods and drifts away.

There are always loopholes I realize as the three of us enter the darkened theater. Unless I set up watch, there is no real way for me to know when Aaron is off the phone or on.

The music swells to near ear-shattering levels. Monet rises from her seat. I grab her arm, ask where she is going. "Bathroom," she tells me as she steps on my toes in her haste. My head follows her until she slips through the doorway. Only then do I look away, Aaron's stare like a coal fire beside me.

The rain has stopped by the time we leave the theater. Everything is sparkly and wet. A tight dampness hangs in the air and the stretch of the Long Island Expressway is divided into two lines, one full of red lights, the other full of white.

We move through the parking lot toward my car. Monet is beside me, Aaron behind. The smell of vomit finds me. Monet's appointment is two days away and I know all the dos and don'ts, but I've had enough. I stop her, grab her arm, peer into her face, my voice both soft and intense. "You got to stop, Monet." She looks at me blinking. "You're hurting yourself more than you are helping. You can't go on throwing up."

"She wants to be me."

The voice arrives phantom quick. I turn and stare at my oldest child. "She can't be you," I turn back to Monet. My words do not soothe her; the indifference of her sister no doubt hurts her. She breaks away from me and hurries to the car.

Aaron shrugs my way. "Can't help it if she's fat."

I resist the urge to smack her.

I have decided not to wait for a stranger to help mend my family. I have decided to bring the matter to the forefront. We all sit around the kitchen table: me, Monet and Aaron. I am trying to do two things at once and feel incapable of either. I want to lay ground rules and dispel skeletons. I am halfway there when Aaron says that she's known forever that Monet was upchucking. That Monet started throwing up when she asked some boy named Kareem if he liked her and Kareem told her she was too fat to be liked.

"Mom, I told her he was way too young and stupid to know better." Aaron's eyes are wide, exasperated. "Ain't no real boys at twelve anyway," she adds. My mouth doesn't work for a minute. I sit back digesting what Aaron has told me, the things I had been clueless about. I am surprised that something so severe never made it to my ears. That Aaron did not bother to mention it to me at all. That somehow she has deemed herself High Mistress of Little Sisterhood and decided it wasn't worth telling me.

I ask Aaron to leave us alone. She goes willingly.

I lower my head, sigh. Look up, unable to offer the briefest of smiles. "Hate to admit it, but your sister is right, you know. At twelve, boys are too young and too stupid to know anything, especially the worth of a pretty little girl like you." My words surprise her. I can tell by the way her eyes widen. I make myself go on, struggling to find hope for her. "I know it seems like a lifetime before you'll have a boy who likes you, but it's so not true, Monet, and you're not fat. Not skinny like Aaron, but you're not fat."

"Yeah, I am."

"You're not, but that's not even the real issue, sweetheart. You want to know what the real issue is?"

Her eyes seek mine. "What?"

"The real issue is not how you look but who you are. People like you for what they see in you, and that stupid boy saw such an awesome power it scared him. Boys do that; they get scared easy. Men too sometimes."

"Daddy?"

I chuckle, relieving the tension thick in the room. "Of course. It's like when God made them, he put in a panic button. Something seems too good to be true to them, they high-tail. Run. Say stupid things, but it's never about you, it's always about them."

She looks away. I've lost her again. I press on. "Look at me. According to the U.S. government I am thirty-five pounds over-weight . . . can I wear a string bikini or show my belly button like Aaron does? No. But does your father love me? Yes."

I feel her thoughts. Know she thinks I am the exception and she is the rule. I have managed the brass ring, but she can't even get up on the horse. "Monie, there's a lot you don't know about life and won't know until you learn it. Right now your whole world is about getting skinny enough for some boy to like you. But you should never have to change to please someone else. And there's so much more to life."

"Like what?"

I draw back, form words in my head. "Like who you want to be. What you want to do." Her head dips. My words are gibberish to her. "Some girls get noticed at twelve. Others at fourteen. Regardless, boys will start noticing you."

She looks at me with earnest eyes. At least the possibility that I know what I'm talking about is there. "But you never ever ask a boy if he likes you. You'll scare them. And when they get scared, they say dumb stuff like 'no cause you too fat to be liked.' If he likes you, he's gonna let you know."

She looks away, frowns her face. "I didn't really like Kareem. I just wanted a boyfriend."

My gut twists. "You will one day, without asking or anything. One day he'll just be there."

"I don't want to throw up anymore."

I reach for her and hold her tight. "I know you don't."

"But now it's like my stomach don't want anything in it and I have to get it out."

"Just your mind playing tricks, Monie. Your stomach wants the food, needs the food. Your body needs it to keep you strong and healthy."

Her eyes implore me for an answer. "How do I stop?"

"We'll find a way," I say, Wednesday unable to get here fast enough.

Emory eases out of his T-shirt, searches the dresser drawer for a clean one. I am watching him without being too obvious about it. I am studying him trying to determine what changes twenty-one years have brought. Gone is the flat hard stomach, the svelte muscles that used to be his arms and chest. Bits of gray seduce his temples and he no longer seems as tall. Eyes that I had considered nondescript have grown deep with age and his chin that I once considered cartoon-character sharp, has softened into something more giving.

"No more T-shirts?"

"Try the middle drawer."

He does, pulling out a white V neck. "How the day go?"

The real question is, Is Monet still throwing up. "We went to the movies. Aaron told me she knew what Monie was doing and why."

His eyes find mine. "Why?"

"Boys."

"Boys?"

"Well, one boy. Monie asked him if he liked her and he said no because she was too fat."

"What?"

I nod my head, in the same place Emory is. "I know. She's just twelve." I pause. "We talked. I told her that she wasn't fat and what the fool boy said was more about himself than her."

"Let me get this straight. My child is tossing her cookies because she wants a boy to like her so bad that she asks some knucklehead and he tells her no because she's fat?"

"Yeah."

"Jesus."

"At least we know why, Em. At least we know why." The guilt glides from my shoulders. I am not to blame.

"When's her appointment?"

"Wednesday."

My husband thinks a minute, nods, gets into bed and reaches for the remote.

Aaron fixes a bowl of cereal and plops into the chair. She must have finished her magazine because a book is beside her now. In that regard she is my child.

Eating and reading. I'm not sure how this habit got started, but I have been doing it for years. It's as if I can't digest food without the aid of written words. I am turning the page of the newspaper when Monet appears.

"Morning," she manages, going to the refrigerator and opening the door. She stands there, frosty white air drifting pass her before she decides to close it. In the freezer she searches, pulling out a pack of frozen waffles. Aaron and I watch Monet, a case study in her own home. To the toaster she goes, dropping in the frozen breakfast cakes. She turns, unaware of our stares and retrieves butter, syrup. A plate, a knife and a fork.

I look away knowing what will come next, look away with sick anticipation. There will be the wolfing down of her food, the sound of the bathroom door closing and the echo of retching that will enter my heart like a knife.

Chapter 10

Tuesday arrives slowly, in no hurry to make way for Wednesday. I go to bed early and toss and turn for a while. Tomorrow is my daughter's appointment with the doctor. Tomorrow she reveals her heart to a stranger.

I am not sure when I finally fall off to sleep, only that it is sometime past midnight. But this time frame has no meaning to my mind as sleep finally comes, and I find myself in the middle of a dream so real, I can feel warm asphalt against the soles of my feet.

I am standing on my old block. I have on clothes, but my feet are bare. There is a car parked and it is filled with things. I see a bunch of faces inside and understand that they are all going on a camping trip.

"You coming?"

I turn and see Philip half in-half out of the driver's seat. His question takes me by surprise. I take a second to say yes and run toward the passenger door. My hand is nearly to the handle before the car speeds off.

I stand in the street barefoot and in disbelief. If only I had moved a little faster. If only there wasn't so much stuff packed inside. If only he had waited.

If only.

I wake up. My eyes are wider than beacons; my heart thrums in my chest. I can still see Philip from my dream, standing there asking me if I was coming. I look at the clock and see it's a little after two in the morning. I am wired and no longer sleepy. I leave the bedroom and go up to my workspace. I search through my junk box and find what I have not looked at in years. There are five of them neatly tied together with a slip of old white ribbon. Their edges have turned ecru and I am careful as I slip them from their holder.

My eyes drift toward the stairs, see it silent and empty. I am in the midst of something illicit and my heart is beating fast. I search the envelopes and find the one that has drawn me. June 23, 1973, says the postmark—three decades ago.

For a moment I feel foolish, desperate. I know the words no longer hold magic, but I cannot prevent myself from taking the walk back in time. Carefully I ease the one-page letter from its encasement. But I cannot open it.

Go to bed, Suvie.

I slip the letter back into the envelope, retie the slip of ribbon around all five of them. I slip them back into my junk box, rise from the chair, click off the light and head back down the stairs to my bedroom and my husband, fast asleep and ignorant of my heart.

Morning comes too soon. The alarm goes off with shattering clarity and the thick slumber I found myself in dissipates into a wakefulness that feels raw. I look over and see Emory getting out of bed. I roll over and go back to sleep.

I awaken an hour later and ease out of bed, make my way toward the bathroom and find it occupied. I knock.

"Yeah?"

"Aaron?"

"No."

"Monet?" Something is plopping into the toilet. Something heavy and wet. "Are you throwing up?"

Her response is strained. "No."

"Then what are you doing?"

"Moving my bow-wills."

"You got the runs?"

"Yeah."

"Cramps?"

"Yeah." Her tone is irritated. Leave me alone, it says.

I stand outside the door, my own bladder ready to burst. The toilet flushes, the bathroom door opens and the smell of feces drifts past me into the hall. Monet looks pale. I feel her forehead. It's warm but not hot.

"How's your stomach now?"

"Better." Her eyes drift from mine.

"Did you eat anything this morning?"

She nods.

"What?"

"Milk and cereal." Maybe the milk has gone bad. "I don't feel good. Can I go lay down?"

"Lay down? You have a doctor's appointment."

"But my stomach is hurting."

My bladder starts to ache. "Let me go to the bathroom." I hurry inside and close the door. The stench hits me like a fist. I grab the Lysol off the tank and spray, wondering how such foulness could come from my little girl.

I open the window and brush my teeth. Take a shower and plug in my curling iron. I go to the kitchen to boil water for my coffee and then go find Monet.

She is in the bed, curled in a fetal position. From the way her body moves I know she is in pain. I sit on her bed, feel her forehead again. "Where does it hurt?"

She points to parts that indicate her intestines. "Bad?" I need to know. She nods, twisting in pain. "Be back." I go and check the milk. It is five days from expiration and a sniff test yields no sourness. I bring it to my lips and take a quick sip. Cool and fresh.

Not the milk.

I am making my way back to her bedroom when Aaron meets me in the hall. Her eyes are heavy with news. "Her stomach's just confused," she says. I blink not understanding. "She ate breakfast and didn't throw it up. It's the food in there. You know, like when you fast or something, you got to be careful about what you eat afterward."

I stare at Aaron. Information Central. I wonder what else is going on of which I am clueless and she knows. I want to laugh. I want to cry. Instead I hug Aaron in a way she hasn't allowed me to do in a long time. She accepts the embrace, but her arms dangle. Pulling away she shakes her head, moves past me and heads toward the living room. I hurry off to see about Monet.

We are late for a lot of reasons: Monet needed two more trips to the bathroom before we could leave, and there was an accident on the expressway. I only share the accident with the receptionist who sits in her chair eyeing both me and my daughter as if we were about to commit some crime.

None of my fears were arrested when we entered the office of glass and wood. Despite tastefully matted reprints on the walls and the wide selection of reading material, the reception area has the sterile feel of a hospital. All that's missing is the antiseptic smell.

I had been trying to determine what it was I was smelling from the moment we entered. It's only after I have handed over the medical insurance card and filled out half a dozen forms that I realized it was vanilla. Not the delicate baking smell but that sweet overt imitation kind that's the rage in upscale stores and body pampering shops.

I watch Monet fidget with the hem of her denim skirt. I feel her embarrassment as her wide thighs spread beneath the short skirt.

Brown and smooth like mine, I am thinking as I find myself staring. She takes her pocketbook and lays it across. Crosses and uncrosses her ankles, wired and anxious.

She does not want to be here. I'm not sure if I want her to be here. There is no one else in the waiting room but us. No other pudgy little girl sitting nervous and fidgety next to her mother, trying to hide flesh she has become ashamed of.

I tried to suggest jean shorts instead. Knew the difficulty in trying to keep meaty thighs together. There is the constant flexing of muscle so as not to give the world an unplanned peep show of your panties.

The top she has chosen is tight about her. It belongs to her sister and strains her chest like cellophane though it mostly bonds fat.

So much I consider as I sit next to her, boredom and fear drawing her to a copy of *Tiger Beat,* a handful of black faces filling the glossy dog-eared pages.

I am thinking about a cigarette. Suddenly I feel the need for some lung-blackening, throat-singeing nicotine. I look at my watch and glance at the bent head of the receptionist. Decide I will sit one more minute before I rise to ask how much longer.

With less than three seconds to spare a fortyish white man appears. His khaki pants and white polo shirt give him a casual look. But as he heads our way, a plastic smile in place, I see the distance in his eyes.

He drifts pass me and extends his hand to Monet. "Hi, I'm Doctor Whitaker, and you must be Mow-net." We both cringe in the mispronunciation of her name.

"Mow-nay," I say crisply. Doctor Whitaker's eyes find mine. Even as he chuckles and offers an apology, I see indifference in his eyes.

"Yes, of course. Like the painter, right?" He is waiting for me to say yes, or show my ignorance of art. But I know of Monet. I have two of his reprints in my study.

"Yes. Claude Monet. *Corn Poppies, 1873* is my favorite," I toss back, letting him know that he is not dealing with some ghetto queen. That my knowledge is as wide and encompassing as his own.

"Yes, of course. Well," his eyes are on Monet again. I see the quick study he makes of her smooth soft brown thighs. "If you are ready, then we can get started."

We both rise. "Mrs. Allen, if you will wait here. We find it best to talk with the children privately."

I know this but in this moment I will not even think of letting my child be alone with that man behind a closed door for a second. "Doctor," I said unable to recall his name, "she is twelve years old and where she goes, I go."

We are staring at each other. A showdown in the making. I have made up my mind that if I cannot be present, neither will Monet.

It takes him a while to concede. Even after he does, he gives me a lecture on doctor-patient confidentiality. I in turn tell him that at twelve there is nothing in my daughter's life I should not be privy to.

With the good doctor in the lead, we head down the long hushed hallway.

The tape recorder makes Monet nervous. The doctor is making her nervous. I do more talking than either of them. I bare what I know of my child's soul in front of a stranger and feel her discomfort and shame in my telling.

I end my monologue with the latest development, a part savored as an ends to justify the means. "This morning she didn't throw up."

Dr. Whitaker looks at me with mistrust. In his eyes I am an overweight black mother from the scrounges of southeastern Queens who has paid so little attention to her child that she has come down with a severe mental illness. That I would sit before him and tell a lie before I would be willing to confront the truth is more than plausible.

"Is that true, Monet?"

She nods. We wait for her to say more, but she is mute.

Dr. Whitaker sighs. Leans back in his two-hundred-dollar executive black leather chair. Behind him I see pictures of his family. They are all white, blond and thin.

"If we want to get to the root of the problem, then you have to be honest and open with me," he insists. Monet studies her hands. The session is going nowhere. I burn to take my daughter out of here.

"Monet?" he calls. I shift in my chair.

"Yes?" she finally manages in a voice so tiny and small I do not recognize it as her own.

"Can you tell me a little about how you feel after you eat."

She looks over at me, at the doctor. Back into her lap.

Dr. Whitaker gives choices. "Happy? Sad? Angry? Mad?"

"Sad."

He nods furtively and jots on his yellow legal pad. We have been here for twenty minutes and there is half a page of notes. I cannot read them from where I sit.

"And then what happens?" She looks at him curious. "You know, after you've finished eating and you feel sad?" Monet blinks but that's all. I know the motion. It means tears. He hands her a tissue. Puffs, the box says.

She takes it and balls it into her hand. Her head hangs toward her chest. Her back rises and falls with breathing. She does not wipe her eyes.

"Okay. Now your mom says you throw up after, is that true?"

She nods her head.

"Okay. So you've just finished with a wonderful dinner your Mom's prepared. Fried chicken, candied yams, collards, maybe?" He has taken the whole soul food issue too seriously.

Monet looks at him like he's crazy. "We don't eat candied yams and fried chicken together." I smile. *Good for you, kiddo.*

"Okay, so tell me what was for dinner last night?"

"We had turkey burgers, corn on the cob and salad."

"Turkey burgers, hmmm." More notes on his pad. I itch to see what he has written. "Okay, so you ate your burger, your ear of corn, your salad, what happens next?"

"I go to the bathroom."

"Okay. Now you are in the bathroom and you're standing over the toilet, what happens next?" We all know the answer, but Monet must say it.

"I throw up."

"How?" Dr. Whitaker wants to know.

She opens her mouth and sticks in a finger. He jots on his pad. "Then I start throwing up," she offers unprompted.

"And how does it feel?"

"My throat hurts and my breath gets choked and sometimes I want to stop it, but I can't."

"Are you still feeling sad?"

She shakes her head. "No, then I'm angry."

"Why?"

"Because it's not normal."

He nods, scribbles and gives my daughter the first genuine smile since he met her. He rests his pen to the side and clasps his hands. His voice is gentle and compassionate. If he is acting, he is doing an excellent job.

"You're right, Monet. It's not normal. So we are going to try and find a way to stop it, okay?"

Monet looks at him expectantly. But the fire fades quickly into a reality only she knows. "Okay." He sends Monet to the waiting room and it is just me and him. Feelings of inadequacy fill me.

"First, let me say, Mrs. Allen, we are both on the same side. I know you are afraid that I will harm your daughter in some way, but I assure you that that's not why I'm here." He turns and points toward the corner. "There is a videocamera that videos everything that goes on in this room. Each session is reviewed by our team of specialists not only to ensure that patients are being treated fairly but also as a means to help decide what is the best treatment.

"Secondly, I know you are feeling responsible for your child's condition as any mother would. But your guilt can interfere with getting her better. Thirdly, we are all not meant to be thin and while Monet is about twenty-five pounds overweight, as are a lot of today's youth, Americans in general are heavier than we've ever been. I'm not here to scold you, analyze you or chastise you. I am here to help Monet." He sits back. I relax a little.

"Now if for some reason you feel I am not capable of helping your child then you have the right to request another doctor or take her to another center. If you are uncomfortable with me, then Monet's uncomfortable with me and in the end nothing will be accomplished."

He waits for my decision. My emotions are oil and water, unwilling to mix. On one hand he has spoken the absolute truth, yet on the other hand I don't see how this snooty white male can really help my turmoiled black daughter.

"I want to check into other specialists for my child." I cannot look at him.

He stands and extends his hand. I shake it, my eyes dusting his. I see much there, none of which I want to dwell on. "It is your decision to make. I will call her pediatrician and perhaps you can check with your insurance carrier for other specialists in the field."

I do not say thank you or anything. I stand up, open the door and exit, the long hushed hallway mocking my quick leaving.

I fish wontons out of the container of soup and pour the contents into a bowl. I place it before Monet and turn back toward the stove.

I fork spoonfuls of fried rice and lay crispy fried chicken wings on the platter, turn and place it in front of Emory. I do the same for Aaron and make a plate for myself last.

Monet downs the soup quickly. Eyes the platters of fried chicken and spicy pork-fried rice longingly. Knows she cannot have any.

After leaving the specialist, I drove over to see Monet's pediatrician. She prescribed a liquid diet for the rest of the day to allow Monet's system to adjust. She listened evenly as I told her of my experience with Dr. Whitaker, waiting until I was done to inform me that the good doctor had indeed called her.

I was certain his spin on things did not congeal with mine and had my opinion confirmed in the cool reception I received after my tale.

"He's one of the best in the field, Mrs. Allen, and you were very lucky to get an appointment with him at all."

A doctor thing. Like the police force, there was some medical white line where doctors do not side against each other, I decide. Still it is hard to comprehend Doctor Medici not believing me. I cannot concede that after seven years of looking after my children, our bond is so weak.

I was full of disappointment when she said she would mail me a list of other specialists that take our medical coverage but it might be a while. That in the meantime I should monitor Monet the best way I can.

I could not believe she did not whip out her directory and give me a better one on the spot. That as Monet's doctor her attitude was so lackadaisical.

When I tried to press her, she briskly cut me off, saying she had other patients waiting and she already had taken up enough time with me. That it was only courtesy that made her see me at all and she had sick patients to get to.

"As if Monet's not," I shot back at her, which made her stand and open the door.

"Good day, Mrs. Allen." I wanted to report her to the medical board. Didn't.

Now as we gather for dinner, a migraine is trying to eat my eyeball. I cannot take medicine until I've eaten so I must contend with the pain as I sit in the silence that is thick around the kitchen.

"Can I have the Jello now?" Monet asks just as I'm about to put the first fork of rice into my mouth. I drop my fork, curse under my breath and rise. Emory places his hand on mine, but I shake it off.

"No, I'll get it," I insist, annoyed, on edge. I go to the fridge, swing the door open wide and search for the Jello cups. I am getting a spoon before I realize I was doing something Monet is completely capable of doing herself. This only adds more fire beneath my pan.

I slam the Jello in front of her, pitch the spoon, its edge nicking her arm. She rubs it as I sit down, my face sharp enough to cut steel.

I am lying in bed, lights off and a cool towel to my head. There is a knock on the door and I am ready to kill whoever wants to enter. Emory knows to leave me alone and is in the living room watching TV. I have been lying here for seventeen minutes as the Imitrex tries to decide if it will or will not work. The nausea has died down some.

"Mom?"

My temples throb anew. "Yes, Monet," I say softly. My world has been tossed every which way but up today, but in truth, none of it is her fault.

She opens the door, bringing with her a shaft of light that falls across my eyes like acid. She sees me cringe and closes it quickly. Head hurting, I try to open my eyes enough to see my child.

She stands in the shadows, not speaking, but I can feel what she needs—a sorry from me. I struggle to sit up as my stomach churns. I lift my arms to her, as my head pounds. She comes to me quickly and swift and I hold her in my arms. I feel her silent hiccups; tears wet my arms.

"Sssh," I say softly against her ear. "It's going to be okay." My words are an elixir, a momentary fix. She trusts me again, something I understand as a question comes from her mouth.

"That man, am I going back to him . . . cause I think I want to."

I take a moment to encounter all of it, all I perceived about the doctor and all that I saw. Recall how he got Monet talking and the sharp annoyance of Doctor Medici. I realize I have dug the hole deep enough. That it is time to climb out of it.

"Sure," I murmur, as pain eats at my eyes. "Sure you can." She hugs me harder. I wait for her to draw back, leave. Slowly I lie down, waiting for the Imitrex to do its job.

I am sleeping when I hear Emory calling my name. "Suvie?" I come to, happy to see the Imitrex has kicked in and the throbbing in my head has stopped. I sit up. Wrap my arms around him as he sits on the bed.

In dribs and drabs I tell him about my day. Reveal the perceived condemnation I got from the doctor but how he was able to get Monet talking. I talk about my encounter with Dr. Medici and having to wait for a list of other practitioners. Last, I tell him about Monet's request to go back.

"I'll take her," he tells me. "I'll call up the doctor and say we've changed our mind, that I will be bringing Monet in."

I nod my head, place it against the beat of his heart. I listen to its tom-tommy rhythm, eased.

Chapter 11

I applaud my daughter's bravery and make amends for my behavior by taking her and her friend shopping.

The whole world is shimmery and green. The humidity is low and it is a surprisingly mild day. In the air burns the hint of autumn, cutting through the heat, the warmth.

Monet and Ayesha giggle twelve paces behind me as we move through the Green Acres mall. It's the boys. They are everywhere. Moving around in groups, pants hanging off their skinny rumps, a certain coolness in their eyes. They stir up adolescent hearts with a fever.

I decided to take Monet on a shopping spree, her friend Ayesha with us. I have bought her new clothes, ones that fit and she seems happy. We spend two hours at the mall, in and out of stores and then we are headed home, some peace inside my soul.

My house is hushed, too hushed I am thinking as I close the door and look around. "Aaron?" I call out as I head down the hall. Monet and Ayesha are in her room taking the new clothes out of bags. Aaron's door is closed. I knock. Hearing nothing, I give the knob a twist.

Her room is neat like always and the teddy bear sitting on her pillow looks at me with beady blank eyes. The rapper DMX glares at me through sun-shaded eyes from a poster on one wall, a bandage under the eye of Nelly on the other. I look around the room knowing my daughter is not here.

There is still another week of punishment and she is not supposed to be away from the house. I turn and call out to her, my voice growing sharp with each sounding.

I check the bathroom and find it empty. Peer into the backyard and move toward my study. Sometimes she goes up to play computer games and I make my way upstairs. My junky workspace greets me, but no sign of my daughter. I make a note to clean it and head back down the stairs.

I move down the hall and see the basement door is ajar. I lean down the darkened stairs and call her name. Rustling drifts up from the dimness and I know what I will see before I see it.

Everything about me goes live wire as I race down the stairs and see J'Qaun adjusting his jeans and Aaron with her blouse inside out.

For a moment I cannot move, cannot think or breathe. I can only stand there before my daughter and the boy I do not like and utter, "Get your clothes straight and get upstairs."

I send Monet and Ayesha to Ayesha's house. There will be words spoken this day I am not ready for Monet to hear. Gawking and stalling at Aaron and J'Qaun, I am forced to move the younger children out the door, locking it. I wait until I see them turning the corner before I tell J'Qaun and Aaron to have a seat.

I say what I saw, what I think, emphasizing the wrongness of it all.

"But we weren't doing anything," Aaron whines. J'Qaun, stiff and hostile, sits mutely beside her. *This ain't cool,* his eyes are saying, but I don't give a damn what he thinks. All I know is what I saw.

There are red splotches on my daughter's neck, her blouse had been inside out and she has on no bra. I came down my stairs and see J'Qaun fixing his jeans. He will sit there pissed off until I say he can go.

"We weren't, Mom, I swear."

I know my daughter is telling a half truth. No, they weren't doing it but were on the road that begins that journey. I understand her embarrassment and her fear. Understand what being caught has done to her own worth. But the larger issue is I now know of her sexual proclivities and I must force enough warning down her gullet so that it will be a long time before she attempts this again.

I stare into J'Qaun's face and understand his lure. He is fine but beyond all that I must press into his thick peanut head that he is not even to think about touching my child like that again anytime soon. I must come off like a Nazi mom who will cut off his dick and send Aaron to a nunnery if they even think about getting touchy-feely, which I know they will the very next chance they get.

"Don't sit there and tell me you weren't doing nothing. You got hickeys all over your damn neck, your blouse was on backwards and J'Qaun was fixing his pants, not to mention being down in the basement when you're on punishment and nobody being home! So don't try and tell me you weren't touching and feeling and getting naked, because you were." I take a breath. "And you are just too young to even be doing things like this," which is so far from my own truth my mouth fills with acid.

"You broke the rules, Aaron, and you broke them good. Now you may think you all grown and know everything but you don't know nothing. You don't have to have sex to get pregnant. A little sperm too close to your cootchie is all it takes, you hearing me? So while you and J'Qaun may not have been doing 'nothing,' that 'nothing' you claimed you *were* doing can lead to something, including diseases that can kill you."

They look at me like I'm crazy. Good, I think, let them think I will take them both out in the backyard and shoot them if it happens again. "And you J'Qaun, you are not to come back to my house ever. You are not welcome here, never have been and never will be. I don't give a fuck what Aaron tells you, you are not to step another foot inside here. You don't give two shits for my daughter and while she may not know it, I do."

His eyes widen. I have touched a nerve. He works his mouth, his first attempt at speaking. "Not even like that, Mizz Allen... Aaron's my heart." He touches his for emphasis. His eyes are imploring me and it clicks. He loves my daughter or at least thinks he does. But I am on a mission and press on.

"Well, tough, J'Qaun cause you won't be seeing her anymore. Let me catch you 'round here one more time and I'm gonna go have a talk with your momma, your daddy and then I'm calling the police."

Definitely not cool. Aaron jumps up from the table and runs off and slams her door. J'Qaun sits there. Hangs his head. When he looks up, there is wetness in his eyes.

"I know you don't like me, Mizz Allen. I know you think I'm some hood rat just trying to knock some boots but that ain't me. I know she too young and I would never disrespect her like that."

"But you disrespect my house, right? You come sneaking in here when I'm not home, knowing Aaron's not suppose to have any company, right?"

He looks confused, shakes his head. "Nah, she ain't told me no stuff like that." I don't want to believe him. "She said she asked you and it was cool."

"Well, she lied." And I can't stand the fact that she did.

"Well, then I'm sorry, Mizz Allen. Had I known, I woulda told her no."

Aaron has betrayed us both. My anger at him eases up. I study him a long time. Take a moment to ask some questions.

"How old are you?"

"Be seventeen come December." Two years older than Aaron.

"What grade are you in?"

"Going to the twelfth."

"How do you really feel about my daughter?"

His eyes light up. I see the lovefire there. "She my heart, Mizz Allen. Ain't no other for me."

"Your boo?" I ask, using the vernacular.

He seems surprised that I know the word. "Yeah, I knew she was on punishment but she told me a week. Today makes the eighth day and when she called me I was like mad crazy." His face twists. ". . . a whole week? I was like dying, Mizz Allen."

I sit back, digest what I can, shifting what cannot be considered now onto a shelf. "You love her J'Qaun?"

He looks away embarrassed. "Yeah, Mizz Allen, I do." He is uncomfortable with such talk.

I smile a little. "So even if I ban you, you're still gonna see her, am I right?"

"Can't not see her. She my everything."

For now, I think. Maybe forever. My next question is hard but I ask it. "Are you a virgin?" He turns red, tightens his lips. Plays with his fingers, the veins in his lean arms tightening. "Are you?" I ask again. He shakes his head no. "But you know Aaron is."

He glances at me, the softness back in his eyes. "I know. And I respect that, Mizz Allen. I swear to God I do."

"So you're not having sex with her, but you are having sex?" He squirms. "The truth, J'Qaun."

"Yeah, but they don't mean nothing."

"To them it does." He looks at me surprised and I go on, milking this moment for all it's worth. "No girl lays down with a boy unless she has feelings for them or wants something from them. Now to you it may just be a booty call, but to those girls, it's all their hopes and dreams. You understand what I'm saying?"

He considers, nods hesitantly. I go on. "Now I'm not saying to start having sex with my daughter. But what I am suggesting is you stop having sex with everybody else."

His face screws up. I've asked too much. "So, I'm just supposed to wait?"

"Yeah J'Qaun you are." It sounds silly in my own ears.

He pulls back, shakes his head. "That's a long time, Mizz Allen."

"How long J'Qaun?" That he will not answer and I respect his need to keep something private between him and my daughter. "You've told me that you love Aaron and respect her, but you and I both know that the time will come when you two will have sex." I pause, attempting to make an alliance with a boy who, up until two minutes ago, I could not stand. "You're older, smarter. So I'm calling on you to do the right thing when that moment comes."

He reaches into his back pocket. Pulls out a fold of Trojans. I cannot miss the size marked "extra large" in the corner. "Never leave home without em," he says proudly.

I shoo at them with my hand. "Put those away." He does. We sit, weighing the words we have shared and what the next step is going to be. I decide for us both.

"As a result of Aaron lying and sneaking, she will be on punishment for an additional week. She cannot have phone calls and certainly no visits." I look at the calendar on the wall. Give a date. "And not a day sooner."

He nods, fidgets. "Yes, ma'am."

I go on. "At the time you will come here and meet my husband. He will want to shoot you but I promise to hide the guns." I am smiling but J'Qaun doesn't see the humor. "Kidding, J'Qaun," but we both sense I'm not. "You will be allowed visits but the basement and bedroom are off limits, you understand? I don't care what Aaron tells you; *I'm* telling you."

"So it's cool?"

"What?"

"Me and Aaron?" he wants to know.

"Already packed and Fed-Ex . . . too late now," I say.

Aaron has been standing in the hallway just out of sight. I realize this as she rounds the corner and throws her arms around me. I fight her embrace and try to keep my face stern, but we all know that we have survived this one storm and are better for it.

I won't tell Emory. I know that if I do, my decision will be overturned and Aaron will go on the sneak again. Inviting boys over when parents are away is as old as time. The trick is to take the situation and give a better alternative and I pray I've done just that.

I had looked upon J'Qaun as a demon seed ready to plow both my daughter's heart and her body. But that wasn't the case at all, and for all the trauma the day had caused, I'm glad it happened.

"Okay, J'Qaun, we clear?"

"Oh yeah, Mizz Allen, very."

"Alright then." I get up from the table. "You two have exactly two minutes to say good-bye. After that you will not be speaking or seeing each other for another eight days." I wave my hand toward the side door. "Now go on out there and get your good-byes."

I stand back from the window and watch. They are intertwined, their lips pliant and taffy soft about each other's. I feel their passion, envy their lust. Force my eyes away, find my Nazi mother mode. There is still Aaron to deal with.

I glance at the clock. Their time is up. I go to the door. "In the house." The sternness back in my voice. They separate slowly, hands leaving sides like molasses down the side of a glass bottle. Aaron doesn't look at me as she goes by. She heads for the hall, but I call her back.

Not getting off that easy, my eyes say as she sits, her joy still with her.

"Did you hear him, Mom? Did you hear?" She is drunk with the words J'Qaun has shared with me.

"Yes, I heard every word. In the meantime you've done something that I never thought you'd do Aaron. You lied and schemed and broke the rules."

Her happiness vanishes. She lowers her head. I raise it sharply. "Look at me." Her eyes dance from side to side. "Now let's get something straight. This is my house and my rules. Now I know you all in love and think you know everything and I don't know squat, but you are wrong, Aaron . . . I know it all."

"We weren't doing nothing."

"We're not going there again," I warn. "You were doing something and I thank God J'Qaun has some decency about him because you obviously don't." I look at her hard. "What kind of boy is going to respect a girl that lies and sneaks? You think what you did today makes you look good in his eyes, especially after I had to read him the riot act over your foolishness? You think about it." I pause, seconds ticking by. I can tell she will only half consider it, but I take it as it comes.

"After things cool down, how is he really going to see you? 'Damn, Aaron lied to me' that's how. You want that? You want J'Qaun to think you're a liar? You think he's going to like you for doing something where he had to sit down and answer embarrassing questions in front of me?"

She looks up. Something is connecting. "Just that, Mom, I hadn't seen him and I knew it was wrong. I didn't mean to go down there, but somehow we were just there and, well, y'know."

"Yeah, I do. I once was your age and feeling just the way you feeling now. But you got to really use your head. You love J'Qaun and he loves you. There's a whole bunch of do's and don'ts you have to follow to keep it that way."

"Like lying?"

"Yeah, and other things. Now he told me he was gonna wait until you re ready. My question is, have you even thought about when you're ready?"

Her answer comes quick. Too quick. "Yeah, when I'm older."

My head is shaking. "Not good enough, Aaron. You have to know exactly when. Cause later could be tomorrow or next week."

She studies me a minute and I feel her question coming. "How old were you?"

"Seventeen, the way I planned it."

"You planned?"

"Of course I did. A lot of my friends were doing it before, but I was holding out until I was seventeen. And like you I was lucky enough to have somebody willing to wait." Sort of.

Curiosity dusts her face. "How long?"

"Did he wait?"

"Yeah."

Lies leave my tongue like water. "Two years, until I was ready."

"So you were like fifteen, too, when he wanted to?"

I nod, caught in the midst of my own fairy tale. Philip never got the chance.

Her face screws. "Was it hard?"

"Sometimes . . . sometimes I wanted to, but I remembered my promise to myself and Philip did too." I didn't mean for that to slip. I had no intention of ever saying that name out loud within my house.

"Philip?" Her eyes widen. She has connected dots that no one in my immediate family is supposed to know. I look away. Aaron laughs. "Philip, huh?" I feel uncomfortable with the conspiracy in which she studies me. "Daddy know about this?"

I need a cigarette but they are upstairs in my office and to leave will admit a guilt I'm not willing to concede to. "We know all about our past lives," I say.

"So if I ask Daddy about Philip, he'll know?" Somewhere along the short span of her life, Aaron has learned the art of deflection. What started out as a chastising session has suddenly turned into an excavation of my past.

"That's not the point, Aaron."

Her eyes are so bright for a minute they look light brown. "I knew it. I knew there was something between you and him. Daddy don't know, does he, and isn't he like married to your old friend?"

"No, he doesn't, and yes, he is."

"Philip was your first?"

"First what?" I challenge, but it is all too late. The horse is out of the barn.

"Love. Your first love."

I have no intentions of bartering with my fifteen-year-old daughter but find myself boxed in a corner. I pull back, give her a careful look. "We'll make a deal. If you don't mention Philip to your daddy, I won't mention you and J'Qaun half naked in the basement."

Her eyes widen. Her smile vanishes. "You wouldn't."

I nod gregariously. "Yeah, I would."

"Daddy'll kill me and J'Qaun both."

My smile is benign. "I know."

She pulls back. Considers. "Okay."

I shift my thoughts back to the issue. "You decide then?"

"What?"

"When you are going to have sex?"

"I guess when I'm seventeen."

"Can't guess, Aaron. You have to know."

"I know that," she whines, the comfort zone gone. It is a difficult thing to decide, even harder to share the time frame with parents because then they'll *know* and will circle like hawks over chickens when the time approaches.

I don't expect Aaron to mark a date on the kitchen calendar, but I do expect her to set some goal. As I sit beside her, I sense both an eagerness and a secrecy and realize we'll both be lucky if she makes it to sixteen.

I take her hands, hold them between my own. "Whenever you do it, be smart about it. J'Qaun carries condoms; make sure you two use them." She pulls her hands away as if mine are dirty. "Don't be getting shy now," I warn.

Aaron looks at me again. More questions I sense and I am right. "How did you feel about him?"

"Who?"

"Philip, before. When you were going together? Did you feel like he was the best boy ever?"

"Yeah, I did."

"Who left who?"

I don't want to tell. I give a half-truth. "I left him."

She seems surprised. "You did? Why?"

I sigh. Think, consider. "Because he chose somebody else."

"Ms. Dorothy?" I nod, the moment surreal. "She stole him, didn't she? Stole him from you?"

I let go my daughter's hands. "Nobody can steal anybody."

"I saw him, Mom. Saw how he was looking at you. After all these years, he was still looking at you hard."

"Was he?"

"Yeah. That's how come I didn't want to leave you two alone."

I shake my head, smile wanly. "Nothing to worry about, Aaron. I love your father and your father loves me."

"Yeah, but he still love you, too." She considers me with wise eyes. "I could tell. Mr. Philip still loves you."

I tire of hearing Aaron say the name. I am afraid now that she knows what Emory never suspects. I wonder if this knowledge will come back to haunt me. "People have the right to love whoever they love. Doesn't mean you have to love them back," my last words as I get up and go find my cigarettes.

I am at the stove making dinner when Emory comes in from work. As he wraps his arms around my waist and nuzzles my neck, I know what it means and where he wants to go.

He reaches in front of me and turns off the flame beneath the sauce. Takes my hand and pulls. I resist.

"Come on," he utters, his eyes heavy with a passion I'm not feeling.

"Making dinner, Em," I say, holding my ground.

"Never stopped you before," he answers, holding tight.

I snatch my hand back. "No."

He looks at me. "What?"

"Period."

"Again?" he asks.

"Yeah. Sometimes it happens that way."

"Since when?"

"I can't," I turn the flame back on beneath the pan. Pick up the spoon and stir. Feel Emory's stare.

"Don't lie to me, Suvie. If you don't want to, just say so; but don't lie."

I turn and stare at him. "I don't," and go back to making dinner.

I'll never be able to venture to our secret place again. Aaron and J'Qaun have filled it with their presence and what Emory and I had there is gone.

I realize there is nothing secret about our so-called secret place at all. That the only thing that hides it is a door. Anyone can open it and find it. Curiosity alone is enough to bring forth such a venture.

I was naive in my choices, thinking that the room next to the boiler would only be used by Emory and me; that a mattress in the basement could be seen as anything other than what it was—a place to make quick, sweaty love. I was naive to think that one day Aaron would not want to use it, too.

I had gone down after the talk and discovered her panties in the corner, all the confirmation I needed. I found myself searching around for used condoms and felt foolish when I found none. I ended up taking the mattress and dragging it to the garage, uncertain as to how I will explain that to Emory.

I will give him a reason later, I think, as I stir sauce and linger as the noodles boil. Later when I put back all the pieces of my life that have become scattered like confetti in the wind.

I study the back of Emory's head, watch him do what he does best, talk to professional people. I can only hear one side of the conversation, but his tone, his words indicate a victory in the making, something that is confirmed when he nods his head, laughs a little and hangs up. "She's got an appointment for next Monday," he tells me. I nod, feelings of ineptness and shame still with me.

"He actually sounds like a nice guy," Emory goes on to say. That he finds Doctor Whitaker okay doesn't surprise me. My take on people and things and Emory's are oceans apart.

"You got plans for Saturday?" he asks suddenly, joviality in his voice.

"No. Why?"

He shrugs. "Haven't done much this summer with the kids. I was thinking maybe we could do a day at Jones Beach or something." He is in high gear now. He has saved the day, family face, and is certain everything will turn out just fine.

"Sounds good. I'm sure the girls will love it. They've been seeing my face all summer. And I know they would appreciate a day with you." Which is true. My daughters adore their father.

He studies me. Eager. "What about you? Would you appreciate a day with me?"

I know what he is searching for, know what he needs. Affirmation. I give it. "Couldn't think of anything better."

"Nothing?" He says with a raised brow.

"Well, yeah, something, but a beach day sounds good too." More than good. It will be an earmark, a visible signal to Aaron that her father and I are still happy, still in love. Still need each other. That the ghost that is Philip cannot touch us, harm us, separate us. That in his wanting me, I don't have to want him back.

I am upstairs in my office going through papers and cleaning out clutter when the phone rings. "Mom, it's Aunt Lisa."

I pick up my extension. Say hello.

"Hey, girl," she begins and I know she has moved past our little disagreement.

Relieved I say "Hey," back.

"How my baby doing?"

"She's fine," I answer, wanting to share it all.

"She see the doctor yet?"

"A few days ago."

"How'd it go?"

I want to tell Lisa the whole thing. Know she will understand my reaction. I sigh. "Girl, I wanted to snatch my child out of there." I sit in my office chair, put my feet up on my half-cleared desk and unburden my soul.

We talk for two hours and by the time we hang up everything between Lisa and me is good again. I needed that; I needed some balance somewhere in my life. Talking with her has revived my spirit, taken the dampers off my heart. Lifted, I go downstairs and take a shower.

Emory is sleeping by the time I get into bed. I ease my nightshirt off my body and press myself against him. He awakens at my touch, turning toward me; I snuggle deeply into his arms.

Day-to-day life carves our realities, becomes our assurance, our beacons, indicators of where we are going, where we are not. Somewhere I think, we are headed, but the final destination suggests rain.

Chapter 12

I am up on my tippy toes, searching the top shelf of the closet for my straw hat. Suddenly the shelf gives way, and an assortment of shoe boxes, pocketbooks and winter caps tumbles onto my head.

I wince, rub my skull and look up at the shelf that has loosened from its moorings. Grabbing a chair, I stand on it at the closet door and grab the wire rack. I ease it gently on its weakened bracket and carefully place the fallen items back on the shelf. Make a note to tell Emory about it.

I slip off my gown and get my swimsuit, step into it and pull up the straps.

My house is full of excitement. It is the type that I have not heard in a long time. Erratic, loud, cheery, it reaches me behind my closed bedroom door, as I stand before my mirror in my five-year-old bathing suit, tugging at the shoulder straps and the fit around one thigh.

It is black, simple, with a one-inch band of white across the bosom but either the cup size has grown too small or my breasts too big. They spill from the armpits, reveal more cleavage than the design should allow.

I turn sideways, see the slight pudge of my belly, suck in my gut watching the roll go unchanged. I turn away from the mirror, pick up my denim jumper, step into it and fasten the hooks as Emery comes in, his Hawaiian swim trunks peaking out from beneath his long sleeveless white tee.

"Ready?" he asks me.

No, I think but nod anyway. I want time to will away the soft belly revealing itself beneath the fit of the suit. I want to conjure up the flat smoothness that was always mine until I had children. I want to look model perfect for this day at the beach.

Aaron comes in, hands behind her back, holding the catch on her two-piece. "Can you hook this?" she asks as I try not to envy the svelte little waist, the way the cups of her bright orange bikini top hug her small round breasts.

She turns and I carefully take the two pieces from her fingers, clasp them, pat her back for good measure, watch her disappear out of my bedroom.

"You think she should wear that?" Emory asks.

"She has the body for it."

"Yeah, but she's just fifteen."

I think about his summation; a smile finds me. "Honey, if I had a body like that, I'd be in one, too."

"You still do."

"Liar."

"This look okay?"

We look up. See Monet standing there in her takini. It is a two-piece bathing suit with a short skirt and a top. Depending on how you move it appears as a one piece, but every now and then a bit of belly will show.

I do not realize just how much weight Monet has lost until now. She looks good. The plump thighs are not so plump. Her hips are nearly the right side of round. Her waist curves in and the buds on her chest have moved to slight swells.

"Looks fabulous, I'd say."

Her eyes seek her father's approval. "Calendar perfect," he intones. Monet smiles, something inside of her pleasing. I know what as she turns and heads back to her room. More good than harm? I can't help but wondering.

*   *   *

The surf is nonexistent as we wade through the bay area at Jones Beach. It is possible to go for yards and the water will come no higher than your thighs. Monet glides beneath the surface like a dolphin. Aaron stands running her fingers through the waves unwilling to get her hair wet. I float on my back, rocking gently as Emory swims farther out.

I hear him call out to me. I stand up and search him out. He is twenty yards away and I can tell by his motion that he is treading water, a depth in which I will not venture.

"Come on," he calls as waves rock him. I shake my head no and wave him back. "Too far, Em. It's too far."

"It's not. It's perfect." But I do not believe him.

Monet breaks through the surface. She pushes water from her hair, wipes its salty substance from her eyes. She spies her father and dives back in, her strokes making splashes as she swims his way.

"Don't go out, Monet. It's too far and too deep." But she does not hear me or pretends she doesn't and soon she is by her father's side, two brown bodies bobbing in the ocean's cadence.

"Good?" I ask my husband as he lies, damp head in my lap, munching a chicken leg. He nods, takes another bite as I gaze out to the shoreline, keeping a watch on Aaron who is engaging with a boy no doubt drawn to the neon orange bikini and the bundled brown skin inside.

They stand in the water, gentle waves lapping at their thighs, four feet apart. I watch Aaron laugh, her head thrown back, thick dark brown hair, now wet and clinging, glistening in the sun.

"The shelf in the closet has come loose again."

"I'll check it when we get back," Emory tells me.

I search for Monet. She is with two girls her own age, water up to their waist. I close my eyes, inhale the sea air. Smile.

"Feels good, right?"

I look down at Em. "Very good. How come we don't do this more often."

He shrugs. Finished off the chicken leg courtesy of NY Fried Chicken. Sits up. "We got anymore A&W?" I shift, roll onto a thigh, search the cooler, melting ice and chilled water engulfing my arm to the elbow.

We are on our way home from the beach when Emory decides to drop by his parents.

I am blessed that my relationship with his mother and father is a good one. Anna Allen has never looked upon me as anything more than I am—a good choice for her son. Elvin Allen has been delighted with me from the moment we met.

I call them at least once a month and we take the drive out to Lawrence, Long Island, often. Summertime has decreased our visits and we are all glad for a chance to see them. We pile out of Emory's car, head up the sidewalk and ring the bell.

The front door opens and Emory's father appears, his smile brightening with every face he sees. "Well, I'll be." He turns, addresses the back of the house. "Anna. Anna, guess who's here?"

Emory's mother comes from the kitchen, hands busy about her apron. I take in her gleaming silver curls uncombed about her head and know she has been to the hairdresser today. I take in the water-stained apron and know that she is in the midst of cooking a Saturday meal.

I am glad that we are not hungry. I cannot stand the thought of Monet going off to the bathroom at her grandparent's house. We have not told any of our parents about Monet and we've decided not to. Our hope is that she will get the disease licked before we are faced with that necessity.

"Isn't this a nice surprise," my mother-in-law intones.

I smile because in this moment, my life, our life feels as good and as perfect as it gets. "We were coming in from the beach and decided to stop by," I say, embracing her as she comes up to me.

"I thought you all were looking a little toasty."

"And ashy," my father-in-law says with a chuckle that says the sight of us does his heart good.

"The ocean makes you ashy, Grandpa Al," Aaron says exasperated.

"I know that, Miss Aaron. I was just teasing you. Can't your grandpa tease you every now and then?" he offers, lightly cuffing her chin.

His touch makes her smile, near shy. "Yeah, you can."

He opens his arms. She enters into his embrace. "That's my girl," he says, kissing her forehead. Monet moves toward them. He makes room within his embrace for her. Hugging his grand-daughters, his face is a beam of delight.

"Dinner's almost ready, anybody hungry?" Anna asks.

I shake my head no. "No, we're fine."

"You sure? I've made short ribs and I know Emory loves my short ribs."

My eyes dance to Emory. Gratefully this time he catches my silent signal. "I'll take some home, Mom. Have it later."

His answer pleases her and she heads off to the kitchen while we all take seats in the living room.

Chapter 13

Philip drives, the streets outside his window hauntingly familiar but emotionally detached. He is home now, but the twists of roads, neon of storefronts and potted asphalt do not recognize him. The world he once knew has grown darker, denser, thick with a communal conundrum he is no longer privy to.

Philip drives, one thought flitting across his heart like dragonflies over a summer pond, quick, erratic, undetermined of a final destination. Suddenly he makes a left, coming up on Clinksdale Avenue. Like a tourist, he moves through slowly, eyes sweeping everything as if for the first time.

He sees the house that had, once upon a time, welcomed him. Wonders if the room is still pink and white. If old albums from the seventies still line its walls. If a grown-up Suvie and her absence have diminished the memories made there.

Philip is in need of reasoning. He is in need of exactness. Returning to his South Ozone Park, Queens, neighborhood has offered him none of the preconceived sanctions. His parents, older than he could ever remember, had greeted him with weary smiles and hesitant hugs; eyes longing for answers to questions they would never speak.

For nearly three decades they waited for him to explain it all. For nearly thirty years Philip's parents had never known if their son loved the woman he had married, only that when a tenth wedding anniversary had sprung up on the horizon they resigned themselves that the nuptials were final.

They never anticipated Philip calling the whole thing off right before that thirtieth anniversary mark. Never considered that their child, closer to fifty than thirty, would return home to "reclaim all that I lost." Mr. and Mrs. Butler weren't certain what misplaced pieces of his life he was referring to, only that their love for him was endless, and as difficult as it was, they supported his choice. Besides, they never cared for Dorothy.

Now as Philip steers his Escalade, mindful of the stares the top-of-the-line SUV is getting in a neighborhood that knew mostly Buicks and Fords, he drifts slowly toward the house that had, once upon a time, welcomed him.

He slows to a near crawl as he takes in the vinyl siding, the shutters of glossy wood. Nearly stops as the need to park his car and get out to ring the bell assaults him. He considers doing just that. Considers stopping to tell Suvie's parents hi, say what he never got the chance to say out loud to Sylvia: that he had been terribly wrong and he was sorry.

But such need abandons him as he spies DeAnna walking up the street, two of her three grandchildren in tow behind her. Philip eases on the gas, looks the other way, feeling the eyes of his sister-in-law on him like fire.

DeAnna Alexander's failings in life are just that—DeAnna's— but in Dorothy's eyes and heart, she carries some of the blame. Dorothy has raised her sister as much as her parents have. When DeAnna was thirteen, Dorothy had been there trying to steer her sister in the right direction. By age fifteen, Dorothy was gone and DeAnna became pregnant with her first child.

Having a second was no real surprise, but the third child that came at the age seventeen was viewed as an outrage and Mr. Alexander had his daughter's tubes tied, damage already done or not.

School, which had never held any real interest, lost all its appeal. DeAnna went on welfare and spent her days watching soaps and yelling at her kids. By the time she turned thirty-two, she was a grandmother living in her parents' basement. Ten years after that, she got kicked off welfare and worked at Key Food, making just enough to pay for her own cable and phone, but little else.

When her brother, Dean, finally moved out, DeAnna moved back upstairs and let her oldest girl, who had had three kids by then, have the basement. Apples falling from the tree, DeAnna's mistakes were living and breathing inside her own child.

A life gone wrong is what Dorothy always thinks when she thinks of her sister. She has tried to help DeAnna find a way, but DeAnna has no interest in that either. This is Dorothy's mindset when she picks up the phone and hears her sister on the other end.

"Philip up here?"

"Dee?"

"Yeah. Philip here? Cause I swear I just saw him."

Relief fills her as his whereabouts is confirmed. "You probably did. He's back in New York now."

"He got one them fly-ass SUV's, Escapades or something?"

"Escalade."

"Yeah, that's it. He got one of them?"

"Yes, he does."

"What he doing on our block?"

Dorothy swallows. "Visiting, I guess."

"Visiting who? Cause he sure didn't stop by here . . . What's going on, Doe?"

DeAnna is the last person Dorothy wants to give the news to first, but she knows sooner or later everyone will know anyway. "We're separating"—a guess because Dorothy has not heard from her husband to confirm or deny it.

"You lying, right?" DeAnna insists in a voice whispery, shocked and scared. It catches Dorothy by the shirtsleeve, tugging her a little. It is in that moment that she understands she has pegged her sister all wrong. Her sister did have dreams. *My own.*

"No, Dee, I'm not."

"All them years you two been together, with that fly-ass house?"

"Marriage is about more than that."

"Like what?"

Like love, Dorothy thinks, but feels no need to say it. "How is Kiefer doing?" she goes on to ask, genuinely interested in her oldest grandnephew.

"Not a bit better. They talking about putting him in a special school for bad-ass little kids."

"But he's smart."

"Too damn smart, that's the problem. I tried to tell them knuckleheads he just bored. But they don't see bored, they see trouble and they'd rather send him to someone else than deal with his smartness."

"What Keanna saying?"

" 'Bout what? That girl don't pay nothing no mind. All she do is run the streets like she still fifteen. I try and tell her she got to get her act together. That she gonna be thirty soon. You think she listen?"

"I thought she was going for her GED."

"For a hot minute, yeah. But then she found out she has to study, do homework. Dropped out. I swear, Doe, you had it right, not having no kids."

"I tried to tell you after the first one."

"Like I was listening. Shoot, I was so happy to have your hard ass hand gone from off my neck, I just ran wild . . . if I had only knew."

"It's not too late, Dee."

"Not too late for what? I got three damn kids and two of them are in jail. I got three grandkids and one is surely on the way there. Now you tell me what's not too late."

Better, Dorothy wants to say, *something better.* But who was she to utter such words?

Philip didn't wake up one morning and decide he wanted to leave Dorothy. That thought had always been there, but time and situations never really allowed it. Bound by responsibility, Philip soon found himself tangled in routine.

Dorothy wore his last name proudly, lifting Philip every chance she got. When he had gone for his first major job interview after graduating from Morehouse, she had taken the money she had personally saved and bought him an expensive new suit and shiny black shoes. She had insisted on how the barber should cut his hair and picked out the perfect cologne for him to wear.

She'd rewritten his ordinary résumé, turning a basic twenty-two-year-old's life into something spectacular. Every day that he left for his job at Mutual of Omaha, she made certain that his shirts were freshly pressed.

She was the one who worked hard to take them out of the cramped studio into a bigger and better apartment. Years later when Philip had mentioned that his boss was taking another position, Dorothy pushed him to apply for the job. Neither his age— twenty-seven—or his years on the job—five—seemed to warrant Philip a chance, but he got the spot.

Dorothy became the grease beneath Philip's wheels, moving him forward, pushing him when he didn't have the ability to push himself. He grew comfortable with her role, came to lean on her support. Found a solid life on the middle class dreams she turned into reality. Though he appreciated what she'd done, the one true emotion remained elusive; an emotion that got pushed away in pursuit of upward mobility.

When that summit was reached, the hollowness returned. Slowly, surely, like sap from a tapped maple tree, it began to puddle at the base of his soul. Philip stepped over it and beyond it, ignoring the growing dissatisfaction that gathered.

When he was facing his fortieth birthday, reflection claimed him and he began to ponder what had been in his heart for so long. A pondering that made him announce to his wife that he wanted a divorce, but somehow the strength of those words failed him and he remained by her side.

But a seed was planted, and ever so often he found himself speaking of breaking up. Dorothy came to take it as just words and more years passed, that was until he talked about taking some time from work to go back to New York. That it was a trip he wished to make alone.

Dorothy protested as she always did, with threats and fast tears, but nothing could change his mind; nothing could hold him back.

He is here now, but he has yet to find what he needs and the reasonable part of his mind does not believe there is a chance.

The reasonable part of his mind does not believe that the sight of him at Suvie's front door for the second time in a little over a week will change his world. But true reasoning was left behind when he got into his SUV and headed to New York. True reasoning is abandoned as he leaves Clinksdale Avenue and gets on the Van Wyck Expressway, old need stirring up like fire.

Philip wishes he had paid better attention to detail. He wishes he had taken note of which car was in the driveway the last time he went to see Sylvia. He finds himself befuddled by the appearance of the Lexus, unable to determine if it belongs to Sylvia or Emory.

He puts his vehicle into park, lets the engine idle, fingers loose about the gather of keys. *You're here now,* his mind stalks, *might as well finish what you've started.*

Philip steps down from the running board, closes his door. Running a hand over his close-cropped hair, he clears his throat, rounds the SUV and stands at the perimeter of Sylvia's house. Evening lights shine like honeyed eyes from the windows.

He swings open the gate, walks the smooth slice of concrete, takes the three steps up and rings the bell. He has no idea what he will say, only all what is in his heart: *I'm sorry, Sylvia. I'm so sorry.*

The door opens with a quiver, the long young face appearing behind the screen door glass. A frown, furrowed and deep, creases its forehead. "Yes?"

"Is your mother home?" Philip mutters, feeling uncomfortable with Aaron's glare, the quick turn of lip, upward, spiteful.

"What you want?" she barks, her voice nipping the darkness. "What you trying to do?" she implores, anger fierce on her face.

Philip is taken aback at her reaction. "I want," he finds himself explaining, "to see your mother. Say hi, let her know—"

"Know what? She ain't got no use for you. Just go away and leave us alone." The door slams hard and fierce. For a few seconds Philip cannot register anything. He stands there blinking, the hiss of crickets magnified as he tries to find his balance, a return to his center. Get his legs moving.

He is heading down the steps when the door swings open again.

He turns, heart pounding, mouth dry as he comes face to face with Emory. "Philip?" He nods, self-conscious, caught, embarrassed and hurt. "I heard the door slam, asked Aaron who it was and she said 'Some man.' " The storm door swings open, warm light laps at Philip, inviting. "Come on in. Sylvia's out, but she should be back soon."

Chapter 14

I don't want to leave Lisa's house. We are in a groove, old friends, best friends, those-were-the-days groove and the ice tea she serves is just the right side of sweet. Cigarette buds overflow the large crystal ashtray and WBLS-FM is playing the oldies straight from my heart.

But we are yawning now moreso than we are talking and Lisa has an early start. She has to be at the New Jersey office by eight in the morning and out her front door by six.

I stand, stretch good and hard. Look down at my friend, swat her leg. "Let me get my butt home."

"Yeah and I got clothes to press." Her head shakes. "I hate going to Jersey." She is a human relations coordinator for a marketing firm and must give a seminar in one of the satellite offices.

"Yeah, but you love the money."

Her eyes grow intense. "What money?"

I look at her confused. "What you mean what money? You getting paid big-time."

She looks away as if my words have offended her. Stands, too. Gathers up the pitcher of ice tea. I get the glasses. We go through the back door, entering her black-and-white kitchen. "Just put them in the sink."

I drain the last bit of mine and do just that. An awkward silence encroaches and I speak to halt its ascent. "We got to do this more often." I see my friend's face soften and am glad for it.

"Yeah, we should."

"Summer's almost over and you haven't been to one barbecue."

"When's the last time you've had one?" she asks.

"You right. But we definitely have to give one before Labor Day."

"Well, let me know." Lisa dumps the ashtray into a square of foil. Crumples it into a ball. Tosses it into the garbage can.

"You still doing that?"

"You know Mack can't stand the smell," she says annoyed.

I shrug. I try hard not to remember just what he likes and doesn't.

The Escalade parked in front of my house takes me by surprise. The Georgia license plate steals my breath. I grow dizzy as I pause by it, take a deep breath as I ease my car past it. I pull into the driveway next to Emory's car and am suddenly afraid to get out.

It's Dorothy, I convince myself as my hands grow damp. Just Dorothy, coming up here looking for Philip, but my heart cannot sustain the lie. I remember Philip getting into it the last time he came to visit and I can't help but imagine my house hurricane-struck as I get out, hit the remote alarm and head toward my front door.

In my head I see Aaron spilling secrets like red glistening seeds of a Chinese apple, staining everything in its wake. I see my husband just behind the door, angry and outraged, waiting for me to enter, demanding the whole truth.

But it's all a mind trick as I step into my own house, catching Philip and Emory shouting to the television. "What you doing?" Emory is bellowing as I push the door behind me closed. The sound snaps up his head, Philip's. My eyes skip the latter. "Hey," I say, controlling my tone, my breathing, my too-fast heart.

"Hey. Phil dropped by."

I have never known anyone to refer to Philip that way. Know for certain he does not allow it, yet he doesn't flinch and I am rooted to the floor.

"Dorothy?" all I can offer as I will my legs to work.

"She's in Georgia," Emory answers for him, eyes going back to the game.

Suddenly it is just Philip and me. Everything else has vanished and we circle each other in a void of smoke and fog. I cannot speak; neither can he as we lock eyes for a lifetime. I am feeling it all over again, feeling him all over again like the first time in the hallway of our old high school.

I am fifteen and breathless as he stands up slowly. "I've been here awhile," he implores.

I nod my head, afraid of how close he will come to me.

"Didn't plan on staying this long. I better be on my way," he offers to both Emory and me. But Emory is engaged in the baseball game and nods his head absently, his eyes glued to the screen.

Philip takes this moment to charge the distance between us. I swear he has flown to me, his feet never making contact with the carpet. He is before me and I have no breath inside. I am dizzy and my mouth parts for air. He touches me, two hands on both of my arms and I feel a fire I have not known in decades.

"It's over," he whispers. "I'm back home. Call me."

I cannot speak. Can do nothing about the hands that move from my arms to engulf my waist, my spine. Can do nothing as Philip draws me near, our bodies magnets of the opposite poles, pulling each other close.

He pulls away, shouts good night to Emory and lets himself out. I blink, trying to settle it all as I find my way toward Emory. Settle on the opposite end of the couch.

"How's Lisa," he asks as a commercial comes on.

"Fine," all I can manage. *It's over,* a scratched forty-five in my head that only recognizes one groove.

Next morning I come into my kitchen and find Aaron at the table. There is no breakfast before her, no magazine or book beside her and everything inside me grows tense.

"I told him to go away."

I swallow, ask calmly, "Who?"

"Philip," the word, venom on her lips. "I slammed the door on him and everything, but Daddy let him in."

Her anger gives way to sadness. All I want to do is allay her concerns. But I don't know how without making it worse. I search for parental words instead. "You can't decide who can and can't ring the bell, Aaron."

"Course not, not if it's Philip, right?"

"Excuse me?"

Her face scowls up. "He come here again and I'm telling Daddy the whole thing."

My face hardens, my words all wrong. "If you do, I'll have to tell about J'Qaun."

She stands, forceful, defiant. "Tell him, I don't care, tell him. Because it's wrong, it's so wrong. Daddy loves you and what you doing ain't right."

She leaves out, a gush of hot wind against my arm. I stand there, my mouth open wide when Monet comes in. "Tell Daddy what?" she wants to know.

I shrug, turn and get a coffee cup.

But my daughter's words haunt me. *What you doing ain't right,* the new skipped record in my head. It loops endlessly as I sit upstairs in my office, staring at the phone, wanting to dial the number I never thought I would dial again.

I try to pick out my reasoning from the mad rush that fills my head. Just what am I trying to do? I love my husband. How can I even think about doing anything with Philip anywhere? But just as quickly as these questions come, the answer fills me.

It is my unhealed soul that fuels me, a soul I thought repaired when Emory came into my life. But now that Philip is back, I understand that it isn't. Understand that it's still as tender and raw as ever. That it hurts when I breathe sometimes. That it hurts when I think about what he and Dorothy have done to me. That the only person who can heal me is Philip, and after thirty years, he is willing and ready to do just that.

I am in my backyard and wishing a trillion things as I prune my roses, pull lush weeds from the soil. I wish I were stronger, wish the life that I've made with Emory were enough. I wish I had come to him differently, not broken, but whole.

I wish Emory had the power, the ability to make Philip unimportant in my life. For years I've felt just that and silently thanked God for giving me all I have, but suddenly it all seems like a lie.

It is a lie that's sticky as a glue trap, snaring any and everything that comes my way. It is what made me search earlier through the white pages for the phone number under the *Bs*. It is what made me pull out the letters I've never read and, save for one, refused to open. Decades later, all five remain unread.

Now it's all I want to do. I want to explore the heart and mind of the boy who wrote them before I can consider the man the boy has become. I want to make sure what I am contemplating is founded in validity, not youthful optimism that should have left me a long time ago.

I want to make sure that the call I make on my cell phone will be worth the undertaking. I want to make certain all that I saw in Philip's eyes, all that I felt in his embrace is worth scattering my present life to the wind in hopes that the pieces will reassemble themselves into completeness for me again.

Jane's Beauty World looks the same way it did ten years ago when I first started going. The hot pink walls have grown a little sooty, and the shiny black-and-white-tiled floor has dulled, but it's basically the same ten-booth walk-in I discovered when hair care became important to me.

I've drifted in and out of various hair phases over my life. I had the mandatory Afro, indulged myself in the Jherri Curl until I grew tired of the plastic caps and wet pillowcases. I went natural for a hot minute, getting my hair shorn to one inch by a professional barber, and last and as far as I am certain, least, was the permanent.

For years I stayed away from it, Revlon being the only brand at the time. I could not stand the burning and scabbing, my scalp too sensitive for the chemicals.

When I abandoned the Jherri Curl, I started using the at-home kits. I'd pick up any box that said no-lye, study the pretty black faces on the cover, go home and do it myself. Sometimes my hair came out good; other times it didn't. Hit and miss, I was ignorant in the ways of real hair management.

Betty, my beautician, told me the error of my ways.

I had come into the shop one spring morning, beating the Thursday, Friday and Saturday crowd. It was my first trip to a real beauty salon in decades and I didn't want the regular customers staring at me and thinking bad thoughts about my hair.

Betty had lifted her eyes up from the magazine she had been reading and waited for me to speak. "I want my hair done," I managed. There was something decimating about her eyes. Plain and brown, they seemed to cut through me like a laser as she took in all of me, lingering on my head.

"You want a perm and condition," she stated, deciding for the both of us. I shrugged.

She took the plastic apron off the chair and snapped it in my direction. I glanced at a younger operator who had paused from straightening out her work station to take in the encounter between Betty and me. I looked at her nails, nicely polished, I looked at her hair, razor cut and healthy and then I looked back at Betty who was waiting for my decision.

I slipped into her chair.

"Perm's twenty-five; conditioner is another ten. A cut is ten more." Her hands were busy in my scalp by then, testing its weakness, its strength, the overall condition. "You got good strong hair, just needs a lot of help," she decided, slipping the plastic apron over me. "Use that neutralizing shampoo, don't you?" My eyes caught hers in the mirror. "I can tell. Lotta women make that mistake, think they doing something and ain't doing nothing."

She extended her hand toward mine. "Betty," she announced.

I took her hand and gave it a light squeeze. "Sylvia." She raised the chair with the foot pedal. "What you use?"

I ramble off the names of the store-bought kits, each one making her grunt. "Worse thing in the world they ever done was make those things. People think they saving time and money. But all they really doing is jacking up what hair they got."

I cringed.

"We gonna have to do a lot of trimming," Betty told me as she worked the wide-toothed comb through the tightness. My last at-home perm had occurred six weeks before, and my roots had grown in so thick I had to use a pick just to comb it.

I turned around in my chair, eyeing her. "You talking about cutting?"

"I'm talking about trimming. Cutting is an inch or more. Trimming is just getting those scraggly little edges before your hair breaks off, and judging by this, breakage is your middle name. So what we gonna do is give you a mild relaxer this time, a deep conditioner and clip these edges. I'm gonna tell you the name of the things you need to start using right away."

I saw dollar bills float out my pocketbook. My thoughts carried to my face because Betty jumped right in.

"You want hair, or you want *hair.*"

I wanted *hair* and told her so.

"Alright then. We gonna get us some."

Three hours later I left Betty's chair fifty dollars poorer and with the best-looking hair I had ever owned. She warned me to enjoy that day, "Cause when you wake up in the morning it might look like a hurricane went through it. But run a little grease through it, touch up a curl or two, and you'll be good to go."

My other instructions were to find the time to stay inside my house with a plastic cap and a ton of conditioner on my head. "Your cleaning day is a good day. All that motion will work up a sweat and heat helps make the conditioner work."

Over the months my hair did begin to grow. I started using the same routine on Aaron and then Monet when she turned ten. Soon we were a family with full healthy hair, Aaron's and Monet's going past their shoulders and never looking back.

Betty explained that to me, too. "Mommas just don't realize all the potential their little girl's hair got at that age. You start treating it right early and, honey, they will have hair for the rest of their lives."

Now as I make my way toward my miracle worker, I plant a smile on my face knowing Betty will not return the favor. She looks up at me, nods and says, "Be with you in a minute," and continues to move a hot comb through an older woman's hair.

The whole place smells like frying hair, hair spray and coconut oil. Nearly a dozen operators in all stages of life are working as *All My Children* plays on the TV.

I want something different from what I've had before. I begin flipping through the various hairstyle magazines in search of something new. I see frosted hair, lemon yellow hair and a concoction that rises twelve inches from the scalp. But I seek full, fluffy and layered.

"Go sit in my chair," Betty instructs as she heads outside to have a cigarette.

The days of smoking in the beauty shop, smoking anywhere indoors were long gone. Even at home I am limited as to where I can puff. It's either the kitchen or my upstairs workspace.

I look back on those days of smoking in my college classroom or in a doctor's office, even the movie theater and find it hard to believe myself. Was the world ever that free? Did we ever really have the power to light up wherever we wanted? Was there really an ashtray at every table in a restaurant, on train platforms?

Betty smokes only half, comes back inside. She tosses her lighter onto her workstation and I see those hands.

Beautician hands.

Old scars, burned markings, nails short and trimmed. *Badge of honor,* she once told me. "You don't ever want to go to somebody whose hands and arms are all smooth and unmarked. Means they ain't been in the business long enough to know much."

Now as she works Vaseline through my scalp, she asks me what I want. By the time she has applied the perm, rinsed and shampooed, she asks me again making sure.

"You never let me do more than a trim. Now you talking about cutting? Took us ten years to get this length, you sure you want it bobbed?"

A true beautician will treat your hair like their own. They will refer to it as "ours" without thought. I knew exactly what Betty was feeling because I was feeling it a little bit myself.

We had finally managed my hair four inches past my shoulders. It had taken a lot of coaxing, conditioning, perming and trimming to get it that length. I could finally do a ponytail and have something hanging from the scrungii; could manage a French bun without any assistance from store-bought hair and now I was asking her to lop off half a foot.

I look down at the hairstyle I selected, catch Betty's eyes in the mirror. "I can always grow it back," I decide, to which she sighs, take up her shears and in a quick motion cuts off three inches.

Betty whirls my chair around toward the mirror. I look at myself and see I look ten years younger.

"What you think?" Betty asks.

I shake my head, the movement sending the soft-layered swirls into motion, the subtle highlights gleaming. "I love it," I say in awe.

"Well, good, cause here's what it cost you." She points toward the floor and there below lies our struggle.

"Just hair," I offer, looking back into the mirror. But the hair on the floor seems to be more hair than I'd ever had in my life.

Now, is how the thought comes to me, but in truth the real word is *soon*. From the moment Philip asked me to call him at his parents, it's all I want to do. I want to stand in his presence and know how wrong he was. I want to stand before him and hear the words that he had made a terrible mistake. That he always loved me.

A reasonable, self-assured woman living my life would not need this. But the reasonable, self-assured woman I thought I had blossomed into doesn't exist, if she ever did. Deep, deep inside I am still fifteen and licking wounds. I am still the hysterical teenager spewing obscenities at Dorothy's front door. I am still the one who wants to place her hands around Dorothy's neck and squeeze until her heart stops.

Seeing Philip has shown me this.

Seeing Philip has obliterated the half-truths and brought forth the reality. Seeing Philip has undermined everything I held dear, has shown my life for the farce it is. There is no doubt I love Emory, but I am still wounded by Philip.

Now as I leave the beauty salon and head toward my car, I try to prepare myself in case Philip is not there.

I am not worried about Philip coming on the line and plans to meet somewhere. I am not even concerned in that moment about all he will say and won't. I am just concerned about his parents hearing me on the other end of the phone after he has left his wife and his life.

The phone rings, rings again. It goes on a third time and I began to sweat beneath my new do. I am about to hang up, courage leaving me when a machine clicks on. "Hello. You have reached the Butlers but we can't come to the phone now. You can leave a message at the sound of the beep. Thanks and have a good day."

But I don't. There is no way I can. I push the red button on my cell and deposit it onto the passenger seat. Take one look at myself and see a stranger peering back.

"Mom?"

I close the door behind me, shopping bags in my hands, a smile fast on my face. "Whatcha think?"

Monet comes up to me, touches it. Marvels at the mahogany highlights, the fluffy fullness. "It's bangin'."

"That means good, right?" I tease.

"Oh yeah . . . Aaron! Come see Mom." she yells.

I try to stop her, but it is too late. Aaron slinks into the living room, eyes gritty, face fixed. Despite trying hard not to be affected, she is. Her eyes blossom briefly, then return to near slits. "You cut your hair."

I know better than to seek more from her than those words, but I cannot help myself. "I think it looks nice," I say with a little shake of my head, wanting to reach out and pull her back to me, reinstill the respect I sense she no longer has. "Doesn't it?"

Aaron does not answer. Just turns and heads back to her room.

"It looks good, Mom," Monet says.

I want to say thank-you, but my throat is locked.

Hours later, I discover my husband is unhappy with my choice.

"What you do?" he asks, coming in the bedroom where I am giving myself a pedicure.

"I changed my hairstyle. You like it?" I shake my head a little, my smile wide.

He comes over, runs his fingers through it. It takes me a minute to realize just what he's doing. "You cut your hair," he admonishes.

"Yeah," I toss back, not liking his tone.

"Why?"

"What do you mean why?"

"I liked your hair long."

I look into his eyes and see the hurt there. "It was time for a change, Emory."

His fingers go back in, their edges moving along my scalp. I pull away. "What are you doing?"

"Looking," he says sheepishly.

"For?"

"The rest of it."

"The rest of what?"

"Your hair."

That he believes Betty has somehow hidden the rest of my hair somewhere inside my hair is a ridiculous assumption. That he is deeply affected by the loss seems a bit much. *It's my hair,* I think, seeing the wounded look still in his eyes. But the wiser me knows better. The wiser me knows that while my breast, my behind, my thighs and my hair are on my body, Emory feels it is all his.

"I like it," I say, matter-of-factly.

"It doesn't even look like you."

"Exactly."

Chapter 15

It's late. Close to midnight. I bring my cigarette to my lips and take a long slow puff. The DJ's voice eases through the radio, heavy and seductive. I close my eyes, think: *We've come a long way.*

Before there was ever a WBLS, WRKS, HOT 97; before black music was allowed on the FM dial and we were consigned to AM to hear our music, there had been WWRL.

Sixteen hundred on the frequency, the end-of-the-line station filled our homes and our lives with music, information and thought-provoking ideas. It was where we heard our voices, our concerns, poets, politicians and activists given free reign in between the Top Ten and the Philadelphia Sound.

I have spent many nights like this in my lifetime, surrounded by the quiet darkness. Back then I'd listen to the soothing voice of Frankie Crocker, LaMarr Renee, Vy Higgesen, speaking soft and gentle over soulful love tunes; my heart filling, yearning to become one with somebody. I would lie in the warm darkness wondering; *Is* he *listening, too, can he feel my thoughts, my heart?*

I have retreated to my workspace, needing a separation from myself and my family. I have come to be filled with music and memory, seduced by a past that shines brighter than any future I can foresee.

It all comes down to love. Lost love, found love, wrong love, right love. Love is the seducer, the charm that makes you want to turn back the clock.

I take another drag of my cigarette, filling up on music. A strange burr comes from the file cabinet behind me. It takes a moment to realize it is my cell, buried deep inside my bag. I dig past my wallet, my eyeglass case, lipsticks, old cash register receipts and a linty comb to find it.

I look at the display. Swallow, connect and utter, "Hello?"

"It's me, Philip."

"I know."

Silence comes, swift, deep; a line in the sand, drawn. I have to decide if I will cross it.

"Your number came up on my folks' phone. They asked me if I knew who it was. I didn't," Philip takes a quick chuckle, "but on a hunch I dialed it back."

My voice looms louder than the whisper I intended. "It was me."

"So much I want to say to you, Suvie." He says my name and I feel old longing. I swallow, glad for the physical distance. "I've been wanting to just sit you down and talk. Explain everything from the moment it happened."

"Talk." My tone has gone from hesitant surprise to angst.

"Face to face."

"Why not over the phone?"

"Because when I tell you, I need to see your face to see."

"See what?" My blood pounds in my ears, so much so I am surprised I can hear his response.

"That you forgive me."

It is not the words that I expect to hear and I find myself dangling, ground gone from my feet. I grapple for footing, struggle to get back on solid terrain. Making it, I pull back. "Forgive you? It's done."

"Is it?"

"Yes, Philip, it is." But I can feel what his question really insinuates and I force it away like I have forced nothing else in my life. "I have to go." I hang up. Light another smoke; listen to Al Green croon about what some woman has done for him. Envy it.

I am about to turn off the radio, go downstairs to bed, when the house phone rings. It's Lisa.

"Suvie, they got Mack."

"Who got Mack?"

"Nassau County. Picked him up for an unpaid ticket." Her voice is thick, low, defeated. Whatever anxiety and fear she had has vanished into a bottom of hopelessness.

I sigh, not wanting to be a part of it, already knowing that this call places me smack-dab in the middle.

"I've been trying to get up some bail money. Been making phone calls all night . . . everybody's broke," she goes on to say.

No, *everybody's* not stupid. It was not Mack's first brush with the law. He has a 1979 TransAm that he keeps up better than his own family. It's a fast car and every chance Mack gets he tests its abilities, usually out in Long Island where the traffic isn't too heavy. He had gotten clocked and ticketed a few times.

Nassau County is not New York City. Nassau County has more than enough officers to handle their crime situation. It is nothing for them to arrest people for unpaid speeding tickets; something Mack miscalculated.

"How much?" I say, thinking of the check I had put in my account the other day.

"Bail is five thousand. Ten percent will get him out."

Five hundred dollars. Lisa had a good job, but she has come to me for money in the past. She does pay it back, but it takes her forever. It is not her doing, it is her gambling-can't-keep-a-job husband Mack's.

Even though it will be a loan, I must look at it as a gift. I must decide if I can afford to give away five hundred dollars; if my family will suffer from its absence, or if Mack needs to spend a couple of nights in lockup to teach him responsibility.

"Suvie?"

I sigh, say "Yeah."

"I'll pay you back. You know I will."

I nod, feeling Lisa's defeat. I scrounge around for other alternatives, ones that don't include me. "What about your house?"

"It's not ours, remember? When we got in trouble before, my parents took it over."

I remember. Mack had gone on a super betting streak, running through their accounts like water. They almost lost the house that time. Lisa's parents came to her rescue but had demanded the title deed.

"Where are you at?" I ask, angry.

"My father just dropped me off. I am at Central Booking on Hempstead Avenue."

"I'm on my way."

I don't feel like explaining anything to Emory and try to get in my clothes and shoes, before he fully wakes up. My plan is to shake him gently, tell him I have to go meet Lisa and dash out the door. But his eyes open before I can leave the bedroom.

"Where?" he asks looking at the clock, confirming the late hour.

"Lisa. I got to meet her."

"Where? Why?"

"Hempstead . . . Mack," I offer, my foot nearly to the door.

He sits up. Turns on the light. "What happened?"

I don't want to tell him, because he will tell me not to. He can't tell me no because it is money I have earned, but he can give me a thousand good reasons why I shouldn't.

"Tickets . . . they picked him up."

His eyebrows rise. "You paying his bail?"

"Yeah." I am out of lies.

"Why?"

I look at him knowing his heart is not my heart. That he does not fully understand the boundaries of best friends and how far it stretches. "Because Lisa's my friend," I say, heading out into the hall.

I drive down Hempstead Turnpike, few cars on the street, the red lights in no hurry to change to green. My anger has not left me, but simmers as I pass by closed fast-food restaurants and mom-and-pop stores.

Decades ago Hempstead used to be the place to live, but like all things time has changed the tranquility into an edgy sort of existence. On the surface all looks calm, but in the air there is a feeling of unsavoriness.

I am preparing myself to speak the words I never have spoken before. I am shoring up in my head the correct way to say them so that I can back Lisa into a corner where she has no choice but to see the stupidity of staying with Mack.

I am going to wage a war in which she must not only admit to defeat but do what she had never considered—leave her good-for-nothing husband behind.

For too long I have allowed the horrors to visit upon her and her son and my heart and mind can no longer take it. I have decided on an alternative and Lisa and Kelvin will move in with me until she finds a place of her own.

I see the precinct ahead, the old-fashioned green globe lights and sandstone building a dead giveaway. I circle the block before I can find a parking space, make my way into the building.

Uniformed officers eye me with distaste. I know their thoughts as I skim past them. No doubt I am here to bail out some drug-dealing son, report the theft of my welfare debit card.

I search the area for Lisa, my words ready. I will pull her aside and talk until she sees reason and is willing to step into a new day. I will speak of her father dropping her off here, but his obvious refusal to bail his son-in-law out.

She is sitting blank face on a bench. The sight of me makes her rise and fall wearily into my arms. She cries and suddenly I understand it all.

She loves him. And that love will make her do whatever it takes to set her husband free. He is all that matters. Mack is her alpha and omega.

"Oh, Suvie," is all she can say and I remember that I love her. That she is my best friend. I cannot ask her to do what now seems impossible. Pushing bitterness away, I whisper words into her ear, hold her for as long as she needs to be held and then together, we walk up to the sergeant's desk.

"Money order or cash," the desk sergeant says without looking at me.

My pen hovers over my check. "I have the money in my account," all I can manage.

His black eyes find me. He does not care. "Then you need to go to your bank on Monday and get some cash."

I'm about to retaliate when Lisa tugs on my arm. She draws me aside, a fevered strumming vibrating her body. "We can go to an ATM," she whispers.

Her desperation surrounds me. I feel a need to pull away. It is heavy and suffocating and I feel as if there is no air. I look at her, my best friend, frenzy deep in her eyes. For a second it is like looking at a stranger and I wonder where the real Lisa has gone.

I go back to the officer, inquire about an ATM. He tells me there's one right across the street, but this time of night, it will more than likely be empty.

True to his word the machine is out of cash. We get into my car and head deeper into Long Island. I spot a blue-and-white Citibank ATM, but I don't like the loosely gathered cluster of teenagers hanging at a pizzeria a few yards away.

I don't stop but continue toward the corner, Lisa's voice disrupting the silence. "What you doing?" her voice, nails against a blackboard. "You passed right by it."

I glance at the worn-down petite woman beside me and realize everything she is is in that holding pen with Mack. I look away. "It didn't look safe; we'll back track to Lynbrook."

"We got to get him out of there, Suvie," she insists.

I don't answer. Just light a cigarette and wait for the light to turn green.

It feels like a million years since I was listening to music up in my workspace, since Philip spoke the wrong words to my ears, but it's only been four hours.

I watch Lisa pace back and forward, hugging herself, eyes filled with despair. It's been two hours since we paid the bail and we are still waiting for Mack. They are doing a background check to make sure there are no other outstanding arrests; that he does not match any other criminals in their system.

I close my eyes, think to call Emory. See Lisa wearing the linoleum bare over a man who should have never owned her. If I don't say it now, I will choke. "Lisa," I manage, but I might as well be talking to the walls. "Lisa," I say with more force. My voice catches her midstep. She nearly trips as she stops and turns.

I pat the chair next to me. "I want to talk to you."

Her head shakes, whirly and fast. She knows what I want to say but will not even consider it. We stare at each other, empty silence between us. "No, Suvie. No."

"Look at you," I say softly. "Look at where being with him has got you."

She is about to defend herself when there is a sound of a electronic lock being released. She dashes up the hall. I sit and wait, hearing her moans and whimpers as she falls deeply into Mack's arms drifting like a ghost in the midst of a haunting.

Mack is hungry, Lisa is relieved and I am tired. Who wins? Mack.

I drive down Hempstead Turnpike in search of an all-night diner. Try as I might I can not stop glancing at them in my rearview mirror.

She doesn't ask a thing. Doesn't scream at him, curse him or anything. Just sits snuggled up under him like a teenager as Mack relays the night.

"Liked ta shit my pants, Lee," he chuckles. "They dragged me out my ride, tossed me on the ground. Put them cuffs on me and hauled my ass to jail. Jail! Can you believed that shit?"

I can, even if they can't. Do the crime and you do the time. But not Mack. Mack has a genie in his back pocket. And I'm the genie's assistant.

He never said thank you.

Hardly even looked my way. Mumbled hey as if that was all that was called for. As if I hadn't left my house in the middle of the night to come and rescue him. As if it wasn't my money that granted him freedom.

My anger is sizzling by the time we pull into Fredrico's, a slightly upscale twenty-four-hour diner where music plays softly in the background and waiters wear little bow ties.

The two of them settle into the booth like new lovers, close, self-consumed and lacking all grace. Mack's lips move off Lisa's face and neck long enough to order fifteen dollars' worth of food. I get up, go outside and call Emory on my cell.

I return, my heart no less heavy and slide into the booth. Even though both Mack and Lisa are staring at me, it is Lisa who speaks. "You got any money? I must of left mine home."

I stare at her, my mouth open. "Five dollars, okay? That's it, all I have." I am yelling and it feels good to let it loose, let it go; send my anger in the right direction for the first time all night.

"Now if you and your husband can eat offa that, then take my last buck. If you can't, then you better cancel all that food." I dig into my purse, fling the bill on the table. Rising, I am a phoenix abandoning the ashes.

"I'm going outside. If you two aren't outside in ten minutes, then I'm going home." I turn and leave, the night heavy with an emptiness that hollows out my heart.

I start a countdown as I unlock the door. Twelve minutes later I start my ignition and pull out of the parking lot. Despite myself, I check my rearview mirror until the diner has vanished out of sight.

Emory is up when I arrive. He sits, the heaviness in my heart mirrored inside him. I cannot hold back my tears, my need to feel his good strong loving arms around me.

He is there in a heartbeat and I lose myself inside the safe warm place that is home, my heart, I think, as he gently ushers me toward our bedroom.

The phone rings for the eighth time this morning. I refused to let anyone answer it. After it stops, I go and check the message. "Can you just pick up the damn phone?" Lisa's recorded message barks.

"Gonna have to talk to her," Emory advises as we have a cup of coffee before he heads for work.

"I know, but I can't. Not now. Every time I think about it . . ." I can't finish, not the sentence, a whole thought, nothing. I am in lockdown. Locked down with Mack and Lisa. Locked down in a way that has nothing to do with putting food on my table, clothes on my back or a roof over my head.

It is so unessential. So not important that I should be able to dismiss it. But I cannot. My friend has hurt me badly and the pain is fresh.

Emory rises from the table. Kisses my head. Heads out the door. Aaron comes into the kitchen. "Who's been calling all morning," she asked, rubbing cold out of one eye.

"Your Aunt Lisa."

"What she want?"

I shrug. Play the innocent.

"We going shopping soon?" she wants to know. "School's coming up." And I know whatever betrayal she sensed on my part has vanished under the burden of want and need. But I am secret with my discovery. I shrug, cool, unaffected. "Haven't thought about it."

"I need some stuff," she announces peering into the refrigerator.

School. Is the summer really almost gone? I know it is nearing the end of July, but there is still August.

"Later next month," I tell her.

"Can I go by myself?"

A mother knows this day is coming but is still not prepared for its arrival. Picking out my daughter's clothes has become a part of my life as much as breathing. It is what I do. But now with Aaron being fifteen, I know my choices and her choices are no longer the same. Realize too she needs to know the responsibility of taking a large sum of money and going to buy for herself.

"I'll be off punishment next week. Figured me and Keisha can do the mall. Take Monet with us if you want."

I don't know what I want anymore. The whole thing with Lisa had robbed me. I offer, "We'll see."

Aaron lets my words linger and fade. She does not moan, frown or blinks. She is becoming wise.

The phone rings again. I motion for Aaron to get it. It is too early for her friends to be calling. She picks up, says hello. Looks at me, says hold on.

With deftness she covers the mouthpiece. Mouths "Aunt Lisa." I shake my head. She says I'm not here. Hangs up and studies me. "You two okay?"

No more lies. "No, Aaron, we aren't."

She makes breakfast and I finish my coffee.

Chapter 16

Best friends.

There is little mystery as to how they are made. We pick people to fill voids in our lives, have a tendency to cling to those who have things about them we ourselves don't possess.

The day Lisa and I met, I never thought we'd become close. I took in the pretty petite coworker and I immediately anointed her a snob. But when we were introduced, her smile was so wide, so genuine, so I'm-so-happy-to-meet-you, that I had no choice but smile back, a knowing coming between us that said we would become fast friends.

Fast friends turned into good friends, good friends, into best. We spent all our free time together, a twosome few could interrupt until Mack happened.

I understood her pleasure and her joy at meeting such a man—Mack was fine. Tall and lean, he had a fast edge about him that women found exciting. They made an attractive couple, but that joining had come at my expense. Suddenly Lisa's time was divided between Mack and me.

Most men weren't threatened by their woman's female friends, but Mack wasn't most men. If I was having issue with him, then he returned the favor twofold. Things always grew tense whenever we shared the same space, leaving Lisa to play the peacekeeper. It was a tough balancing act, but she managed to keep both of us in her life. Still, I missed our times together.

When she told me they were getting married, I pretended to be happy for her, understanding that he had become her love of all loves. Lisa was happy and I went out of my way not to tap-dance on her joy, but always in the back of my mind I knew Mack wasn't good enough.

It was easy not to like him. Easy to turn my nose up at what Lisa perceived as the best thing that had ever happened to her. Maybe it was the fact that he didn't like me; maybe it was the way he seemed to overshadow her life. She could not pass gas without Mack demanding to be there smelling it. Whenever she wasn't with him, she had to constantly check in to let him know where she was.

It was true love as far as Lisa was concerned, but all I saw was a manipulator. When her own mother complained she hardly saw Lisa anymore, I knew it wasn't just me.

Still on her wedding day I was right there as maid of honor. Allowed her joy to reach inside my heart. Mack was not the man I would have chosen for her, but he was the one she had chosen for herself. I made myself respect that.

I had met Emory by then and he helped fill in the gaps Lisa's new life had carved. By the time Emory and I had said "I do," Lisa had settled into her new role with ease. She seemed peaceful and happy. I came to look upon their life together as something Lisa not only wanted but needed. Then three years into her marriage she came to me with a confession that blew the lid right out the water.

"He stays out, won't keep a job. Gambles away our money. Says nasty things to me." I did not expect those words from her. Despite my own reservations, I could not believe her life had come to that. I did not see how Mack could not see the jewel Lisa was, that he would treat her so badly.

Leave him, I was thinking. *Just pack your bags and go.* I had been working up the courage to say those words when she beat me to the punch. "Can't even leave because I'm pregnant."

It was bad timing, plain and simple. Lisa had been one of the few women I knew who never had to make that trip to the clinic to undo what nature had planned and they hadn't. Her womb had never been scraped out, sucked dry. No baby had ever begun and ended life still inside her.

I asked her if she still loved Mack even though we both knew the answer. Asked her if she thought he would change. She had the hope he would and I left it at that. She went back home that day, no less saddened, no less disillusioned. Went back to the husband who caused her grief.

That first confession freed her up to share more of the drama. At least once a month she called me upset about what Mack was putting her through. Even though I never said it, all I wanted was for her to leave. All I knew was how she wanted to stay.

Before last night I had never even suggested it. Before last night I had learned to turn my heart and my mind off from even speaking those words. But last night happened and everything is changed because of it. It's cleared me of keeping silent and has allowed my anger to manifest.

The doorbell rings.

I know before I even answer who it is. I know that she has not gone to work and has chosen instead to come and confront me. What I am not sure of is what words will be spoken. If she will be apologetic or continue to play the hand that began last night.

I open the door. The multicolored bruise around her eye, the swollen blackberry mark about her mouth, a startling discovery.

"Happy," she says, outraged. "This what you wanted?" she demands as she forces her way into my house. "He beat me, Suvie. He beat me good. Ain't never laid no hand on me ever, but last night he kicked my ass."

That she is dry-eyed amazes me. The fire in which she speaks the words is amazing, too. She is not hurt; she is not belittled, just pissed. That anger she lacked last night now sizzles.

"Wanna know why?"

I don't. It's not important. All that matters is he did. But I allow her her words. Know she needs to speak them. "Because you left us out in the boondocks, like that's my fault."

The ridiculousness of it finds me, but the notion also fills me with terror. I no longer know what Mack is capable of and fear rushes me.

"I tried to tell him it wasn't my fault. Tried to tell him you got your own mind, but he wouldn't hear it. We called a cab and he cursed us both all the way home." She pauses, shakes her head, the ludicrousness of it with her. "Cabby told me not to get out. Said he'd take me somewhere 'safe,' which just pissed Mack off more." Caught up, she is back to last night and sadness flows through her. "For a minute I thought about doing just that. Thought about not getting out and just riding off forever."

Tears glimmer in her eyes. "He grabbed me by the back of my neck. Hauled my ass into the house and threw me on the couch. He finds my stash of money, goes out and pays the cabby and comes back yelling. All his yelling and screaming woke up Kelvin. He came into the living room and saw us. Tried to intervene and Mack knocked him into the wall. My baby was lying there hurt and scared, and something in me just snapped. I started swinging and Mack started swinging back. When he got too tired to beat me, he kicked me. And when I was too hurt to even whimper, he stormed out the house."

Lisa stands there, the horror still fresh. She is a woman done in by her own heart. "He ain't never done nothing like that before," which I know is the absolute truth. He has cursed her, spent their money, refused to get a job and just taken up space, but he has never struck until now.

"Where's Kelvin?" I managed

"At my mother's. He won't come back, you know. Told me he was going to his nana's and he wasn't coming back until Mack left for good." Years in the making, the war has began.

"Can't blame him," I mutter.

"What you mean you can't blame him. That's his daddy."

Yes and the worst kind, I think. The absolutely worst type of father any youngster can have. It forces children to take sides, be silent against the abuse. It tears at the fabric of their very soul with little possibility of healing.

"Let him be, Lisa," I said softly. "If he wants to stay with your mother, let him. When he's ready to come home, he will. He deserves that much."

She begins to protest, but her energy is draining fast. She plops down into a chair and I go off to make her some coffee and retrieve an ice pack for her bruises.

Lisa has been pushed into that corner. Now she has to decide if she will stay or make her way out.

I don't know what I will tell Emory, but I know I will have to tell him something. His alliance with Lisa is not like mine. He thinks she is a fool and has little patience for her.

Lisa has agreed to stay with me a few days. I have pulled out my portable cot. I put it in my workroom upstairs. Pray.

Our dinner table is unusually quiet. It is the fifth chair squeezed at the edge that does it. I see Emory staring at Lisa and wish he will stop. But he is too far away to kick and I doubt if it will do any good.

Monet is the first to finish and she rises, headed toward the bathroom. It has become routine, old hat for us, but for Lisa it's all brand-new.

"She going to throw up?" the first words Lisa has spoken since we sat down.

"She's sick," Emory insists, his anger apparent. Lisa starts to say something, decides against it. Instead she leaves her half-eaten plate and goes and sits on the front stoop to have a cigarette. I finish up my meal and join her.

"Don't pay Emory no mind," I say, easing down next to her. "Men don't understand."

Lisa looks at me. "What about you, do you understand?" Her eyes are boring into me in search of my truth. "I didn't plan this," she says after a while. "I never said, 'Let me marry Mack so he can spend my money, yell at me all the time and beat me.' I never thought I'd end up here, but I'm here already, y'know? And I know it's not where I am suppose to be, but I am."

"What about your son?"

Lisa sighs. "Fifteen? Those formative years are gone. He has already seen, witness. Learned. What difference would it make if I left Mack now . . . damage is done."

"You not going back to him?"

She does not answer. Looks away.

"Why?"

"Because despite it all, I love him, Suvie. I love him like I ain't never loved anybody before."

"But does he love you?"

Her eyes find me again. "You know that doesn't even matter. A heart don't care who be loving who, only about who it loves." She looks away, drags on her cigarette. I stare out into the night.

I am in the kitchen doing dishes when I hear noises from upstairs. A little while after Lisa comes down, folded linen in her hand. "Where you want me to put these?"

It is the sheets and blanket from the cot I made for her. I know without asking that she is going home. I turn back to my dishes, indicate up the hall. "Linen closet by the bathroom."

She leaves and I hear a door open then close. Her footsteps are muffled as she backtracks my way. We stare at each other, unsure of what it all means, of how our lives will or will not intertwine from this point onward. We both know what the other wants, but there is no middle ground. We are at absolutes with no room for compromise.

"You know I love you, Lisa."

She nods, eyes glistening.

"And you deserve so much more."

"I know," her voice barely a whisper.

My mouth moves but no words come. I have said it all.

"I'll be okay," she utters, her voice cracking. "Don't worry about me, I'm going to be fine."

But never happy, I think.

She slips her pocketbook onto her shoulder and I just want to chain her in my basement. My stomach is sick with worry and fear. I do not want her to leave.

"Give me a hug," she says and I go to her, embracing her hard. We are both teary eyed as we ease each other, our fingers quick about our cheeks.

"I love Mack, but I love my life, Suvie. I got a son who needs me and I'm not going to let anything bad happen."

But it already has and she is still there. I tell her so, knowing it is not the parting words she needs to hear.

"No man's gonna beat me. He hit me one more time, then I swear on my grandmother's grave I'm gone." There is a fire in her eyes. I just hope it remains.

I wanted Lisa backed into the corner but find it is myself who is there. My mind is exploring my world of what if. What if it were me in that situation? Would I be able to walk away? Just say no?

There should be an out. Some in case of emergency switch to flip when staying is no real choice at all. There needs to be a device, some pill, a special prayer that untangles the heart and sets you fully free.

Love shouldn't be so cruel, so unkind, unjust. Love should recognize true love and leave the imposters alone. Love is supposed to be wise but in my world, it is just a lie. Love has no allies, is true only unto itself.

I am barefoot, standing in the street, looking at the car packed with things and Philip is standing by the driver's side. He has already asked me if I am coming, but this time he is waiting patiently for my answer.

I feel someone beside me. I turn and it is another Philip except I know it's really Emory. "Are you going?" Emory/Philip asks me.

I look back at Philip who is waiting patiently by the car. I can see his face, but I cannot read his thoughts. "Are you coming?" he asks again and I know in my heart the words I must speak. My answer bubbles up my throat but can go no farther.

"He's waiting for your answer, Suvie," the Emory/Philip beside me is saying. "He's been waiting and time is almost up."

"But I'm already beside him," I manage, confused.

"No, you are beside us both," Emory/Philip tells me and then I am awake, my heart beating in my chest, Philip's face fading slowly from my mind.

I don't want to analyze the dream. Don't want to know its true meaning, but the significance is already there. It takes awhile but soon I am sleeping, and like a two-part movie, the dream goes on.

I am in the car now, things crammed up against the back of my seat, Philip at the wheel. We are on our way upstate and it is fall, my favorite time of the year. The leaves stand out in bright surreal colors of orange, brown and yellow.

We have been driving for a long time and I am tired of the ride. *I just want to get there,* I think, the winding road scattered with fallen leaves.

It takes a second to realize Emory/Philip is not with us. That somehow we left him behind. I ask Philip where he is but Philip ignores me and stares straight ahead.

"Suvie . . ."

I turn around in my seat and see nothing but things. I sense Emory/Philip is back there somewhere and I need to find him.

"Suvie," he calls again and I go to climb into the back, but the seat belt restrains me and I began fumbling with the release.

"Won't work," Philip says.

"Why?"

"Because you really don't want it to."

But in my heart I know better and fumble some more.

"You got to want it, Suvie," Philip says, the road endless and Technicolor with autumn.

"But I do," I respond, wanting more than ever to get there or get out.

"You don't," Philip answers with a chuckle and I come awake again, the eerie laughter echoing inside my head.

I look at the clock. It is thirty-three minutes after three in the morning. The witching hour. The house is filled with the creepy silence that remains after a bad dream. I go to wake Emory *and tell him what?* Resist the idea.

I get up out of bed, turn on the hall light as I go. I get a glass of water and go upstairs to my workspace. I turn on the radio, smoke cigarettes, thinking.

Chapter 17

A strange electronic melody invades the quiet of my bedroom. I look toward my pocketbook hanging on a door handle and know its source. So does Emory.

"Who's calling you on that? Don't they know your home number?"

I shrug. "Probably a wrong number."

"You want me to get it?" he asks, taking a step.

I sit up, feet hitting the carpet. "No." I reach into my bag, find the slim device, feel it *brrrr* against my palm like a kitten stroked. Press the off button. Bring it to my ear. Dead air greeting me as I say "Hello? Hello?" In the middle of my performance, I pull the phone away, stare at the digital display, see the number I've purposefully forgotten. Shrug. "Nobody there."

Pitching the cell back into my bag, I get back into bed, nestle into pillows as if sleep is the only thing on my mind.

I am expecting the call. I knew it would come but wasn't certain if it would be while I was paying for dry cleaning or checking the freshness of meats at Key Food. I am nearly to the dry cleaners when my cell rings.

"Suvie?"

"Yeah."

"It's Philip."

"How are you?"

"I could be better."

"Oh?"

"I have to talk to you, Suvie. Alone."

"I'm alone now. I'm in my car."

"Not by phone."

I know this. Agree on a meeting point. Disconnect and head for the place I thought I'd never go again.

I fiddle with the radio as I drive down the North Conduit. I have WBLS, WRKS and CD101.9 programmed, but what I seek cannot be found on any of those stations. I hit the search button, music and voices slipping from my speaker like a waterfall of disconnected emotions.

A lot of it is Hispanic, with talk radio and hip hop coming in a close second, none of which I need. I am searching for *before*. Not the R&B of my youth before, but the other music that found me back then. The ones that were infused with sixties' hopes struggling against seventies' realities.

I am searching for America's "Horse With No Name," Joni Mitchell's, "Help Me." I need Maria Muldaur's "Midnight at the Oasis," Carol King's "So Far Away." I yearn for Bette Midler's "Do You Want to Dance?" Songs I loved in secret. Songs that touched my heart differently than Stevie Wonder, the O'Jays, and the Delphonics.

I am searching for the other me, the wounded me, the one who crawled into the hole of despair, licking my wounds as soft melodious white voices surrounded me, full of guitars, horns and no bass—airy, cloud-filled bittersweet joy, dipped in sorrow.

A reckoning is before me, one that I have hid from for decades. One that makes me take the right toward the Van Wyck Expressway a little too sharp. One that races my heart, pounds my head. Allows me to do this.

Allows me to meet Philip.

I am punching the search button of my radio like a mad woman.

When John Lennon's "Woman" fills my car, my finger stops, my ears buzz as a much-needed peace fills me. I sit back and light a cigarette. By my sixth puff, the song ends and the call letters of WNEW fill my car reminding me of how much times have changed.

I remember when WNEW was a news radio show and the only music you heard were from commercials or the station's call letters. An unexpected sadness comes into me. There is no going back. Is that my hope? That Philip and I gather up what remains and move forward?

As I zip beneath the Rockaway Boulevard underpass, I refuse to answer that.

Traffic flows quickly until I reach Atlantic Avenue. Construction ahead brings everything to a slow crawl. Cars move at five miles an hour. I look at the digital clock on my dash and see that I have four minutes to get there. I will be late.

Will he wait? Will he think I've changed my mind? Too late I realize I should have taken the side streets, but somehow I've chosen the long way. I don't ask myself why as my car crawls twenty feet. The sun is high in the sky and its beams sizzle inside my car despite the air conditioner being on high.

I flip the visor, but it does little to take the rays of the sun off the left side of my face, my bare arms. I begin to sweat a little and my car fills with cigarette smoke. I crack the window to allow some of it to escape.

The crotch of my white shorts pinches me. I shift and tug at the hem. Aaron calls them "wannabe booty cutters" though they are three inches too long to qualify. Still they are shorts I usually only wear around the house

A white sleeveless mock turtle completes the picture. I glance at myself and see a vision in white. Virginal, something I will always be to Philip.

A break comes in traffic but just as quickly the car in front of me slows. Following suit, I apply my brake.

It is seventeen minutes after one by the time I pull into the empty staff parking lot behind Jamaica High School. I see Philip rise off the bleachers. He is moving toward me before I can undo my seat belt, extinguish my cigarette and pop a Tic Tac into my mouth.

Philip moves toward me before I can swallow the huge rush of relief that he is still waiting. Before I can unlock my car door and put one foot onto the hot asphalt. I tell my eyes to stop studying the still muscular legs, the rippled brown of his arms, but they don't obey. His indigo denim shorts, sleeveless Carolina Blue T-shirt, an irresistible lure.

Not quite August and the sun burns into me as I close my car door. I want to move, but my feet won't go, so I stand and wait, my heart triple-beating in his arrival. His face is older, his hair contains smidgens of gray, but it is the same Philip I fell for so long ago. After weeks of his return, we are finally alone.

I'm not sure what will happen, but I have to make a quick determination of all that will not. Yes, I want this moment, but I must be clear within myself of the emotion and physical boundaries.

Sweat races down the side of my face and I wipe it. I try to smile as he draws near, but old pain stiffens my face. I see the life we could have had, the deep love we could have shared. I set the perfect fit of us—two spoons cut from the same mold, but what he has done changed all of it.

I look beyond him and see the huge oval of dry grass surrounded by the track. I spy graffiti in Technicolor along the cement wall and lastly I gaze up at the towering structure of mortar and stone that is Jamaica High School.

"Still looks the same," Philip calls out to me, the distance between us growing short.

I nod my head, longing for shelter, a cool breeze. My back is damp and I feel my shirt sticking to my skin. I become conscious of my white shorts, my white top. Even my white canvas open-back Keds have me feeling conspicuous. I resist the urge to tug down the edge of my shorts.

"I didn't think you were coming."

"Traffic," I say. Before the word is finished, he is before me, his cologne riding the hot air, his arms reaching out to hold me but I sidestep his attempt.

Philip accepts the unspoken boundaries. Looks about him. "I didn't think it would be so hot out."

"Me either."

He points toward the bleachers. "Over there?"

"No shade." He continues to scan the perimeter, settling on an old oak tree some thirty yards away. "Under the tree. We can sit." It looks cool, but I have on white and tell him so.

"There's a comforter in my car," he offers.

I nod my head and move toward the shade as he trots off. I stand under the spread of the tree's leaves and wait for Philip's return, wondering what words he will speak and how they will change my world.

I sit Indian-style on the comforter that has seen one picnic too many, pushing my thoughts away from who has lain here and why. Philip stretches out on his side, legs crossed as if we are picnicking.

I look around me, wondering what picture we present, glad that we are far from my neighborhood. I think about leaving Aaron at home while she is still on punishment, tap-dance on the image of Emory sitting at his desk at work. "I can't stay long," I find myself saying.

Philip catches my eyes and it is lightening strike twice. Everything in me goes live-wired and I forget how to breathe until he looks away. Reeling with so many emotions, I feel punch-drunk. But his next words sober me.

"She planned it."

I am not surprised, but it hurts to hear what I always thought. "But you were a willing participant, right?"

My cell phone rings snatching me from my anger and I fumble in my purse. I see my home number. Connect. "Hello?"

"Mom?"

"Yeah."

"Where are you?"

"Running some errands, why?"

"The leftover meat loaf, is it for dinner?"

"No, Aaron. I'm picking up something on the way home."

"So I can eat it, right?"

"Yes, you can eat and I'll be home soon."

"Okay." She disconnects. I put my phone away. Try to remember what Philip was saying, what I was feeling. Can't.

"Yeah, I was," he tells me.

"Was what?"

"A participant, but I can't say how willing."

I remember now. He has told me Dorothy planned it. I want to know everything. "How?"

Philip looks behind him, back at the high school that had held his secrets. He closes his eyes, sighs a little. "It started one day after class. I'm leaving, off to meet you by the flagpole and suddenly she's there. There and talking about what she wants to do to me, things I'd never ask you to do."

"Fuck?" the word bitter from my mouth.

"No, yeah, I mean. No, no right away. She talked about giving me a blow job."

I cannot stop the laughter that comes from my mouth. Cannot stop the feelings of anger that course through me. "A blow job? You left me, went with her, my so-called best friend, married her and spent nearly thirty years with her because of a blow job? You broke my heart, denied me my best friend because you needed your dick sucked?"

He reaches for me. "Suvie." But I dance away from his attempt. I stare at him, eyes blazing. "That is what you're saying, right? You left me, quit me, because I wasn't ready but good 'ol Dorothy Maynard was willing to put your dick into her mouth."

Philip hangs his head, shame on him thick. When he lifts it again, his eyes are awash in sorrow. "I was sixteen."

"Sixteen and stupid. Sixteen and selfish. Sixteen and too damn horny for your own good."

"You weren't doing nothing for me."

His words sting like a slap. I blink, mouth moving, but no sound comes out. In a heartbeat there are tears in my eyes. One spills down my cheek. He reaches over and wipes it. I allow him to, his touch, healing.

"I'm sorry. I shouldn't have said that." I say nothing, cannot say anything. I am too numb. "But the truth was I couldn't wait," he goes on to say. "And it was the biggest mistake of my life."

His words draw my eyes. I see so much in them, myself included. But the past cannot be undone and my sympathy shifts quickly. "But you stayed with her, Philip."

"Yeah, I did. And I know how, but I don't know *how.*"

"Some part of you must of wanted it."

He chuckles. It is a bitter sound. "The moral side, yeah. The religious. But later on, it just became life, my life, Dorothy's. Ours . . . I never stopped wanting you."

"But you didn't come back to me."

"I tried but you weren't giving me the time of day. Then Dorothy started talking about being pregnant and I knew I was done."

"Pregnant?" I'm stunned. The Dorothy I knew never wanted children.

"That's what she said. Till this day I don't know for sure, but the Catholic in me said we had to get married."

"So why now?"

"What do you mean?"

"Why did you leave her now?"

There is sorrow in his eyes and need. It is the need that answers my question.

Silence comes and in the hush, we arrive at a bottom line, a bottom line that Philip never wanted and one that I am fixed squarely in. I lift my left hand, the gold band shimmering softly. "Nineteen years of a good marriage and twenty-one years with a wonderful man is what this represents. Emory is everything to me."

It takes him awhile to understand all that I've said and the things I haven't. It takes him a hot second to see that the little girl he has longed for is gone. In her place stands me, Sylvia Allen, with a life he can neither touch nor re-enter.

"It could have been different," I find myself saying, "So very different. But you made a choice, Philip, and everything changed because of it."

"So why did you agree to meet me then?" His eyes are burning into mine.

"Because some part of me is still fifteen years old and broken-hearted and I need answers. I need to know why. I need to know if somewhere inside of you, I still matter. That Dorothy could not do away with all of me . . ." My confession takes me by surprise.

"So you do still care?"

I swallow. "I never stopped."

"Loving me." It is not a question.

I make myself look at him, hiding nothing. "Yes, loving you."

Something shifts around us. Something quick and unexpected. I never see Philip sit up or reach for me, but suddenly his arms are around me, his lips are pressed to mine and his tongue is making long-ago music inside my mouth.

I am dancing with him, dancing emotionally with him like we used to. Rainbows spin my heart. A sweet completeness fills my soul, so absolute that I never want his hands to stop their glide along my spine. Suddenly I am no longer Sylvia Allen, but Sylvia Morrow, fifteen and smitten. Fifteen and in love for the first time.

My heart feels as if it has known no greater joy. I don't want to stop, even though what I am doing makes me a liar, wiping away the last thirty years of my life.

I lose track of time. Seconds, minutes, hours? I'm not sure as we have found our way to our knees, one-skinned, and kissing, my wounded heart healing beat by beat. Philip's hands play music along my hips, my arms, the small of my back. His cologne fills my every breath. His fast-beating heart matches my own rhythm. It is heaven.

A car horn blasts. A shout of "Get a room!" breaks the spell. I pull away. There is a rekindled fire in Philip's eyes asking a question his mouth will never speak.

I force myself back into the future. Answer it. "It's too late," I offer, struggling to get beyond this moment. "Much too late," I say, all that is, coming to light. "I never stopped loving you. Not once. But the possibility of that love died in nineteen seventy-three."

"How do you know that, Suvie? How do you really know?"

"Because when you should have left Dorothy, you didn't."

I stand up, gaze toward Jamaica High. Philip rises, too, and reaches for me. But something about me makes him halt the attempt. His eyes are soft and wounded. I resist stepping inside of his sorrow "So this is it?"

My face moves into a weary smile. "*It* was it a long time ago. This?" My arms lift out. "This is the good-bye we never really had the chance to say, so I am saying it now. Good-bye, Philip."

I turn and walk away, whispering the past a hushed farewell, ready to embrace my future.

I enter my house and Aaron meets me at the door.

"Watcha buy?"

Her question confuses me. "Buy?"

"You said you were running errands. Was going to bring back dinner."

I've forgotten. Forgotten about picking up the dry cleaning, milk and bread. Something for dinner. I blink and blink again. Stumble for an answer. "We're having KFC. I'll run out later." I move past her, go to my room and close the door.

Hours later as I stand in my kitchen taking out plates and getting glasses, I hear Emory pull into the driveway. A sharp guilt fills me and I try to fix my face into something normal, but I don't know what that is.

I hear the front door open and close. Go to the freezer to get ice for the glasses. Wait for my husband to discover me and pray that nothing different shows on my face.

Emory comes into the kitchen, pecks my cheek. "Hey."

"Hey back," I said, dumping cubes into the glasses.

He leans towards the red and white bucket. "KFC?"

"Yeah. Too hot to cook."

"Where are the kids?"

"In their room. Dinner is almost ready."

Emory moves out of the kitchen and heads down the hall. I hear a rap on a door, the twist of a knob. Then "Hey, Monie."

"Hey, Daddy."

A few seconds later there is another rap on another door, the twisting of a knob. "Hey, Aaron" is all I hear. I strain to hear a reply but the only sound that comes is of the door being gently closed.

I am pouring ice tea into glasses when Emory appears. "What's up with Aaron?"

"What do you mean?"

"She looks like something's wrong."

I swallow, fake casual indifference. "You know that child. When's the last time she looked like anything was right?" But I know Aaron has sensed my deceit this day and my heart strums as I wonder if she will hold up her end of the deal.

"I forgot the dry cleaning, but I'll get it tomorrow," I tell Emory as we settle in for the eleven o'clock news.

I fight off a yawn, the long day coming to an end, the mask of normalcy heavy on my shoulders. Betrayal floats around me, something I did not anticipate and I try to emotionally shoo away.

"The charcoal Dockers are in there?"

"I think so."

He sighs a little, but not enough to sting. It is not the first time I've forgotten something and he knows it will not be the last.

As I watch Emory ditch his basketball shorts and slip into pajama bottoms, a new fear finds me. If we make love tonight, will he know another man's lips have touched mine?

I put my eyes back to the television as Emory gets into bed. I tense as he turns toward me, his lips against mine brief. My breath lets go as he utters "Good night" and burrows into his pillow, ignorant of whom, this day, his wife has become.

Chapter 18

Remnants of the day before are still with me the next morning.
I awake to an empty room, Emory off to work and I'm not
able to remember just when he left or if he kissed me good-bye.

I get out of bed and make my way to the bathroom. I hear a television coming from behind Monet's closed door, whispers from behind Aaron's. Despite my full bladder, I knock and open it before
she can call out.

She is quick, but in a split second I see the cordless phone being
slipped beneath her pillow. I start to scold her, but something in
her eyes stops me. Dare and knowledge. They are powerful tools
that halt me. But only for a moment.

I march across her room and with deftness, slip my hand under
her pillow. Retrieve the phone. "No calls," I bark with an anxious
bitter fire.

She says nothing as I turn and leave her room, but I feel the
words inside of her. They press against my back like an maelstrom,
hungry for destruction.

The dry cleaning I forgot yesterday demands my attention today.
The last thing I want to do is leave Aaron at home but asking her
along will magnify my guilt.

I leave and am back home within twenty minutes and am re-lieved that my household is the way I left it—Monet watching TV in her room, Aaron playing her music. But there is an elephant in my house and I know the cards are going to fall and soon.

I go to my room, hang the dry cleaning in the closet, startled as the shelf tilts, sending items to the floor. I stand there for a mo-ment, staring at the fallen pile, fuming. Emory was supposed to have fixed it.

I leave everything out, the shelf tilting, so that he can see it for himself when he gets home.

I decide to work in my garden. I go into my backyard and tend my flowers, working up a heavy sweat. I take a long cool shower, change my clothes and take up camp in the living room. I watch television, flipping channels before I decide on the Discovery Channel.

I watch a woman have hip replacement surgery, feel the pound of the hammer as they replace bone with steel. Afterwards, I move to TLC where two sets of neighbors decorate each other houses. When *A Wedding Story* comes on, I change the station.

I get up and make lunch. Monet asks if she can go down to Ayesha's house and I tell her yes. It's just Aaron and me in the house and she hibernates in her room.

The phone rings and for a moment I think it may be Philip. But it's Chelsea, wanting to know if we still planned to come up before the summer ends. Emory was supposed to call her and give the bad news, but it's obvious that he hasn't.

"I'm not really sure, Chell."

"I haven't seen you guys since last summer."

"I know, but there's so much going on now."

"Like what?"

I realize I've said too much. No one outside of our immediate family knows about Monet's eating disorder, my own personal dilemma. I am not about to tell any of it. I lie. "I have a ton of grants I have to finish by the end of August and then school starts and you know how that is."

But Chelsea doesn't, something I forget. I'm not certain if Chelsea never wanted kids or could never have them. Foot in my mouth, I struggle to recover. "Endless hours of school shopping, hair appointments, the whole nine yards."

There is silence on the other end. I imagine Chelsea in her big rambling museum of a house, all by herself for days on end and feel a tinge of guilt. "Listen," I say quickly, "I'll check with Em when he gets home. Maybe we can squeeze in a weekend before now and then."

"That would be great. I really miss you guys." There is longing in her voice and I know why. In her eyes, our family is completion. In her eyes, we have reached life's peak.

But there are fissures in our foundation, cracks that grow wider each day. A deep rumble reverberates and soon it will implode.

I can't remember the last time Aaron wanted to go to Home Depot with Emory. Years perhaps? There is no doubt the wire rack shelf in our closet has to be replaced and Emory has to make the trip. What surprises me is that Aaron wants to tag along.

"Can I go?" she asks quickly as she runs water into the sink to start her after-dinner chores.

Emory is as surprised as I am. He looks at her funny. "With me. To Home Depot." It is not a question.

"Yeah. I've been cooped up in this house for days."

My mouth opens. "You have a kitchen to clean."

She avoids my gaze. Seeks her father's eyes. "I can do it after, right, Daddy? Can't I do it after we come back?"

"I guess she can."

"She's on punishment," I said quickly.

"Taking a ride with me to Home Depot doesn't means she isn't," Emory says back.

My eyes dance to Aaron's and what I see steals my breath. The elephant is ready to charge and when Emory returns from his short shopping spree, who I am to him, how he sees me will be changed forever.

I am upstairs in my office. I am trying to prepare my soul for battle. I hear Emory's car pull into the drive and my heart triple-beats.

My palms grow sweaty, adrenaline races through me. I hear car doors slam but nothing else. The animated voices that left here half an hour ago are absent.

I hear the front door open and close, hear footsteps coming my way. I reach for a cigarette and light one with trembling fingers. Tell myself that I didn't do anything wrong. That if anything, I did what was right. That I took brave steps to close the door on my past and in the process I have freed up myself to love Emory with all of my heart.

I tell myself that the good-bye kiss was as innocent as a handshake. I tell myself it was nothing more than a real good-bye.

Then Emory is standing before me, his body blocking the ceiling light outside the door. I try to meet his eyes but am unable to. I inhale and blow out a stream of gray.

"Where were you?" he says with trepidation.

"When?" I answer as casually as I can manage.

"Yesterday afternoon."

"I just went to run errands." I turn on my computer and wait for it to load.

"Aaron says you told her you were running errands, but when you came home you were empty-handed."

My eyes shoot defiantly toward my husband. "Is she my keeper now?"

"Did you go meet Philip?" He is looking at me and I see the fire raging. Looks at me and I see hurt stirring up in the mix. I try to find a response but nothing comes. Emory fills in the blanks. "All these years we've been together and I have to hear from my own daughter that Philip was your ex?"

"Because it didn't matter."

"What do you mean it didn't matter? I come home to find him sitting on my couch, find out you snuck away with him and you talking about it didn't matter."

"Who did I marry? Who am I with now?"

"Who did you sneak off to see?"

"Number one I didn't sneak."

"So why did you lie to Aaron?"

"I was trying to avoid just this, that's why."

"Avoid what, me finding out?" I hear the absurdity in his voice.

Feel it like a wall of water. It crashes down on me. Swirls me around. Drags me with its undertow as I struggle for breath.

Emory is silent, still, but I can feel his body vibrating. I know what I must do, tell the whole truth though nothing inside of me wants to speak it.

"I was fifteen," I began, trying to remove my soul from the telling. "Fifteen and he was sixteen and Dorothy was my best friend." I am trying to be impartial, trying to tell the story without claiming the emotions. But speaking the words rushes me back to then and sorrow takes a fast hold. "She wanted him. Wanted him and took him from me. My best friend in the whole wide world took Philip and it hurt."

Tears glisten in my eyes. I don't want anyone to witness the sadness. But Emory is there and I must finish. I push through it all and get the tale told. "I went on with my life; they went on with theirs. They got married, moved to Georgia, the whole nine. I tried not to make it matter anymore and after a while it didn't. Then I get that letter from her. Then she and Philip show up that day, and bam, it's all back."

"What's all back?"

My voice grows soft, wounded. "The hurt . . . it was like I was fifteen all over again and they had just done it to me yesterday, you know? Sitting up there with them like that, it was hard. But it was the past and I made myself forgive them. I thought I did. I thought none of it mattered until Philip came here that last time."

"And?"

"He told me him and Dorothy was getting a divorce. That he wanted to talk to me. I didn't want to. Didn't want to know a thing. But it was like I was running from it and I got tired of running. So I went yesterday. I went and we talked. Met at our old high school. I spent all of fifteen minutes with him."

"What did he say?"

"He told me how it happened between him and Dorothy."

"And?"

I see the questions and suspicions brewing in my husband's eyes. Struggle to squash it. "And nothing. I told him that I was happy with you and that was that."

"Happy. Not love. But happy?"

"Of course love," I defend.

"But did you tell him that?"

In truth I haven't. Wrangle with a lie; go for the truth. "No."

"Let me get this straight. You sneak off to be with some guy, 'your first' as Aaron puts it and not once did you tell him that you loved me?"

"It's not how it sounds, Emory."

But he is not hearing me. His mind is full of a scenario that has not taken place. "And all you two did was talk, right? At your old high school, right?"

"Yes," I say, but Emory has headed back down the stairs.

If asked, it would have been me on the couch, me on our old sofa that has stood the test of time. I have spent enough evenings dozing in its nubby corner and would have been able to spend the night there. But Emory beat me to the punch.

He is already there, a pillow, summer blanket placed on one side, as he sits, stone faced, eyes toward the television. The remote is in his hand and he is flipping channels as I come down the stairs, blue light flashing like thunder about our darkened living room.

I pause to say something, but no words come out of my mouth. I ask God for a quick time to heal us, that by morning's light we will have taken some emotional step closer to forgiveness.

But even as I ask this, as I move past my husband, I cannot find the belief that my prayer will be answered, cannot find the comfort I need.

Chapter 19

Morning comes and I am exhausted. I have not slept much, my body finally giving away to sheer exhaustion around two in the morning. At a quarter after seven Emory's movements wake me and I play possum, waiting for him to get dressed and leave for work.

I wait until I hear the sound of his engine starting, then count to twenty before I get out of bed. I make my way toward the bathroom, the smell of aftershave full in the humid after-shower air. I breathe deeply, wondering if I will ever get the chance to know it against his skin.

I use the toilet, brush my teeth, splash my face and head to the kitchen. Encounter Aaron who is sitting at the table eating a bowl of cereal.

I mumble good morning. Do not hear a reply and don't expect one. I put water on to boil, get a coffee mug, the jar of instant coffee. My movements are quick and agitated as I try to escape the penetration of her gaze, but there is no escaping and I feel her words bubbling up before the sound reaches my ears.

"Why'd you do it? Why'd you lie and sneak to see that man?"

I turn, drawn by the heartbreak in her voice, taken back by the tears streaming down her cheeks.

"It's not like that," I say carefully, calmly, though nothing in me is calm.

"Yes. It. Is," she screams at me, standing, fists balled, live-wired. "Yes, it is!," she releases again as if her life depended on it.

I go to hold her but she pushes me away so hard I bang into the counter. "Don't touch me. Don't you ever touch me again! You ain't nothing but a liar," she bellows, running out of the kitchen.

I can't move. Can't think. Can't breathe. I can only cry, silently and forever, awash in a thousand guilts.

The day is lonely. No one speaks to me, looks at me. Not even Monet. I am invisible in my own home and Emory's silence when he comes home from work is the worst punishment. His anger brushes me everytime we cross paths. I want to reach out and touch him. Want to sit him down and try once more to explain. But I cannot get my hand to lift or my mouth to work.

By bedtime I am beyond my breaking point. The silence is about to smash me to bits. I sit on the bed as Emory comes into the room, grabs a pillow, retrieves a blanket. Sit there, wanting an in.

"Emory," I say, so overwrought I cannot think straight. He doesn't answer, just heads out of the room. I find myself hot on his heels, my footfalls fast behind him. I nearly bang into him as he dumps the bedding onto the sofa.

"Emory," I plead again, voice cracking, tears flowing like rain. I touch him and he pulls away with such force, it hurts my fingers.

"No, Suvie. Goddamn it, no!" He throws his body onto the couch. Stretches out, back to me.

I fall to my knees. "Emory, please. You have to know. It's not what you think." But my words fall on deaf ears and I collapse to the floor, the sound of my children's footsteps stirs up the pain.

I imagine the picture we present—Emory on the couch, me on the floor. It is not how I want them to see us, but we are too thick into the drama to stop it.

"I'm sorry," I mutter to the carpet, mucus sliding out of my nose. "So sorry," I say again, meaning it with everything I have.

"Mom?" I hear Monet cry. "Mom?"

"Leave her, just leave her," Aaron decides, condemnation full in her voice.

I cannot stop crying. Cannot answer my youngest daughter's call, defend my oldest's denunciation. I can only lie there at my husband's turned back until all my tears are gone. When my soul relinquishes the last tear, I get up and go to bed.

I did not think sleep would come, but hours later banging awakens me. Dresser drawers open and close with such force it sounds as if a giant is moving about my room.

"Goddamn it," I hear Emory mutter. "Where are my clean undershirts?"

There is a pile of clean clothes in the basement, but I am afraid to open my mouth. Emory slams another dresser drawer shut and leaves the bedroom. I hear the shower going and quietly get out of bed. On tippy toes I make my way to the basement, dig through the basket of whites and find a clean undershirt.

With the same care, I knock on the bathroom door, open it, wave the undergarment like a white flag. It is snatched out of my hands quickly, the closing door nicking my forearm. Stunned, I rub it wondering how far this journey will take us.

Will Emory hit me like Mack? Leave me forever? Suddenly I can't stay here. I throw on clothes, get into my car and drive. Without a real destination, I try and convince myself, but soon I am urging my car up the long hill of 168th Street, Jamaica High School filling the horizon like a monolith.

I park my car, get out and walk toward the bleachers. Early-morning joggers race by me as I hold my head and cry. The sun rises higher, washes me with its hot brilliance. I move to the shade of the old oak tree. My face nestles into the space between my drawn knees. Tears glide down my leg, dampen the gather of my socks. I stay that way until my legs begin to cramp, my spine aches, the world goes by me, inaccessible.

By the time I pull up to my house, it is past ten in the morning and I have no more answers than when I left. A migraine the size of Montana is with me. I take Imitrex on an empty stomach, knowing all of it will not stay down. I throw up minutes later and retreat like a recluse into my bedroom.

I don't sleep, don't move, just lie there, twisted like hot metal. I take the time to flay open my choices. I could have told Emory who Philip was a long time ago, but didn't. I could have refused to meet Philip, but didn't.

The phone rings. No one comes and says it's for me. I hear Aaron's voice drift down the hall. She is on the phone, breaking curfew, but I'm too drained to care.

I am in my kitchen making dinner, pretending that life is fine. I wash lettuce, cut up cucumbers and flip turkey burgers with skill. I wash down countertops, unload the dish rack and find four forks in the drawer. I lay out napkins, fill glasses with ice and set four places for the meal.

"We're going."

I look up, the sound of my husband speaking to me, surprising. Monet is beside him. "Going where?"

"Her doctor's appointment. It's at seven."

I blink, blink again, nudge myself back to Monet and her illness. I cannot believe I've forgotten. Can't believe the whole day has passed and she never mentioned it to me. I look at the table setting, ice in glasses, forks on folded napkins.

"It's dinnertime."

Emory looks at me like I've lost my mind. Monet doesn't look at me at all. "We have to leave now or we'll be late." The front door opens and in a heartbeat they are gone.

I remove two settings. Wrap burgers in foil, put buns back into the plastic bag. I call Aaron to come to the table and get no answer. A thorough search reveals Aaron is gone.

Daughters of mothers may be the best of the friends, but sometimes the mothers of those daughters will barely like each other. This is the reality I have come to know, remember, as Keisha's mother comes to the door.

It has to do with how we perceive our children's friends. I think Keisha is too grown for her own good. No doubt Keisha's mother thinks Aaron is too fast. Still I push the conflict aside as I smile nervously at Keisha's mother. "Deidre. Is Aaron here?"

She looks at me surprised, then surprise turns into something else. *Always knew that daughter of yours was trouble,* her eyes say. "No, Sylvia, she isn't."

"Is Keisha here?" I ask, peering into her showroom of a house. That Keisha's parents have more money than Emory and I ever will is a fact. Their home is a rolling expanse of professionally managed lawns and a sunroom in the back.

"No, she's not."

"Well, if you see her or my daughter"—only desperation makes me say these words—"please have them call me."

"Alright." Deidre steps back and closes the door. I stand there a second feeling that she knows more than she is saying.

.

"Gone? What do you mean *gone?*"

I don't want to be me anymore. Don't want to live in my skin. I want to be somewhere else, anywhere else as I tell Emory of Aaron's disappearance. "Weren't you here?" he asks, closing the door behind him. "How did she get past you?"

I have a thousand answers, all them standing before me but I shrug. "I don't know, Em, I don't know." I have not cried since I discovered my child missing, but now the tears come.

"Tears aren't going to find her," Emory barks, cutting my sorrow in half. "Every time I turn around there's some shit going on." He turns toward Monet who stands quietly in the corner. "You know where you sister's at?" There is enough fire in his words to burn the hairs off her brow.

"No, Daddy, I don't."

"Some boy she likes?" he goes on to ask. Monet's eyes find mine and I know my grave is about to be dug deeper.

I sit in the car, foot bouncing and in need of a cigarette. I watch my husband talking animatedly to a man I just know is J'Qaun's father. I see the father shake his head no, see Emory insist with the back of one hand against his palm.

He is seconds from losing it.

I get out of the car even though I have been told to stay put. I move up the walkway and up the steps. I move in front of Emory, hoping to cool his heels. Smile a smile I am not feeling and speak in calm tones. "I'm Aaron's mother and we're just trying to find our daughter. She left the house and we don't know where she is. Figured she might be here with J'Qaun."

It is easy to see J'Qaun's father is both patient and level-headed but Emory has whittled away both. "I already told your husband I have not seen her."

I believe him. I need to get Emory to believe him, too. "Come on, Em, let's go." But his alliance to me is gone.

He shrugs off my words, my attempt to usher him to the car. "No. I'm not going anywhere. I'm going to stand right here until that boy gets here."

"Em, please," I say, aware of people on the street watching. But my husband is lost, caught up in a fever. His wife has been living a double life and his daughter, his *Aaron,* has been leading one, too. "Come on, Em," I implore, "let's go."

"I'm not going, Suvie. He has to come home sometime and when he does—"

J'Qaun's father leaves the doorway for the first time. He drops down to the top step and glares. "What? What you gonna do to my boy?"

I wedge myself between them, but my height is no match. I turn, nearly knocking Emory backward, pleading with him to let it go. "Em, please. It's not J'Qaun's fault. Come on, let's go home."

But the fire is in him, volcano spewing. Any second it will erupt. "His son knows where Aaron's at and I'm not leaving until he tells me."

"Daddy, please . . . please, Daddy." Monet's voice comes, shattered and desperate. I see her standing outside the car, her eyes filled with tears, her palms up, opened. "Please, Daddy, please," she begs, her voice too twisted with pain to ignore.

I hold my breath, wait for him to heed her words. He looks away, still angry, turns and heads back toward the car. I look up at J'Qaun's father, my eyes brimming. "I'm sorry for all of this. I am so sorry. I've met your son and know he's a good kid. Just that my husband didn't know about him until today."

"You need to handle both your kid and your husband, bringing all this nonsense to my front door. I don't appreciate this, not one damn bit. If he ever shows his ass here again, I swear, I'll have him arrested."

I believe him, can speak no more. I turn and head toward the car, wondering where Aaron is, and with whom.

We sit in silence, Emory and I. The minutes going by like hours. We are on parent watch. We have combed the neighborhood and rung doorbells. None of it has yielded our child.

I tell him the rest of the Aaron and J'Qaun tale, determined that no more secrets remain. I speak of my bold discovery of finding them in the basement, the firm warning, the plan to have J'Qaun formally introduced.

"You just full of secrets, aren't you? What else is going on around here I don't know about?"

"Can I tell you why I didn't tell Philip I love you?" Emory looks away. "Because there never was any doubt that I do. Saying it didn't even seem necessary."

Emory is about to reply, but the sound of a key in the front door steals his words. Up in a heartbeat, his feet take wings as his hands work loose the belt from his pants.

"No," I scream, running after him. I latch my hands around his wrist. "No, Emory, no." The door swings open and Aaron is before us, eyes defiant, mood intent. She does not see the belt. Emory shifts away from me and the strip of leather flies free, cutting into her arm like a laser. Aaron yelps in surprise and my house erupts into madness

Aaron is screaming and running, Emory is screaming and lashing and I'm screaming trying to curtail the belt. The bathroom saves her. She hurries inside and locks it. It takes thirty seconds of shoulder pounding before Emory realizes he cannot knock the door down, cannot beat his child insensible. Cannot change what has been done.

It is his moans that draw her out.

Aaron has never heard her father cry and it squeezes out all the air from the house.

Emory has slid to the floor, belt forgotten, hands to his face. I sit on one side, Monet on the other, our arms about his shoulders as he lets loose his pain. The bathroom door opens. We hear, "Daddy?"

He does not look up, does not stop his tears, just keeps on with his anguish.

"Daddy?" Aaron says again, dropping down to the floor, scrambling in front of him, wedging herself against his chest. "No, Daddy, no. Don't cry. Don't."

His arm slips around her; unintelligible words fall from his mouth. They weep together, Monet and I, muted with our silent sorrow. Time passes before he can stop his crying, before things settle down enough for Aaron to explain.

"I was angry," she confesses. "Angry at Mom, at you, everything. So I left, just snuck out the door because I couldn't stay here anymore. Everything was just wrong. Nothing was the way it was supposed to be."

We are silent, respective of Aaron's need to share. "First thing I did was call J'Qaun, but he wouldn't meet me. Told me to go home. That I was still on punishment." Her head shakes. "I hated him then, more than I hated anybody in this house. Was just crazy with hate." She looks off. "I went to Keisha's but her mom said she wasn't home, so I just started walking. Walked all the way to the mall, got there and walked some more, trying to figure things out. Trying to understand why Mom did what she did. Trying to understand how my happy life turned out not to be so happy."

She looks up at her father. "I didn't mean to hurt you, Daddy. Just wanted away from here. And I'm sorry, sorry for everything."

Emory hugs her, holds her tight. "It's okay, baby, you're all right, that's all that matters. Anything happen to you, I don't know what I would do."

Monet looks at me and I, at her. We don't say it, but we know. We are out of the mix.

Your husband will love you, but sometimes he will love his children more. It is something I realized when Aaron was first born. Emory would come in after a twelve-hour day and breeze right past me to pick her up.

She would be the first to get the kiss hello, the one who would fire up his eyes whenever he spoke of her. He turned her into a die-hard Jet's fan and Sunday it would be just the two of them in front of the television eating popcorn and yelling at the screen.

When Monet was born, Emory followed a similar routine but it wasn't hard to see where his heart was. For years I stood by in silent knowledge, convincing myself it was the way it was supposed to be. For years I stood by on the sidelines, jealous of their bond.

But like all things it became buried beneath the day to day. Got pushed away under the healthy growth of our children and the good life we carved. But now our children are not so healthy and our life, not so good. There is nothing to push back the bitterness and I find myself angry.

"She's been through enough, Suvie," Emory insists as he hangs up his slacks, tucks his shoes beneath the bed. "I can't see any more punishment."

"Well, I can. She broke the rules, Emory. You can't let her slide."

"You broke the rules, too, yet you expect me to let you slide."

"Let me slide? Let me slide? Since when do you call your silence and indifference sliding?"

"You were the one who cheated, not me."

"I. Did. Not. Cheat," I said firmly.

"What do you call it? Telling lies about where you're at. Sneaking off to Philip." He says the name like it's diseased.

"I did not sneak off to see Philip. I met him to talk. I needed to know why, that's why I went. I needed to hear from him how he ended up with Dorothy."

"Something that happened over thirty years ago?"

"Yes, as crazy as it sounds, yes. I did not go to *get* with him or cheat on you. I went because I needed to hear it. After all these years, I still needed to know."

"You could have told me, Suvie. You could have told me a long time ago who he was. But you didn't and then you snuck off to meet him . . . so it's got to be something more."

"We talked. Want to know what was said? He told me. Told me how Dorothy got him. He was the first boy I loved, Em," I say breathless, "the first my heart ever claimed and it was taken from me and I had to find out why."

"Did he touch you?"

"I did not sleep with him, Em."

"That's not what I'm asking you."

"We talked." I am beginning to sound like a broken record.

"And he didn't touch you, at no time. Not a hug hello, good-bye?"

"He tried to hug me hello, but I would not let him."

"What about when you left, did he try to hug you then?"

I don't want to go there. Don't want to delve into the sweetness that charged through me when my lips touched his. I don't want to disclose that how, for the briefest of seconds, I felt such complete-ness. But I must go with the whole truth. "He kissed me . . . good-bye."

"Kiss kissed or a peck kiss?"

My mouth goes dry. *"Kissed,* kissed."

Emory's voice comes, hysterical, near giddy, full of a madness that wounds. "I knew it! I knew it! Trying to tell me nothing hap-pened and all the time you still wanted him."

There is a crazed fire in his eyes. I have to put it out. I throw my arms around him. I hold onto him for dear life. "No, Emory, no. Not him. Just you." I say this over and over, my voice a whisper. I hold him and whisper until my arms ache. Hold him and whisper until my voice grows hoarse. I hold onto my husband, my all, for dear life, drowning and desperate to save us.

We are making love. It is voracious with little hint of tenderness. We are wounded drones, attempting to repair the hive. We are using everything we have, all the strength we can muster. Beyond exhaustion, we plow on.

I come in a maddening rush of explosion. Blood rushes my head so quickly, I see stars. I wait for Emory to finish, but he is stal-lion hard. His lunges shift me along the mattress; my head begins to knock the headboard.

It takes awhile for me to realize he is hurting me. I try to temper his rhythm, try to get him over the hump, but he seems content in the body slamming, his quest for pleasure given way to something else.

With all my might I shove him off me, his sperm hitting my belly, my breast. I spin around, sit up and stare at him. It takes awhile for him to see me. He blinks, getting his surroundings, drawing deep shuddering breaths.

His eyes are wide, stunned. He shakes his head, confusion in his eyes. "Sorry," he mutters disorientated. "Don't know what got into me."

I don't believe him.

Chapter 20

There is a calm in my house, flat as glass, mocking all truths. It hangs in the air, drifts around doors and assembles into corners.

It is there while Emory dresses for work and speaks no words to me. There as Aaron straggles off to the bathroom and Monet hides inside the thickness of sleep.

Three weeks ago I knew all that my life was and wasn't. I could have whipped off a five-page typewritten report on the life of Sylvia Allen. Three weeks ago I had few doubts, a wallet full of hope and a husband who cherished me. That's all changed now.

For the first time in my life I didn't want to lie in the same bed with my husband. For the first time ever I did not trust the arms, legs and hands of the man beside me. I lay awake most of the night convincing myself it was not attempted rape.

I never thought I would live my life in lies. Never thought that I would have to go away from myself and pretend a better world. Say, *We'll be alright, we'll survive this, get back to where we used to be.*

But I am and it's a hard thing to swallow.

"If you got something to say, Aaron, then say it."

She has been stealing glances at me most of the day and I've had enough of her stares.

"Why?" Aaron implores. There is no respect in her eyes, just a need to know and I debate with myself whether to answer or not. I have shared enough of my life with her and it has bought me nothing but heartache. "I thought you loved Daddy."

"I do."

"You don't. Cause if you did you would have never done it."

Done it. I realize what she is implying. I want to get that point straight. "I. Did. Not. Sleep. With. Him."

"So you say."

"Who the hell are you? Just who the hell do you think you are?" My voice is fire. "I'm your mother. You don't have the right to accuse me of anything." But I could have just read her a grocery list, told her the sky is blue. The look she gives says it all.

I have lost her respect, and my power.

The day slips into evening as I stand in the kitchen washing down countertops, removing bits of dried rice from the stove. I look at the plate of food covered in plastic wrap, look at the clock. It's eight forty-seven. Emory is nearly three hours late.

I visualize a flat tire, a broken timing belt. I search out hope, comfort, some affirmation that his lateness is excusable, and any second he will come through the door.

"Mom?"

I look toward the doorway, see Monet. "Yeah?"

"Daddy coming home?"

Tears. They fall from me quick and furious. My daughter's arms are around me before I can take my next breath. I feel incompetent with the need I feel for her embrace, her empathy, but I cannot stop holding onto her. It is the first bit of kindness I have had in days. The first affirmation that I am not the bad guy.

I hold onto my youngest and play her question over and over in my head. *Is Emory coming home?* The truth is, I don't know.

I am tired, wearied to the bone, but I refuse to turn off the television or leave the couch. I refuse to stop waiting for Emory. I look at the little red numerals on the cable box and place them into tangibles. Seek excuses as to why.

Twelve-seventeen. Six hours since he was due home, fifteen hours since he has left. My husband is somewhere out there and I don't know where.

The phone is cradled in my palm. I have been holding it since the eleven o'clock news. I have made endless calls to his cell, but they go unanswered. I have fought with myself not to call the police, check with his parents or call his best friend, Ralph.

I have debated all of these options as the need for answers rides me. My mind flits over the past few days as Dave Letterman tells a joke.

Was meeting Philip worth it?

I have staved off this question for days now. I have been running and ducking and doing a mad dance refusing to answer. I am about to answer myself when a key slips into the front door.

I am on my feet and at the door before it swings open. I search my husband's face for signs of the last six hours of his life. I search for excuse, apology, his forgiveness, something that says he loves me still.

But his eyes are blank. He moves past me and goes to our bedroom. I am halfway there when the door closes in my face.

Not a word did Emory speak last night. When I woke up in the morning, he was gone.

I call him at work and leave a message. I give him two hours to call me back. When he doesn't, I go out and run errands.

I end up at Forest Hills. I comb the bookstores, the GAP shop. I check the discount store to look over items I don't need.

I go to a matinee, try to lose myself in the darkness of the movie theater, aware that I have left Aaron at home and unsupervised. I know she is breaking the rules. The principles I have maintained have become all smoke and mirrors. In her eyes, I am a fraud.

Monet is at the stove when I return. It is nearly five-thirty.

"Making dinner," she says, a pot of water boiling on the stove, a package of pork chops resting on the counter. "Daddy will be home soon and I know he likes to eat when he gets in."

Her innocence churns my heart. She is trying to repair what only Emory and I can fix. I do not shoo her away as I want to. Instead I thank her and go put down my bag.

I come back, wash my hands and get a frying pan. I instruct her on how to stir up the noodles as they boil. As we move around the kitchen preparing a meal, I realize this is the first time we have ever shared such a moment.

I take it for all it's worth showing her how to properly wash tomatoes and rinse out the seeds. She smiles as she dices them up and carefully sprinkles them over the bed of lettuce.

For those few minutes, our world grows brighter, closer. I am setting the table and she is turning over the last batch of pork chops when Emory comes through the door.

"I made dinner, Daddy."

But he ignores her. Latches his eyes into mine. "Where's Aaron?"

I don't know. I assumed she was in her room but something in Emory's eyes says she isn't.

"Do you even know, Suvie? Do you even care? She's suppose to be on punishment but I saw her on the boulevard."

"So why didn't you stop and make her get in the car?"

Emory looks at me and I understand why without him saying a word. Aaron is a branch of our family tree, sucking off the bitter root. Until Emory and I reach some agreement, defiance will be her middle name.

Dinner is a silent affair. The three of us gather, bow our heads, say prayers and begin eating. Monet forks up salad, places it into her mouth and lays the fork to rest. Her eyes are off and away, but I see she is thinking, no, not thinking, counting.

Mentally I click off numbers, my notion confirmed as I reach the number twenty and she picks up her fork again. It is an old device in the battle of weight maintenance. I am happy to see that something has come from her session with Doctor Whitaker. Silently I applaud her effort.

"I'm going away next week."

The sentence falls from the sky even though it comes from Emory's lips. I know it's probably a business trip, but the very idea fills me with dread. I nearly choke on the pork chop. Cough, hold my chest, swallow, cough again. Monet is up getting me a glass of water. I take it, say thank you. Resist the urge to scold her. *You can't fix things,* I want to say.

"Where?" I ask, knowing it doesn't matter, only that he will be gone away from me.

"San Francisco."

I see something in his eyes. Relief? Need? I'm not sure, only that he wants to get away from here, away from the cheating Suvie, the bulimic Monet, the disobedient Aaron. "When?"

A coldness creeps into his eyes. "What you mean when? I told you next week."

Inexactness is not one of Emory's traits. He has spent a lifetime being explicit and precise. By now he would have run down his whole agenda, from the time his plane left to the time it would return.

He is lying and I cannot let it go another step further. I sit in silence finishing my meal, my stomach churning, my thoughts in a million directions.

Monet asks if she can be excused. I nod, glad to see her go. My appetite has vanished but I pick over my food as Emory finishes his. The moment his fork hits his empty plate, I reach over and touch his wrist. He pulls back, but my purpose has been served. I have his full undivided attention.

"We have to talk, Emory."

My heart is beating fast and I have no idea what I will do if he refuses as he has done in the past few days. But something shifts in his eyes and for a hot second I see a glimpse of the old Emory. Know I have not lost him yet.

"Really talk," I say waiting for him to grant or deny me.

He looks around the kitchen. "Here?"

"No, not here. Somewhere else. Somewhere private."

"Where?"

"We'll get in the car and go somewhere."

"What about Monet?" he says.

"She'll be fine." Words more faith than fact.

We are silent on the drive to Valley Stream Park. It is nearly dusk, the sun low in the sky and the whole world is stained brilliant orange. Emory is driving, I am in the passenger seat and the whole of our existence is crammed up invisible behind us.

I remember my dream.

Remember Philip behind the wheel, the back of the car packed with things and Emory somewhere within the clutter. I find myself glancing toward the backseat half a dozen times before Emory pulls into the parking lot.

There is no other car there. Far away is the whisper of traffic on the Southern State Parkway. We have chosen the park so that we can shout, talk and cry in private, do whatever needs to be done to get through this.

I light a cigarette as I step out on the asphalt. I scan the perimeter listening to the hiss of insects, the click of cicadas in the trees. The car doors slam, echoing about us. I wait for Emory to start walking; I follow his lead.

I know my first sentence but don't know Emory's. I'm not sure to start or to let him begin. But as we walk into the park, tree leaves high above our head, he is silent. I was the one who asked for this talk, therefore I must speak.

Somewhere inside me the question I'm about to pose has lived forever. It has sat behind a box of glass with a little red hammer attached. I am certain there is a label affixed that says, *Break open in case of emergency.*

Emotionally I lift it and with all my strength shatter the case. Reaching inside, I pull out the words, "What do you want to do?"

It is a question heavy with implication and life-changing consequence. It is a question that reveals nothing of my desires but simply an opportunity for Emory to share his. The question purports a willingness to abandon my own wishes and make his my own. It is a fate sealer in which I have no control.

Emory does not answer and a small bit of relief fills me as I realize he is not certain. He has not made up his mind to leave me, to go on ignoring. He hasn't made up his mind to forgive me either.

I go on. "Because this whole thing about you going to San Francisco, this whole thing about ignoring me and hating me and treating me like air cannot be the end all." I am on fire. "It is not fair to me, not fair to our kids and not even fair to you. Now I've made a big mistake, the biggest one I've probably made in my whole life but you need to decide how you are going to handle that."

He chuckles; it is a weird demented sound. "Handle? Handle? You want to talk about handling shit?"

That he curses surprises me but I have come prepared for all types of Emorys, good, bad or indifferent. "Yes, Emory, I would."

"When you came to me, said you wanted to be an at-home mother, a *grant* writer, the last thing I wanted was for you not to have a steady job. But it was what you wanted, and I told myself, she'll be there for the kids. Our kids will be safe, so I buckled down and worked my ass off supporting us. Going without, doing without because Suvie wanted to stay at home and the money wasn't constant."

I knew this, but it had been years since we had actually discussed it. I thought it was forgotten but soon realize this day will be an excavation into our past. I try to prepare myself for all the skeletons.

"I wanted to quit my job a thousand times, you hearing me, Suvie? A thousand. Didn't know that did you, no, of course not because I never complained. Never said a word. Just went to a fucking job I hated day after day, year after year because you didn't want to work full-time."

Emory is screaming, sending nestling birds off in startled flight. "I'd come home, stripped of everything, tired, worn-out. Come through that door and see my babies. I told myself, it's worth it. It's all right. I can do this for my kids. For my Suvie."

I know where this conversation is headed and my eyes fill with water. I blink, blink again.

"But then I find out everything isn't alright. Find out Monet has had bulimia for months and Aaron's been sneaking boys into the basement. And I'm like, well, fuck, where the hell is Suvie? Where she's been and what she's been doing? Isn't that why I bust my ass every day, so she can stay home, look after them, keep them happy and healthy and straight?"

His voice has lost some of its anger, a sorrow has filled the void. I want to hold him, but I know he will not allow it.

He looks at me, his eyes wet with unspent tears, a desperation heavy in his voice. "Where have you been, Suvie? Where have you been that you couldn't get a handle on it?"

A tear rolls down his cheek. He does not interfere with its jour-

ney. "How long you been seeing Philip? How long have you been
lying next to me and living another life?"

"No, Emory, no. It's not like that. Wasn't like that. I saw Philip
that one day and twice at the house. That's it."

But he doesn't believe me. "It can't be. Not with what's been
going on with Monet, Aaron . . ."

"But it is, I swear, Emory, I swear."

"So how come our children's lives are so screwed?"

Silence. Nothing moving but the rise and fall of our chests. No
birds tweet, no insects buzz. We are at the end of the world.

With deftness I take an emotional knife and split my gut wide
open, my truths pouring out visceral, steaming and unstoppable.
"I was there, but I wasn't there. I know that now. I wasn't paying attention, just wrapped up in my own little world. Up in my attic, visiting friends, on the phone. There but not there, y'know?"

I stare at him, splayed open and bleeding. I stand before him,
stripped as I have never been stripped before. Waiting for him to
do what he used to do, take me up, hold me, make it better. Lift
the burden.

"How could you let something so important slip away, Suvie?
How could you ignore your children for the sake of yourself."

"Because I did not know, Emory. I thought I had it under control."

His eyes pull away from me and it hurts like a slap. His voice is
low, rumbled, without weight. "I swore I'd always be there for my
kids. Swore it up and down, I did. I thought you felt the same."

"I did, I mean I thought I did." My neck twists. I am confused,
hurting, lost. "I thought I was. But I wasn't. I know that now. All
this time and I'm just realizing it now. I ruined everything for
everyone and I just want to make it better."

I need to hear him say that I can, that we will. That we will take
the very next second of our lives and make it better. But too much
has been taken from Emory and he doesn't have the strength to
lie, or hope.

"I wasn't going to San Francisco," he admits. "I was just going to
go away for a week and think." I nod my head. "But now there's
not much to think about, is there?" His eyes have found me and
they are peering without mercy. "Our whole life has been a lie.

One big gigantic falsehood. You weren't taking care of my children; you didn't love only me. You were still in love with Philip."

I dismiss his words, his summary of who we are and aren't. "It is not a lie, Emory. It is not a lie that I loved you enough to marry you and have your children. It is not a lie that our children are not perfect, but we love them. It is not a lie that I needed to confront Philip about my past. It is also not a lie that I need you and can't see living life without you there."

"How come you didn't know this before you went and met him?" he asks as he turns and heads toward the car.

Finished. He is done with me. Done with words, sharing, everything. I cannot let him escape, cannot let him go back without something final. Things need to be decided before he steps through our front door and nothing has.

I toss my cigarette to the ground. Mash it with an angry foot. "You can't walk away!" He turns, surprised by the attack of my voice. "You cannot walk away without telling me if you are willing to work it out or not."

"I don't know, Suvie."

"Bullshit, Emory, bullshit. You got to make a choice right here, right now. I will not let you go home with the indecision over us. I will not put my children through another day of this."

"Your children! Your children? Since when they became only yours? They're my kids, too."

"Well, damn it to hell, act like it. Stop hiding behind what I did and didn't do and act like they're yours. Decide if we are worth working out or if what I did was so unforgivable you're ready to step."

I am panting again, breathing hard on the moist warm late-summer air. Gnats flicker in a cluster around my face; I swat at them absently. "I know what I want. I know what Aaron wants and I know what Monet wants. What do you want, Emory? You leaving or staying? You forgiving me or holding it against me forever?" Suddenly I don't care what he decides, I just want him to make a decision.

"I can't trust you, Suvie."

I have mishandled the two most important things in our lives, our children and our marriage, and I accept my unworthiness. "I know you can't. But after twenty-one years, aren't we at least worth a try?"

He hesitates, uncertain. "A try?"

"Yes, Emory, a try."

"What about Philip?"

"It was never about Philip," I say softly and in hindsight. I take a step toward him. Make myself go on. "These past few days I've been wanting to fix something that was broken long ago. But I can't go back and fix the past. There's only the now and I want us to have a now." My hand lifts toward him. He does not take it.

My hand drops; my heart breaks. We were so close, were almost there. But almost does not cut it. I nod, concede. "Better head home."

I get into my side of the car, Emory into his. I stare out the window on the ride, Emory silent and lost in thought beside me.

Aaron is sitting at the table, picking meat off a pork chop bone when we return. I say nothing and head toward Monet's room. She is lying on her bed watching television. My face at her door fills her with expectation.

"It is worked out?" she asks.

"We talked, Monet, that's all."

"Is he gonna stay?"

I still have no answer. Do not try to find one. Direct her toward the source. "You have to ask your father." I turn away, feeling her desires like rain about my shoulders.

I tried, I tell myself as I head toward our bedroom. I change into my pajamas, come back into the kitchen and see Emory and Aaron talking. They stop when I enter. My eyes skim over Aaron. "You have kitchen duty tonight and for the next week." I leave before she can protest. Hear Emory say, "There is no choice here."

Wonder if he is talking about Aaron's duties or his leaving.

Chapter 21

Dorothy Butler lies on the top sheet, the whir of the ceiling fan a circle of haze above her. It is early evening, nine o'clock arriving a few minutes ago but she can no longer sit up in her family room and watch television.

Weeks since she has heard from Philip, she is certain at least a letter is coming her way, telling her that he's not coming back. That the house and all its possessions are hers to keep, that their life has been a lie. These are the things her mind tells her even as her heart tries to press a different truth.

It is no lie that she loves him. No lie that there is no other man for her. No lie that she gave her soul to the devil to have him, no lie that for over thirty years he remained steadfast and faithful by her side.

This is what Dorothy strains to hold onto as the night slips into darkness, as the ceiling fan whirs above her, her house sighing softly, awaiting a final end.

Morning arrives bright and sunny. A humid day, Dorothy can feel it the moment she enters her garage. A few seconds later she is pulling her car out of the driveway and making her way through her subdivision.

She bypasses lawns and mailboxes and two-storied homes of brick and stacked stone, the beauty escaping her, the sameness blatant. When she first moved in, she had marveled at the sloping streets, the tall pines and the tempered Georgia-style homes that would become her neighborhood.

Now it's a prison of Bermuda sod and Halloween festivals where all the residents dress up, decorate their lawns in skeletal remains and celebrate trick or treat like some major religious holiday.

Dorothy drifts past the THANK YOU FOR VISITING MILL CREEK ROAD SUBDIVISION sign. Two lanes of morning traffic zoom by her as she watches for an opening. Some mornings it comes quickly; other mornings it doesn't. This morning the cars are tight upon each other and she guns her engine, swinging wildly into the flow of pickup trucks, SUVs and Hondas. A passing driver shakes her head. She's crazy, the driver's expression says.

Dorothy is in no position to disagree.

The mug, old and faded, is the same one Dorothy has used since she started her job over a decade ago. As she stands in the break room, stirring Cream Mate into the cup of weak coffee, she doesn't mind its antiquity as she searches the plastic container for a pack of Equal.

She has just ripped open the little blue envelope when from behind her comes the whisper of nylons and the smell of CK Cologne. Dorothy knows it is her coworker and somewhat good friend Lauren. Meeting up in the break room before the start of the workday is a ritual for them.

But in the past few weeks, the meeting has grown hard. Dorothy has donned a mask of happiness for these brief gatherings and she does not know how much longer she can pretend.

Her smiling friend, with crinkly blue eyes, sable hair and thin lips painted in combination shades of magenta appears before her. The words, "Morning, Dorothy," comes too.

Dorothy forces a smile and returns the greeting. "Morning, Lauren."

"How's Philip?"

Dorothy lies quickly. "Just fine." Lauren has been to her home, has sat in Philip's company and thinks he's charming. She has been swayed by his stories and longs for the perfect picture he and Dorothy present.

She does not know what Dorothy knows. Has no inkling of the acid that washes through Dorothy's gut at his mention. "Lunch?" Lauren wants to know.

"Sure," Dorothy answers, leaving the break room and making a hasty retreat. The coffee tilts wildly inside the mug as she heads to her office. She opens the door and closes it, glides past a picture of Philip as she takes a seat.

In five days Dorothy will attend the company picnic sans Philip. She will be forced to pretend that he is just out of town on business. But for now as she takes a sip of swill coffee and turns on her computer, she is still Mrs. Philip Butler, whole and complete in her coworker's eyes.

There is much uncertainty in her life. Much that is standing on shaky ground. But there are still absolutes that Dorothy can cling to, certainties she knows will never change. Listening to Cassandra Wilson's "New Moons Daughter" is one of them. Her love of Chinese food and anything by James Baldwin is another.

The twelve years she has put in at the job, going from a receptionist to a manager is also a part of her assertions. She is a good and fair manager, loved by staff and considered favorably by the powers that be.

It is something she doesn't think about so much as know. It is as much a part of her as breathing—effortless. She does her job and does it well. A hard worker, this morning is no different as she finishes reading a letter and signs her name.

There is a knock at her door. Before she can ask, Sarah, her administrative assistant pokes her head in. "Dave wants to see you." Dorothy is about to ask about what, but Sarah has vanished behind the cracked door.

She takes a sip of her coffee, pushes back from her desk and heads out of her office for her boss's. She raps twice, hears "Come in," and steps inside.

Twenty minutes later Dorothy leaves in a fog, her mind unable to comprehend all that was said to her. She goes back to her office and stares out in space, numb.

Half an hour after that, Sarah is standing by her desk weeping. Dorothy's layoff has shaken her.

"Sarah," Dorothy says firmly. But Sarah just shakes her head and continues to cry. "Sarah," Dorothy says once more. "There is no time for tears. There are still things to be done." And though Dorothy would love to join the weep fest, she knows that how she leaves is just as important as her first day hired. Besides, she will not let them see her cry.

"But I don't understand. I just don't understand. How could they do this to you?"

"It's business," Dorothy says evenly, giving the performance of a lifetime. "The company is downsizing and my position is being eliminated. It's as simple as that."

But it is not and Dorothy knows it. She knows that her perceived importance to Kintron Electronics was just that, perceived; that her position, her importance, her place in the company held no importance. That she was just a cog in a wheel and her departure won't stop the machine.

"I've been asked to finish up as much as I can today and so we got a lot of things to do." Dorothy takes up the pile of letters she has signed. "Make sure these get out and bring me the Marcadia file. Then look around and see if you can find some boxes."

Sarah nods, leaves out.

The Olde Sports Bar and Grill located on Highway 17 has red vinyl booths and is barely filled. Dolly Parton's voice wails from hidden speakers as Dorothy stares out the smoky picture-glass window. It is not the type of place she frequents, but this afternoon she is in need of a sympathetic ear and an alcohol buzz.

"Moments like this, I swear I miss New York," Dorothy muses while Lauren tries to catch the eye of a waitress.

"Been there once," Lauren says with a flash of blue eyes. Lauren is Southern born and raised. Originally from Kennesaw, Georgia, she moved east to be closer to the shore. *Love the ocean,* she would say, *and Lake Allatoona just don't git it.* Dorothy doesn't know Kennesaw or Lake Allatoona, she has never ventured that far north.

A small town, Kennesaw is, was anyway. A real one-horse town. Then they started building on every bit of red dirt, chopping down trees and putting up subdivisions. But we got the Civil War Museum and of course the Big General. You know the Big General. It's that train y'all Yankees stole from us Confederates during the war, she once told Dorothy with an exaggerated drawl and a fast smile.

But Dorothy didn't know. Her knowledge of Southern history is the Civil War, slavery and the Ku Klux Klan, none of it pretty.

"You want to order food?" Lauren asks, digging into her bag for her cigarettes.

Dorothy picks up the menu, everything fried and greasy and decides on a burger. Lauren orders sautéed zucchini topped with mozzarella. Their drinks arrive and Dorothy's is nearly gone before Lauren takes a third sip. Her eyes dance to the half-empty glass of vodka and club soda and Dorothy knows her thoughts. She feels the need to defend herself, but she is not sure what her defense could be.

"Maybe it won't be so bad," Lauren begins. "I mean it's not like you're going to be hard up for money. Philip makes a good salary."

"Philip is gone, Lauren . . . it's over."

Lauren's face takes a swift journey, arriving at utter disbelief. "You're kidding me."

Dorothy picks up her drink and finishes it. Sets the glass on the table hard. "No, Lauren, I'm not. Philip left me weeks ago."

"But you never said anything."

Dorothy can see the pain in Lauren's eyes and the fear. Philip was the dream she aspired to. He has robbed them both. Dorothy pauses, looks away, back at her. "How could I?"

Lauren flips loose hair behind one ear. Her eyes study the lines of the hardwood table. She does not look up for a long time. When she does, her eyes are wet. "Dorothy, I am so sorry."

"Not as sorry as I am."

Lauren head shakes. Those blue eyes, intense. "No, I mean I'm really sorry . . . you don't have a job."

One of Dorothy's eyes raise. "And no Philip, right?"

On Monday, Dorothy was let go. By Wednesday she is interviewing for new jobs.

With Philip gone, she does not have the option of taking some time to figure out where she would like to work. She applies wherever the need for an office manager exists. She has gone on one interview already and it yielded no results. She is hoping this second one will.

But she has caught her interviewer by surprise.

The faxed résumé spoke things about Dorothy, but it did not speak the whole truth. On the surface she is the perfect candidate from her Rafaella suit and Anne Klein shoes, to her Dooney & Bourke pocketbook. But beneath the superior work history and the fashionable clothes is a woman a decade too old, and six shades too dark.

The interviewer smiles condescendingly and widely, knowing the next six minutes will be a waste of both their time. Dorothy senses this but refuses to bow down. She sits erect in her chair, maintains eye contact and keeps her hands demurely in her lap.

She makes her smile easy, her answers conventional and becomes all that she professes to be—highly qualified. But one second beyond six minutes, she is cut off midsentence.

"You have a very impressive work history and it looks like you have all the requirements," her interviewer tells her. "Unfortunately we still have more candidates to see and won't be able to make a final determination till then."

The interviewer rises, extends her hand. Dorothy rises too, mindful of the letters of recommendations still tucked inside her portfolio. "Would you like to see my letters of recommendation?"

Eyes dance away from her. The head shakes itself no. "Oh, that's not necessary. We have all the information we need."

Dorothy shakes the hand firmly. Nods and leaves the office. She walks with her head high, her smile fixed in place, so much so everything beyond her shoulders ache.

She takes three more interviews the next day and two more on Friday. By week's end, she has had seven interviews and not a single one offer her the slightest promise.

With no job and no husband, Dorothy is in her car heading toward Alpharetta, Georgia.

She is driving to her best friend Belinda's house. She is going to unburden herself, going to share her woes. Dorothy is going to spill beans she has not shared with her best friend, but can no longer face alone.

The condo she pulls up to looks like the other sixty-something units in the complex. There is hardiplank siding and decorative stack stone. An arch in the middle towers three stories tall.

Dorothy has not spilled a word about what has become of herself and Philip, but she is ready as she parks her car, gets her pocketbook and steps out into the bright Georgia day.

She is ready to tell it all, the whole sullied tale as the door of 2614 opens up and Belinda appears in khaki shorts and a white sleeveless T-shirt. She smiles brightly Dorothy's way and opens her arms to hug her.

Dorothy's eyes drink in the array of magnolias that are placed in half a dozen glass vases throughout the living room. Magnolia trees are native to Georgia. There are half a dozen behind Belinda's condo and she helps herself to their blooms often.

"How was the drive?"

"Not too bad."

"Thirsty?" Belinda wants to know. Dorothy nods her head. Ducking into the galley kitchen, Belinda comes back with a tall glass of ice tea.

Dorothy takes it and finishes half before she rests it on the coaster. She waits for Belinda to take a seat. Considers her friend with heartbreaking eyes. "I want to tell you something, Belinda. Something I never told anybody."

It is then that Belinda notices it, the sadness. It clings to Dorothy like spider webs, shimmery, faint, resilient. "Everything okay?"

"No, Belinda. Everything's not okay. Philip is leaving me and somebody besides myself needs to know why."

The eyes that eagerly awaited the tale are not the same eyes once the tale is finished. They have been replaced with fear, hesitation and surprise. They have been replaced with fiery mistrust and deep angst. "But he was your best friend's man."

Dorothy nods, deep, quick. Her head moving up and down so hard it looks like it is about to snap off. "I couldn't stay there. I had to get out and Philip was the way out."

"But your best friend's man? Your best friend?"

Dorothy understands why Belinda is stuck on that point. Belinda has become the Sylvia in her life and not once has she ever considered Dorothy capable of such knife-stabbing treachery.

"I know she was my best friend, but she didn't know what she had. And if it hadn't been me, eventually it would have been somebody else."

"Even if that was the case, Dorothy, it shouldn't have been you." Belinda grows silent, but even her muteness cannot stop what her eyes are saying. The chickens have come home to roost.

"But it was me and it's done and Philip's leaving and I've been laid off."

"You've been let go?"

Dorothy looks at her pocketbook. Longs for a smoke but Belinda doesn't allow it in her house. Her eyes graze the glass patio door. "Can we go outside?" Belinda gets up, her movements quick, sharp edged. She is annoyed and angry. Her best friend is full of deceit and lies.

They step out onto the patio, the heat of the day surrounding them the moment they do. Dorothy lights a Virginia Slim, inhales as if her life depends on it. Lets it go in a smoky rush.

"Last week, can you believe it? No notice or anything. Dave just called me into his office like I hadn't given twelve years of my life there. As if I wasn't the best damn manager they ever had."

"They offer you a package?"

"If you can call it that. Three month's salary, then I'm on my own."

"Does Philip know?"

"I haven't had a chance to tell him. I haven't spoken to him since he left almost four weeks ago."

Belinda looks off, digesting the words her friend has spoken to her. She does not change the direction of her glance, only the intent of her heart as her hand snakes out, finds Dorothy's. Squeezes it.

Philip sits behind the wheel of his Escalade. He doesn't feel the super suspension, the lushness of the leather seats. His ears do not register the crispness of the superior audio system; he barely glimpses the tree-lined highway.

Philip is trying to connect old dots. Trying to come to terms with where his life had led. His struggle forward has only led him backward. Back to what took thirty years to flee.

He makes two stops along the route from New York to Georgia. Fourteen hours later, he pulls up to the expansive ranch in Mills Creek Subdivision.

Phillip hits the garage remote. Sits transfixed as the sight of his own garage. Dorothy's car is not there, but she will return eventually. What words can he speak? What words does he want to speak?

He eases his SUV inside, gets out and heads toward the kitchen door. The security system beeps out its warning and he punches numbers into the keypad.

He moves through the family room. Makes footprints on the freshly vacuumed carpets as he enters his bedroom, continuing on to the master bathroom. Relieving himself, he turns on the faucet, glad for the spill of warm water against his hands.

Philip picks up the phone and dials Dorothy's job. Is told she no longer works there. He goes and takes a shower, changes his clothes, calls his parents, letting them know he arrived home safely.

Philip goes to the kitchen, looks in the fridge, unprepared for its barrenness. Outside of a small container of milk, two ends of bread and a bottle of water, there is nothing there. He goes to the family room, flops onto the sofa, remembering Dorothy's decision not to have children and how he hadn't wanted any either.

Because I wasn't supposed to stay.

But he has stayed. Has stayed longer than he was supposed to. Twenty-six years ago he should have taken the trip back. Right after he graduated college, he should have returned to New York, returned to Sylvia.

But he didn't and as he sits there, waiting for Dorothy, he knows he is on a whole new journey but to where, he cannot answer.

It has been a long drive from Alpharetta. Dorothy is tired by the time she reaches home and is glad when her car makes the final turn into her driveway.

She hits the button on the remote and the garage door glides up, the sight of the champagne-colored Escalade shocking. She puts her foot on the brake, studies the vehicle that has been missing for almost a month. Tries to gather clues from the mud splatters across the license plate, the dusty dried raindrops nestled on the back window.

She extinguishes her cigarette and carefully pulls her car into the other side. She lowers the garage door and gets out, her car door slamming shut.

She goes to the SUV, presses her face against the glass, searching out more clues as to why he has returned. She is still there, breathing against the tempered glass when the door to the kitchen opens wide.

"What's wrong?"

She looks up and sees Philip. She doesn't understand the question or perhaps understands it too much. She pulls back, smudges of car dust clinging to the front of her blouse. Dorothy glances at her husband, looks away. Moves past him as if he is air.

"You okay?"

She stops in her tracks, turns and faces him. "You're not serious."

"I called your job. They say you don't work there anymore."

"They fired me."

"You're kidding."

"Does it look like I'm kidding?"

Philip, uncertain of what to say, switches gears. "I was looking for something to eat." He points to the refrigerator. "There was nothing in there."

Disbelief fills her face. "You disappear for weeks and all you want to know is why there's no food?"

Philip hadn't been certain just which words he would speak, but as Dorothy stands angry before him, he goes for the simple. "I made a mistake, Doe, a terrible mistake."

"No, Philip, you didn't make a mistake. You've just discovered that what you've wanted for all these years isn't yours to have. Well, welcome to the club." There is fire in her eyes and brushes of pain. "Did you really think she would leave her husband to be with you? Did you really think that after all this time and what you did to her, she would give up her life for you?"

"I thought wrong. I know that. But I'm back now. Isn't it enough?"

Dorothy glares at him. "You want me to be glad you're back? Well, let me give you a newsflash. You could have stayed right there in New York, because I'm done. Done with you and done with living this lie."

Philip finds himself speaking words he never thought he would speak. Finds himself feeling things he thought he would never feel. "It wasn't a lie."

"Wasn't it? You off for weeks without so much as a phone call? What do you call it?" Philip reaches for her. She cannot believe his gall. "Don't. You. Dare."

But he ignores her warning, reaches for her again, every fiber in his being trying to connect with what he never wanted, but suddenly needs.

Dorothy twists away from him, surprised and affirmed in the same breath. "You think there's something left to us?"

His voice comes tight and pain-filled. "Yes."

She stares at her husband as if he is from Mars, things coming from him, through him at the speed of light. Dorothy goes on, fine-tuning her impressions, disbelief in her as she senses all of it. "Not enough to count." She turns and walks away.

Dorothy sits on her deck, the sun a near memory, nighttime coming fast. She smokes cigarettes, sips from her glass of wine. Tree frogs croak incessantly. Loons keen mournfully. A peaceful moment, but inside her there is turmoil.

She has left Philip.

She has not left him physically, but emotionally, she is gone.

She has reached a clearing in her life, a view uncluttered by self-esteem, a new worth. Once upon a time she had believed that Philip could "make" her, but she realizes that she has "made" herself.

This life, the way she lives and how she lives it, has been her doing. She is the one who struggled and scrimped and saved. She is the one who pushed Philip to apply for bigger and better things. She was the one with the abilities, not Philip.

She has made this world for herself and there is no way she is going to hand that over. With or without a job, she cannot maintain it by herself, so in that way she still needs Philip. But it is the only way she will need him, despite his new-found emotions, emotions that have been carved from a rebound.

He is trying to cling to what is because he can't have what was. Dorothy knows this. Knows that if Suvie had thrown her life away to be with him, he would have never come back here.

But Suvie hasn't and Philip is back here with me, Dorothy thinks as she sips wine and tries to see fully all that will mean and all that it won't.

The guest room has seen few visitors. Its bed still feels showroom fresh, the pillow's store-bought new. A room for the occasional overnight visitor, this is where Philip lays his head.

His first night there, he twists and turns, mindful of Dorothy down the hall. Mindful of the decree that they will continue to live under the same roof, but as far as she is concerned the marriage is over.

Mostly Philip is mindful of the silence she gives like breathing—constant.

Attempts to talk to her, engage her, go unheeded. She will not even share a meal with him. Instead she uses the barely used dining room, the large table dwarfing her as she eats in silence, the sight of her filling him, a new waiting taking up residence in his soul.

For years Philip withheld his heart from her in hopes of reaching what has turned out to be an unreachable summit. With determination, he placed a fortress around his soul, refusing her admittance. But the walls have crumbled and he finds himself unsheltered and open.

There is nothing for him in New York, so his eyes have turned back to what was. Philip never suspected that that has vanished too. That nothing remains, not his present or his future.

Chapter 22

It is the morning after the great talk. The morning after Emory and I returned from the park with no more answers than when we left.

Emory doesn't say much to me as he gets up and gets ready for work. Having mastered the art of playing possum, I burrow under the covers as if sleep is all I know.

I wait until his car leaves the driveway, make my way to the bathroom. I ignore my reflection in the mirror as I wash my face. I head to the kitchen in need of morning coffee. Brewing some, I drink it. Stare at the yellow walls.

Aaron comes in, eyes everywhere but on me. In no mood to argue with her, no mood to begin a new war, I leave the kitchen and give her space. We are wounded enough.

I go up in my workroom. Pull out the letters from Philip. I study the postmarks and run a finger along the edges. In a heartbeat I am heading back downstairs, letters in hands, the gas grill out back—my destination.

I lift the black glossy lid, lay the letters down near the burners and prime it. I strike a match, turn on the gas and watch flames eat through all of them.

Tendrils of smoke rise from the grill. I watch them drift, feeling neither better nor worse. I watch the smoke, refusing to ponder words I will never read. They've taken up enough space in my life and I welcome their riddance.

Life has become scattered but I cling to some of the broken pieces. At five-thirty I head to the kitchen to begin dinner though my appetite is gone. I am standing at the stove, stirring up canned stew when Emory comes in. His weariness is like a banner about him, his hello to me brief and empty.

He heads down the hall and soon the bedroom door closes. Minutes later I call out that dinner's ready and dump the brownish mix onto my plate. I sit at my table and fork up a spoonful. It is near tasteless in my mouth.

Monet appears and gets a plate. She fills hers and sits across from me. Aaron comes in, serves herself, retreating back into her bedroom. Emory is last and I am hungry for eye contact but his eyes are everywhere but on me.

He takes his meal to the living room. Seconds later canned laughter drifts from the television. I take up a few more forkfuls, but I am unable to finish the rest. Scraping my plate, I hear Monet wolfing her food down behind me. I look at the time. Wonder if Lisa is home. Go to my bedroom and make a call.

Lisa and Kelvin are sitting on their front stoop when I arrive. It is an unusual sight but nothing in my life is usual anymore. I get out of my car, wave, smile, make my way.

"Getting some fresh air?" I ask, studying faces.

Lisa shakes her shoulders, a soft painful smile arrives. "No, we're just having some spending time together."

"Hey, Aunt Suvie," Kelvin offers.

"Hey yourself." I tap his leg, indicate for him make room for me to join. But he stands up, kisses his mother's cheeks, gives her a fast hard hug.

"You call when you get there," Lisa asks.

"You know I always do." His eyes find mine. "Good seeing you, Aunt Suvie."

"Good seeing you, too, Kelvin." My tongue burns to ask questions, but I wait until he has headed down the block. "He still at your folks?" Lisa sighs, nods, reaches for her cigarettes. "We're going inside?"

Her head shakes no.

I don't ask why. Pull out a cigarette, too. Together we blow blue jet streams into the late-summer afternoon.

"I have some things to tell you," I begin.

"*Things?*" I've caught Lisa by surprise. My life has always been an open book, with few secrets. "What kind of things?"

I swallow back the lump in my throat. "You remember Philip."

"Philip, Philip?"

"Yeah, Philip, Philip."

"What about him?"

"A few weeks ago, he just shows up on my doorstep. No Dorothy. Just him."

"And?"

"He was there for about two minutes and then Emory came home from work."

"So what happened?"

"Nothing then. But he came back a second time." This is the hard part of the story for me; the part where things get murky. "He told me him and Dorothy weren't together, that I should call him at his folks. That he was back home."

"Call him for what?"

"To talk."

"About what?"

"About what happened, I guess."

"You didn't, did you?"

"Didn't what?"

"Call him." She is looking at me hard, searching out my truth. Finds it. "Oh no, Suvie, tell me you didn't."

"Yeah, I did."

"Why?"

"Because I was still hurting, Lisa, that's why. Still hurting over something that happened so long ago it shouldn't have mattered. But it did and I didn't want to hurt anymore. I wanted the pain gone."

"And you thought having a conversation with him could do it?"

Or something. "Yeah, I did."

"Did it?" My head shakes yes. "Did you do more than talk?"

"Yeah."

Air leaves her like a deflated balloon. "Damn."

"He kissed me."

"Kiss or *kissed* kissed."

"*Kissed* kissed."

"Emory knows?" I nod my head. "And stuff's just been jacked since, right?" I nod my head again. She considers me for a long time. So long, I know her question before she asks. "Was it worth it?"

"No."

She looks off seeking the answers I can't find. "You and Emory, you two can survive this. The love between you two is too strong not to."

I nod my head in slow agreement, but I do not possess her faith.

I come through my front door. Lock it. My house is thick with shadows. Not a single light burns.

"How's Lisa?"

I do not see Emory sitting on the couch and his voice catches me by surprise. It is the most words he has spoken to me in days, the only thing he has asked. "She's doing okay."

"We need to talk." I nod my head, go take a seat.

"I'm trying to get beyond this, really I am, but it seems the harder I try, the less I can."

"So what are you saying, Emory?"

"I think we should separate for a while."

I am stunned but not surprised. I am taken aback but not shocked. Still it takes awhile for my mouth to work. "Break up." It is not a question.

"Not break up, break up, but give each other some space. Time to think about where we headed."

"I don't need space," I defend, making sure he knows all I want and don't.

"Well, I do."

"Then say that. Don't put me in it."

He looks at me. I see he is too weary to battle with words. That he simply wants out. "I won't be able to afford two households," he goes on to say. The fact that he has thought it out so carefully tells me that he has taken the first steps to separation. But his next words inflict a new pain. "You'll have to go back to work."

My eyes widen. "Back to work?"

"Yes, Suvie, back to work. You grant writing isn't enough and I can't pay for two places."

"So don't," a solution that fills me but doesn't touch the place Emory stands at now.

He moves past my suggestion "We should try and make it as easy on the kids as possible, so I think we should tell them together."

"And you think us both saying it is going to make it easier?"

"At least they'll know we both agreed to it."

His words make me chuckle. "I haven't agreed to anything."

"Might as well tell them now," he decides, standing.

"We can work this out," I insist, though in truth, I am not sure if I believe those words.

"Work it out how?"

I shrug caught off-guard by it all, by his need to just give up, walk out. "We can go see someone. A marriage counselor, or something."

He snickers at my suggestion. His face twists as if I have truly lost my mind. "A counselor."

"Yes," I said quickly. "Sometimes outside people can help. Just look at Monet." But it's a bad example. She has been seeing the doctor for weeks and she is still bingeing.

He heads for the kitchen and the olive branch I've extended goes up in flames. The fire is back in my soul. "You won't even consider it." His muteness gives me his answer. "So wait, let me get this straight. You'd rather break up our household, cut our finances and send me back to work so you can have some space, something the children are supposed to not only accept, but understand, yet you won't trying counseling first?"

Again my question is ignored as he calls out to the children to come to the kitchen.

It is neither a pretty scene nor a benign one. There are tears, outrage and rapid expressions of personal desires. Aaron wants to go with her father. Monet wants her father to stay and all Emory wants is to go.

Everyone's wants are expressed except mine. I am not given the opportunity nor do I expect it. In their eyes, I've already abused that privilege. In their eyes, I deserve no say.

I toss and turn most of the night, the empty space in my bed, a physical calamity. Emory is back on the couch. He will sleep there until his move becomes final.

Around four in the morning I finally drifted off to sleep, awakening some six hours later to the sound of my daughters arguing.

"He asked me."

"So, I still want to go."

"He ain't asked you though, now did he?"

"So? I can still go."

"But he ain't asked you."

I don't know who asked what and who hasn't but I get up, go to Aaron's room to find out. "What's going on?" I ask them both, knowing only Monet will answer.

"Daddy going to look at apartments today and I want to go."

"He ain't asked her. He asked me."

"So why can't you both go?" But I don't want anyone to make the trip.

"He asked me specifically, that's why." Aaron is snippy, snappy and my hand itches to make contact with her face.

"That's only because I was sleep," Monet defends.

Aaron gets into her sister's face, head tilting from side to side. "No. He don't want you along."

"Stop it!" The intensity of my voice takes them by surprise. "Nobody's better than anybody else around here, you got that? If Monet wants to go, she's going. Unless your names are Emory or Suvie, then nobody has the right to tell anybody else what to do."

A slim caramel wrist flips my way. "Yeah, whatever."

My hand lifts and makes quick hard contact with Aaron's face. She is startled, but that is all. Her widened eyes recess as she barely blinks. As she tells me, "Hitting me ain't gonna change a thing for you. Daddy's still leaving here and it's your fault."

My hand tightens, but I resist the urge to strike out again. Instead I take a deep breath, let it go. "Monet, go get dressed. You're going with your father." My eyes find Aaron. "As for you? Forget it. You're not going anywhere."

Her mouth opens in protest. My eyes narrow, daring her, looking forward to a knock-down, drag-out with her as my opponent.

Sensing this, Aaron shuts her mouth. Turns and flops on her bed. I leave, the victory more bitter than sweet in my mouth as I go to the living room to find Emory. I let him know Aaron will not be accompanying him this day.

"What do you mean she's not going?"

"She doesn't get to roll her eyes at me, tell me 'whatever' and still go."

"I really need her to come along with me."

"Monet's going." Silence. We share the first real eye contact in days and I don't like what I see. Deceit resides there. Deceit like I've never witnessed in his face before. "What's going on, Em?"

"Nothing. I just wanted Aaron to spend some time with me, that's all."

"Until next week, you'll be seeing her and have been seeing her everyday, so that can't be it."

"I figured since she'd be there weekends, she might want to help choose what apartment I get."

"What should it matter to her? She'd be happy in a shack if it meant being with you." Those words hurt both of us for different reasons. I press on. "And Monet's going to be there too, so why can't she decide?"

"Fine, Aaron won't go."

"You haven't answered the question." But there is no need. Monet is his daughter, but Aaron is his heart.

I am sitting in my living room, curled on my sofa watching a Lifetime movie. I am not there because I particularly want to be, but because I must keep a watch on the front door to make sure Aaron does not slip out.

I've listened as Aaron took a shower. Heard the music blasting as she got dressed, signals to me that she plans to go somewhere, slip out when I am not looking. And so I must keep watch until Emory and Monet get back.

I look at the wall clock, see they have been gone for nearly two hours. Wonder how their search is going and ponder the magnitude of what it all means. I know Emory is leaving me in less than a week, but the reality is someplace that I'm miles from reaching.

A part of me wants to believe it is a bluff. A part of me wants to say he is not really going, but that part cannot do away with the lonely nights I've spent in my bed. Cannot do away with a husband who barely looks at me.

I find myself thinking of Philip. Wonder if he has any idea of what my life has come to. I force myself to the next step and wonder if Em and I will move so far apart that there will be room in my life for Philip. I make myself ask if my situation is a gift horse I am looking in the mouth.

Before the thought is halfway finished, the answer comes. What I want is my family whole and together again. What I need is for Emory to stay.

Monet is giddy when she returns home. Gushing, she comes to me and describes the new place her father will live. She is ecstatic as she describes the bedroom that will be hers two days of the week.

"The place is awesome. It has a patio and you can see forever and me and Aaron's room have their own bathroom."

I try to smile. Try to fit myself in her joy, but I don't reach the mark as my too-bright expression hardens on my face.

Monet senses it, pulls back. "I mean, it's okay. I still like it here better."

I look at Emory, in need of confirmation. "So you found one."

"Yeah, rent's kind of high, but it right up there on Hillside. Not too far, even though parking's going to be a monster."

I nod, murmur, "That's good." Feel nothing good about it at all.

I feel his stare. Find his eyes. See glimpses of the old Emory there. "I don't want to go, Suvie. I swear I don't. But I can't stay here feeling what I'm feeling. I can't."

Monet sensing the change in the room leaves. It frees my tongue to speak up. To toss out one last olive branch before the inevitable. "You don't want to leave, Emory, then don't. Do the hard thing. Stay here and fight, for us."

His head shakes. "I can't."

* * *

I've confided in Lisa that Emory is leaving and I have to find work. She tells me about a position for an administrative assistant that is coming up in their LeFrak City office. She is friendly with the manager there and says I'm a shoo-in.

One less straw off my back, but it doesn't grant me relief. In four days my husband will pack his things and go.

No one in my house is prepared for that departure.

Chapter 23

We have always been private with our business, what little there was. But my daughters are making spectacles of themselves in our driveway as they cling to their father, the last of his things packed into his car.

I've given up calling out to them to let their father be. Given up insisting that they will be seeing him the coming weekend. I've stepped back from the front door and closed it, my own good-bye forfeited to my children's sorrow.

I wipe tears from my eyes, feel the injustice of it all, Emory's absence filling every room. I cannot stay in the house and take refuge in my backyard. Tend the garden.

My roses are wilting. Weeds are having a field day. Something has nibbled away at my pansies and the grass is half an inch too high. I am glad for the diversion as I get my kneepad, grab a thick weed and give it a tug.

It snaps halfway up its stalk. I toss the broken piece aside, grab what's left and pull, but the roots are deep. I gather strength and tug again, the force sending me sprawling backward at an awkward angle.

"Tough one."

I look up and see Emory and for a hot second I forget he is leaving me. I smile, self-conscious, and right myself. "Very."

I wait for him to close the distance, but he remains at the edge of my garden. "I'm going." I nod, unable to speak. "So this weekend, I'll be by Friday night. Pick up the girls. Don't make them dinner. I'll take them somewhere to eat."

I toss the hard-gotten weed aside. "Okay." Grab another.

"I'll keep my cell on till my phone gets put in. And you can always reach me at my job in case of an emergency."

I nod, pull another weed, this one more giving as it gently lets go of its hold. I blink and blink. Hold back a loose tear. I grab another weed, give it a tug. Like the first one, it is stubborn and won't let go. I decide I won't struggle with it. That I will dig it out with my spade.

"Suvie."

I don't answer. Can't answer. No words I can speak will change this moment and I don't see the point in trying.

"Suvie," Emory calls again and I hold up a hand.

My voice cracks, moves barely above a whisper. "Just go, okay?" I hear his footsteps fading. Refuse to watch his retreat. I sniffle up mucus, wipe at my eyes and immerse myself in my garden until I am sweaty and spent.

Our first night without Emory.

Physically, nothing is different inside the house. Not the layout of the furniture or how the ceiling fixtures and table lamps cast their shadows. The refrigerator still hums its familiar rhythms and the glow from the television set still maintains its blue-ness.

The toilet bowl hisses as always as it fills and the fluorescent lights in the kitchen offer the standard *pop!* when turned on. The colors of the walls are the same pale beige and the third step from the bottom going up to my office hasn't lost its squeak.

I am upstairs because the silence down is too complete. I've lost a dozen games of solitaire because my mind cannot compute strategies to win. I play until my right wrist starts to hurt and my thumb begins to lose feeling.

I've considered calling my folks, calling Emory's, but I don't want to believe this is permanent. I don't want to consider that we will never heal. I want to talk to my children. I know I need to, but what more can I add? What more can I say? What hope can I offer them when there is none for myself?

Something says try. Something says even if you fail, you have to at least talk to them. I search my soul for a bottom line to this madness as I head down the stairs. Find it.

Aaron does not want to leave her bed; Monet comes willingly. It is Monet's face that tells me that talking with them was the right choice. She sits at the kitchen table, eager and expectant, and as I wait for Aaron to join us, I realize she is looking for something I cannot give. She is looking for the answers that will bring her father home.

But I am not Emory. I cannot climb into his head or reveal his soul. I can only talk about this from my own experience. Allow what's inside of me to lead my thoughts. "The last thing I ever wanted was for us not to be family, for us not to be together . . . I didn't want your dad to leave."

Aaron rolls her eyes. Monet sits, drinking in my every word. "But your father has left and I can't make him come back. I know you both probably think you know why this happened, and I am not going to go into all the details. But I want you to understand that us sitting up here with your father gone was *his* choice. I never wanted him to leave. In fact, I asked him to stay, but he has decided otherwise."

"Couldja blame him?" Aaron interjects.

"Nobody is perfect, Aaron. Not me or your dad and despite what your father thinks, I did nothing wrong."

"Nothing wrong? Daddy's gone because of what you did. How can you say you did nothing wrong?"

I resist the fire in Aaron's voice. Refuse to rise up with her. "Because it was important to me. There were issues I needed to address and the only person I could address them with was Mr. Philip. I've been with your dad for over twenty years. My love for him is absolute. But he couldn't see that or wouldn't. And that's not my fault."

Aaron's head shakes, "He wasn't the one who went sneaking around." She looks at me and I taste her pain. We stare at each other a long time, out of words, far apart. She looks away, asks, "Can I go now?"

I nod my head, glad she's at least asked to be excused. I fix my eyes on Monet, the one I perhaps can still reach. "It's not as simple as it sounds, Monet. Life isn't just black and white, you know?"

She nods her head, reaches out a hand of understanding. I grab it, grateful.

The first week after Emory was gone, I held stubbornly to the belief that he would be back. The second week the hopes die when Emory's parents arrived at my front door unannounced.

I feel hijacked as I realize Emory has told them without consulting me. I feel sucker punched as I realize that, for him, the arrangement is more permanent than it will ever be for me.

But these thoughts slip away as his mother opens her arms to me, as her words, "Oh baby," mix with the sorrow in my heart. Too greedy for comfort, too desperate for her support, I fall into Anna's arms, my weight heavy against her. "Why didn't you call us?" she wants to know. I don't answer, just cling to her.

"Let's get inside," Emory's father says, ushering us past the threshold.

They sit on the couch heavy and weary. I try to look at them, but my eyes refuse instruction. I look at the wall, the TV, the drapes that hold a fine gathering of dust. I look everywhere but at them, guilt, a hot brand in my heart.

Emory and I have never gone to either of our parents with our troubles. For over two decades we have shown them that our life was nothing but smooth sailing even when it wasn't. Our separation has taken everyone by surprise.

Aaron appears. She sees her grandparents and rushes to her grandfather's arms. She gets on his lap and clings to him. Her long legs dangling over his, the sides of her ankles nestle on the floor. She is nearly as tall as he is.

I want to tell her to get up. That's she's not a little kid anymore. I want to tell her that she is entirely too big to be there and she looks ridiculous. But I bite my tongue as her sorrow fills the room, her tears slipping easy between her cheeks and her grandfather's neck.

"It's going to be okay, Aaron," he tells her softly. "Don't worry about a thing. It's going to be just fine."

"He called us," Anna begins, her voice full of the confusion that she feels. "He said that he had moved out and that you two were separating. He didn't tell us why."

I want to speak, but I can't. I want to implore her with my eyes, but I can't do that either. I look away and Aaron's voice fills the void. It scrapes us with talons of fury, inflicting injury with every word. "She did it. She's the one." She finds her grandfather's eyes; her whole body quivers. "It's all her fault, Grandpa Allen, all her fault."

"Now wait one minute, young lady. You don't know whose fault it is. So you stop it right now."

"But Grandpa—"

His voice is stern and unyielding. "What did I say? This is a matter between your mother and your father. So whoever's fault you think it is, keep it to yourself." He eases her off his lap. "Now go over and give your grandma a kiss. She sitting in here, too."

With great reluctance she gets up from his lap, goes to Emory's mother and loosely hugs her. She looks heartbroken at her grandfather and glares at me. Leaves.

"It's going to be hard on them, especially that Aaron," Anna says.

I find my voice. "Not easy on me either."

"Life never is, Suvie." I look at her fully for the first time. I see compassion and sorrow in her eyes. No, Emory has not told all of it. "So how are you making out?" she goes on to ask with a careful smile. "Are you doing okay?"

"As okay as can be expected."

"Don't you worry too much," Elvin decides, "these things have a way of working themselves out. You and Emory have a good life together. You two can get beyond this."

I can only pray that he is right.

Emory's parents don't stay too long. They say that they are there for me if I need them. I thank them for their offer but I will never seek it. I haven't in the past and have no plans to start now.

What I find myself able to do is make the phone call I never wanted to make. With Emory's parents knowing, it will only be a matter of time before my own find out.

I call my parents and before I get the first sentence out— "Emory and I have separated"—my tears wash away my voice. I cannot answer their questions of "why?" I cannot begin to respond to their inquiry of "what happened?" I can only sob into the receiver for what seems a lifetime, unable to find my voice.

I refuse their offer to come over. Having Anna and Elvin here has taken too much from me already. I don't have the strength to look my parents in the eye, give Aaron the chance to tell all that she knows.

I promise to come by in a few days and hang up the phone. Lying across my bed, I feel, for the first time in my life, that I have failed everyone.

Rush hour traffic.

It assaults me from all sides. In front of me, behind me, on my right, my left as car after car sludges its way along the Grand Central Parkway.

I am nearly to my exit and as I've discovered every single morning since I started my job, I don't know how good or how bad the Long Island Expressway will be until I am about to get on it.

Most mornings traffic is so slow I could walk to the next exit with time to spare. A main thoroughfare into Manhattan, millions of cars each day use the LIE and though they'd expanded the lanes, it always remains clogged.

I inhale my third cigarette as I inch my way toward the off ramp. The office I work in is on the fourteenth floor and the building is totally smoke-free. I am trying to adjust to working without smoking. My first few days I felt a nicotine withdrawal as I've never felt before.

Five days a week, nine hours a day, I leave my children home unattended. I've attempted to milk Monet for every move Aaron makes, but Monet only know she leaves before noon and comes back home before five. Questions directly to Aaron aren't very helpful because all she says is she's with Keisha.

I thought to call Keisha's mother to confirm this fact, but saw no sense in calling on someone who will never be my ally. Whatever

Aaron is up to, she's up to. Out in the workforce to support my family, I leave it in the hands of the Almighty.

Friday afternoon has never felt so sweet.

I stand in my bedroom looking out the window, taking in the decline of my garden. For four days I have stood at this window wishing for the strength to tend to it, but I couldn't do more than make a fast dinner, and let the television watch me.

My first forty-hour workweek leaves me exhausted and I find comfort in the exhaustion. Wearied, I don't feel as much. Wearied, I don't think as much. Wearied, I don't miss as much. But now that the weekend is here, there is little to distract me.

Mentally I plan my weekend.

I'll tend my lawn. Visit Lisa and shop. My wardrobe is too casual for the office environment I work in. But even as I lay out the next two days, I am edgy about them. Monet and Aaron will be with Emory. It will be just me.

They say there are four steps to resolve: anger, denial, sorrow and acceptance. I don't know where I am at—anger or denial. All I know is it hurts to see my children leave every Friday night. That the completeness they make in my life vanishes.

I hear a key in the front door and know it's Emory. I rap on my children's bedroom doors, tell them their dad's here. I go back to my room and close the door. Monet always comes to say good-bye. She hugs me, and I hug her back, kiss her soft cheek. I hold myself together as she draws back, utters, "We're going."

As always I nod, try and keep the wetness from my eyes. This is my third Friday of their departure. I have not quite mastered the stoicism this moment calls for. Still I manage a weak smile, urge her toward the door, call out "See you later, Aaron," and get a mumbled "Bye."

I sit and listen to doors open and close, each connection, a shudder in my heart.

A month on the job and I hate it. Seven weeks without Emory and I hate that too. But not even that can match the flame lit inside of me when Aaron lets it "slip" that Emory has a friend.

"She alright," she adds, "nothing spectacular." Aaron does not look at me when she says this, but I know she is anticipating a response.

I say nothing. Simmer quietly refusing to have any more battles with my child. Monet appears, her face washed and her clothes changed. It's Wednesday and she has a session with Dr. Whitaker.

A few second later Emory pulls up. Soon he is coming through the front door.

"I hear you have a friend?" I begin. He looks away from me and I wait for him to look back. When he doesn't, I press on. "This was supposed to be about getting your head together, this time away from me. But it looks like you've already gotten it together and you're on a different direction, which is fine. But I should have heard it from you."

"It's not serious."

"Oh, like that even makes a difference?"

"She's just a friend, Suvie. Nothing serious to it."

"So you aren't sleeping with her?"

"No."

Relief fills me, but not enough to do away with the unease. "You want out, Em? You want to start a life with somebody else? I won't stop you. But don't think I'm going to stand by and let you act like you're already gone."

"Didn't I tell you it's not serious. That it's not like that."

"So what is like then?"

Pain flashes in his eyes. Disappears. He changes the subject. "Listen, Dr. Whitaker wants to see all us."

"All of us?"

"Yeah. As a family."

"Family? Oh, is that what we are?" My eyes are hot on him, but it takes a second for them to focus. I see a man I once loved and no longer know. Accept that I am desperately in need of answers, ones I can't find for myself. I nod my head and say, "Okay."

I have only been to the office that smells of vanilla once and the memory is not very pleasant. I am nervous as I sit in the waiting room, Aaron on one side of me, Monet on the other. I am terrified of what this first session with Dr. Whitaker will yield.

I glance at my watch for the twelfth time, praying that Emory will not be late. Though we are still apart, as Monet's parents we can show a united front, both be responsible for her illness.

"Mrs. Allen?" My head shoots up and I see the nurse. She is smiling my way, but it doesn't ease my tension. "The doctor said all of you can come in now."

I swallow. Look around. "My husband's not here."

The word *husband* catches me off-guard. I cannot remember the last time I used it. There is something powerful and connected in that moniker; something hopeful in being able to invoke it. I want to say it again and again. Shout it into real existence, but there is the sound of a buzzer and the door swings opens. Emory comes through, out of breath.

"Sorry I'm late."

I wish those words were for me but they are for his children, the receptionist and the nurse who is waiting with a Madonna smile. I purposely hang back, allowing Monet, Emory and Aaron to go first.

Feeling like an outsider looking in, I long for admittance.

The session is about Monet and how we see her fitting into our lives. Emory and I are careful with our words. Only Aaron seems up to the truth. "I think she can stop if she really want to. She just don't want to." She cuts her eyes at her sister.

"Why do you think that?" Dr. Whitaker asks.

"Cause she don't always throw up. Sometimes she eats and she don't be heading for the bathroom. Other times, she can't get there fast enough."

"Why don't you think she doesn't want to?"

"Cause of the attention she get."

I look at Dr. Whitaker, waiting for him to condemn me. But he doesn't. He simply nods. Makes notes on his paper and then asks Monet how she feels about all that was said about her. By the time the hour is up, no one feels better about anything.

Chapter 24

"How are things," my mother asks me as I tie the apron around my waist. We are having a family dinner at my parent's house sans Emory. It was my mother's idea, one that I think doesn't help.

"Things are going, Mom."

"Aaron tells me this is about Philip."

I nearly drop the glass salad bowl. Take a breath and turn toward my mother slowly. "Why am I not surprised," all I can manage.

"Is it? Is it about Philip?"

"No. It's about me."

"So you didn't have an affair with him behind Emory's back?"

The look in my mother's face hurts more than the question. Like Emory, the possibility is very real for her. I don't want to have this conversation. Don't want to evoke his name in my mother's house. Decide not to.

"It's not about Philip."

"You haven't answered the question, Suvie."

"And I'm not going to answer either."

"That was so long ago and I thought he was still married to Dorothy."

It's a can of worms that I refuse to tamper with. I stare at my mother. "Regardless of what Aaron says or doesn't, this is not about Philip."

"So if it's not, why are you and Emory separated? How would Aaron even know Philip's name to speak it?"

It is tempting bait, but I force myself not to nibble. "You want me to make the salad now?"

Fall is deep within itself. The children have started back to school, I am looking at my eighth week at work and Emory is still living elsewhere. But this evening we will all be together, if only for an hour.

It is our fifth meeting as a family with Dr. Whitaker. During the third session, discussions moved from just Monet to all of us. I've begun to look forward to relieving burdens and exploring old wounds. Every other Wednesday, between the hours of seven and eight pm, we become one again, if only to cry, complain and hurt.

I take the expressway, steal glances at Monet quiet in the backseat, catch a glimpse of Aaron's bent head, the magazine more important than I will ever be even though it's too dark outside to read.

I get on the off ramp, wait out a red light. Light my cigarette and inhale blue smoke. Aaron sucks her teeth and rolls down her window even though air is chilly. Monet says nothing, shivering in silence as we make our way to our appointment.

I ease into the parking lot and we get out of the car in silence. Emory is waiting for us outside the building and I linger as my children run to him.

My heart overflows as I watch them share hugs and kisses. I try and steel myself as I approach, but it has become difficult just to say hello.

He should have known me better, should have realized that yes, I went to see Philip but it was him I loved. Emory should have realized I was just plagued by a ghost, an ethereal past and there is no embracing of specters.

He, in all his wisdom, should have truly understood my need to set myself free, instead he has chosen the lesser road and has deemed me unworthy. As a result, Emory has gone on with his life in a way I could never go on without him.

I cannot fake a smile, can do nothing to remove the sadness from my eyes as I look at him. I swallow, say, "Hello." He returns the favor as Aaron sidles up underneath his arm.

Her eyes glimmer like jewels in the sun. "You coming, Daddy?" she asks, with little girl wonder.

"Where?" Emory responds, half distracted.

"My game. Tomorrow. We're playing Jackson."

She has become the cheerleader that her father did not want for her. I see hesitancy as he replies. "What time?"

"Game starts at five, but it's okay if you're late."

He nods absently, says "Let's go inside."

I sit in my car, Monet in the backseat and Aaron is outside clinging to her father like cellophane. We have gone through another hour of soul searching and as is often the case, I feel no better or no worse for it.

"You promise, Daddy, you promise?" Aaron asks. "It's okay if you're late, I don't mind," she repeats for the fourth time this evening and my heart twinges with envy.

He urges her toward the car, opens the back door. Guides her by the shoulder to get her into the backseat. He kisses her forehead, comes around the other side and kisses Monet. Says he'll see them later and heads toward his car.

This is the hardest part for me, watching him leave. I can never manage to pull off before him, I always find reasons to stall.

I fish in my bag for my cigarettes, adjust my mirrors, find the right music on the radio. I let my engine run though it needs no warming up and only when Emory pulls away, do I.

Together we exit the hospital commons. We will both make a right and then a left. Together we will ease onto the highway but the speed at which Emory drives is always the same: no matter how much I push the petal to the metal, no matter how hard I summon a will to reach him, he always leaves us fast and far behind.

I am beating Aaron senseless. Blood splatters the walls, coats my face in drippy redness. She is not screaming, is not speaking, just standing there allowing me to lash her.

I go on screaming and beating but make no real impact. I come awake with a gasp, lay there panting, my hand clenched around an invisible belt.

I get out of bed, move quietly down the hall. Ease Aaron's door open and find her bed empty. I look at the clock, see it is after one in the morning. I search my house and she is nowhere around. Know I have her lost forever.

"She just got here," Emory says over the phone, relief making my legs tremble. "I was going to call you as soon as I had a talk with her."

"She just left."

"Figured that much." Emory pauses and I know what's coming; it is a thought I have entertained myself. "Maybe it would be better if she stays with me."

I nod, concede, half glad to see her gone. She has brought war into my home and I am weary of the battle. I love my child, but most of the time I can't stand the sight of her. I find myself endlessly blaming her for everything wrong in my life.

I think of what I will tell Monet. Am unwilling to add more stones to her stack of sorrows. But I realize there is no choice in the matter and pray that we will all survive.

My house expands and contracts on a daily basis. Some days Monet and I can fill it completely; other days we are dwarfs in a castle of giants.

I have settled into both the emotional and mental reality of my nine-to-five. Added to the money Emory gives, we are doing okay. But financial security is just the tip of my iceberg. Below the surface little else is complete.

I have enrolled Monet in basketball, still continue the family sessions with Dr. Whitaker and her bulimia comes and goes, but it seems to be receding a little more each week and for that I am thankful. Weeks will pass where she does not purge, but then there are times when she is back in the bathroom sticking her finger down her throat.

Doctor Whitaker tells me that there is a good chance she will have the problem licked and I am happy to hear that. She had lost a dress size, is no longer quite so chubby and has grown two inches, which also helps to thin her.

In many ways my children's lives are better, but I've come to face the fact that mine will never be the same. But it is a bed I've made, a thought that comes to me as I come in from work and see Monet at the door, news on her face.

"Daddy wants you to call him."

"About what?"

"I don't know but he said as soon as possible."

I put down my bag and pick up the phone. Punch in numbers and Aaron answers. "Let me speak to your father."

The receiver is dropped. I hear her call him in the background. Soon he is on the phone, his voice filling me like sunshine breaking through a cloudy day.

Is this the day? I ask myself. *Is this the day he will say he loves me still, wants us to be a family?* I have never loved my husband more, have never stopped needing him but I push aside such wants. Grown good at the masquerade.

"We need to talk."

Just like that, the words are there, running through me, around me, about me. I swallow, still my heart. Ask. "About what?"

"This arrangement," he offers. "You gonna be home later?"

I resist the urge to chuckle. My life ends and begins at my front door. "Yes," I tell him, "I'll be here."

"I'll come by, drop Aaron and we'll go somewhere."

I swallow again, say okay. Hope.

There is something magical about the moment Emory steps through the front door, the whole house seems to sigh a sweet sigh, the table lamps seem to glow brighter and the very air goes serene.

He looks around as if he has never been here before and something painful dances in his eyes. I feel his thoughts, have gotten keener in my impressions of his emotions. I know what he is feeling. He misses being here, too.

Aaron drags in solemn behind him; her face aged with the disruptions of her life. I want to hug her, but I have become off limits.

She looks at me, tears there, a surprising emotion from the daughter who has become stone. I sense some secret, some unbestowed knowledge and wonder what she and Emory have shared.

"Hey," she finally mutters softly. I am not sure if she is addressing her sister, myself or the both of us. Still Monet and I both say hello back as Aaron looks around, another stranger in the midst. She starts, stops herself and looks at her father. He nods his head and she goes off to her old room.

Monet moves into the void Aaron has left behind. She goes to Emory, arms wide and he embraces her, holding her tight. There are tears in his eyes, which he wipes absently, releases his daughter then asks me if I'm ready.

I tell him yes.

"Well be back in a little while," Emory tells Monet, turning and walking out into the chilly autumn night. Getting into the car, he starts the engine, and soon we are on our way.

I have come to this front door a few times, but I've only entered twice. That we are coming back to his apartment is surprising, that we have shared no words on the drive is not.

It is difficult being with Emory now; who we have become mocks all that we were. I am not sure how to feel, where to put those feelings as Emory indicates a sofa I would have never picked, and I settle on its nappy too-hard surface waiting for him to end the mystery.

My absolutes are all gone now. Poof, vanished, they have disappeared into thin air. There are only a few things I know and a thousand of which I have no clue; the biggest is if any of the love Emory felt for me remains.

I realize this is the answer I have come in search of. I look at him and can't help but love what I see. Our life wasn't perfect, but it was worth much. I don't understand how I sacrificed it all for unimportant answers. Cannot see the motivation that drove me, only what I have lost.

"You want something?"

His question takes me out of myself, catching me off-guard. That he is asking, showing even a tiny bit of concern waddles me in soft painful bunting. I shake my head no, ease my soul from his eyes.

"Gonna get a beer," he decides, leaving me in the space that has become his life. I look around at the bare walls, the minimal furniture and get no sense of the man I was married to for nineteen years. It could be anybody's place, any single man's pad. Nothing here invites me to stay, makes me want to linger.

Emory returns, damp bottle in his hand, and takes a seat in his armchair. He rolls the bottle between two palms, studying some space beyond my head.

That he is thinking fills me with dread. That he is uncertain of what he wants to say makes my heart pitter-patter. I had assumed he has come to some decision and telling me is just a formality, but his indecision speaks otherwise.

"Never knew life could be so hard," he begins. "Never thought I'd wake up one morning and find nothing the way it's supposed to be. It's like some bad nightmare I can't wake up from and I don't know what to do."

He looks at me, expecting me to deny his assumptions. But I cannot because he has just described my world to a tee.

"Aaron . . ." He takes a deep breath, adjusts emotions. "Every day she's becoming somebody I don't know. I thought her coming to stay with me would be better. Thought I could get her under control. Said to myself I can do what you couldn't." He laughs, shakes his head, his bewilderment filling the room. "Well, I found out I can't. I can't help her, can't control her, nothing. I tell her to be home by seven. She comes in at nine. I tell her to clean her room; she leaves it dirty. I tell her no company when I'm not home, but I've found things saying someone's been here . . . she's having sex."

My head lifts. My eyes grow wide. A deep cold fear slices my heart. My mouth is dry, my tongue thick. "Sex?" It is hard to say the word.

"More than once. Found the empty condom packs in the garbage. Guess they flush the condoms down the toilet."

"Who?"

"I don't even know, Suvie. I asked her; she denied it. Said she wasn't having sex. And even when I showed her the empty condom pack, she kept on denying it."

"J'Qaun?"

Emory shakes his head. "Aaron says he won't see her anymore because of all the troubles she's been in. Said he has no time for no wild female, quote, unquote."

Wild female. This is what my child has become.

"I just can't handle her anymore, Suvie. I just can't." He is looking at me and it has been years since I've seen such a look in his eyes. He is asking me to intervene. To come in and do what he can not. But I am not up to the challenge, feel a sweet victory in his defeat.

"And you think I can?" I remember his words, his accusations. Recall how he saw me as an unfit mother and remind him of that fact. "I ignored my children for the sake of myself, remember?"

He looks away and anger finds me fast. "Ain't easy, is it? Ain't easy raising children who don't want to be raised. Can't just reach in a box and pull out solutions. Can't fix things with a snap of your fingers can you? You want me to take Aaron back, why should I? She acts like I'm a fucking wall. What do you think I can do that you can't?"

He looks at me again and for the first time in months I feel a connection to the man who was my husband and then decided not to be. More than history, more than pain, more than children and vows and whispers of infidelity. More than lies, half-truths, dead dreams, unhealed wounds, we are joined in a way time will never erase.

"Maybe if I came back home."

It is one of those sentences that falls from the sky. It arrives without warning and I am totally unprepared. If the words had come months ago, I would have reached out and latched onto it. But too many months have passed, filled with lonely days and bouts of dread. I feel no relief, only anger.

"Come home to do what?"

It is his turn to be stunned. That I am questioning this long-awaited decision is not what he expects. "What do you mean?"

"Just like I said. You want to come home and I want to know why? Because if you're just coming home to 'save Aaron,' then you might as well stay right here." I breathe, wait for Emory to understand all that I will not say. I breathe, wait for him to expose his insides as I have exposed mine.

"But that's what we want . . . to save her."

"Says who?" I snap back. "That little girl has caused more heartache than a little bit. I tried but my effort wasn't good enough. You decided to be super dad and came and snatched her up and I let you. But now that you've discovered you can't. You just can't hand her back."

"But she's your daughter."

"I bore her, but she was never mine." The thought makes me tremble. She had deemed me unworthy and as a result I free myself from her. She wants to live her life; then I will do nothing to stop her pursuit.

"That's crazy, Suvie."

"Is it? From the moment Aaron was born, she was 'your little girl.' Now that's she's grown into some wild ass child who don't do what's she's suppose to that's not my fault. My child?" My head shakes.

I sit back spent, exhausted, relieved. I've held onto those words forever and experience contentment in their release.

"So you don't want me to come back?"

I look at my husband wanting so much and feeling incapable of even attaining a tiny bit of it. "I never wanted you gone, Emory. That was your choice. And I've taken your choice and was forced to go on with my life, with Monet's. Our lives had been torn to pieces. We're still married, but you're seeing other women. You have gone where I never have."

"That was over before it started."

"Doesn't matter. All that matters is it did start. And that says a lot about how you really feel about me."

"You snuck off with Philip," he throws back and I see something in his eyes.

"Oh, so it was payback?" He looks away. I wait for his return glance. When it doesn't come, I go on. "I made a mistake and you've taken that mistake and stuck a knife in my heart because of it. Just left me bleeding to fucking die. Now you talking about coming back? Why? So you can help Aaron? What about me? What about Monet? Don't we matter?" I take a breath, on fire and sizzling with hurt.

"It's got to be for all of us, Emory. All of us. And if you can't forgive me, can't love Monet the same way you love Aaron, if there is not enough of yourself to share equally, then no, I don't want you back."

I wait for him to say it. Wait for him to confess that he can do that. That we are all important, that we all matter. But it's all in his eyes. He can't.

I stand, adjusting my pocketbook on my shoulder. "I'm ready."

"Wait, Suvie."

"For what?"

He does not answer. Can't answer. Things grow clear in this moment, clearer than they've ever been. Our life together was put together with bits of glue and dabs of spit. Ill-prepared for the storm that came our way, we've become shipwrecked.

"Take me home, Emory," I say, heading for his front door, knowing all that I am leaving behind, the hope, lost, never to be regained.

Chapter 25

Thanksgiving takes me by surprise.

I knew the holiday was approaching but never thought it would catch me as it does. Emory and I are still separated. Aaron is still living with him and Monet goes there on the weekends. Even within this great divide I never expected to be separated from them for the family holiday.

While I wasn't up to carrying on the responsibility of a holiday feast, I did anticipate that we would be sitting at someone's table together. I had a few places in mind—my parents, Emory's. But his folks are heading south for the holiday and he has decided to go along for the trip. Aaron wants to go too, so does Monet.

"I'm going to Carolina, with Daddy," Aaron tells me over the phone.

"Carolina?"

"Yeah. Grandpa and Grandma Allen are taking the drive down. Daddy's going too."

My knee-jerk response is hurt but I swallow it quickly. "If your father says it's okay, then it's fine with me."

"Monet wants to go too."

Pretense leaves me. Surprise claims me. "Monet?"

"Yeah, Mom. She really wants to go, but she doesn't want to hurt your feelings."

"She can't."

"That's what she said you'd say." Condemnation ladles Aaron's voice. I bite my tongue, making myself back down. "Well, if she wants to go, let her." I don't mean a word of it.

"Can I talk to her?"

"Hold on." I put the phone on the kitchen counter. Shout "Monet, it's for you." Turning, I head upstairs, my hurt, a newborn I cradle close.

I am trying to work on a proposal I took on simply because I must stay in the loop. I have no plans of abandoning my real career and dreams of returning to it is all I cling to.

I reach out, place a hand over the heating vent. Draw my sweater around me tight. There is a draft that comes from the window that I had been meaning to tell Emory about but always seem to forget. The cold blustery day is making its way through and I am writing a Post-It note to myself when Monet appears at the doorway.

"I don't have to go," she begins.

Even before I look up I know that everything in her wants to. I try to see myself without even Monet on Thanksgiving and the vision crushes my heart. Yet, I can't hold her hostage. Know that I must let her go.

"No, you don't have to go, but you're going, okay? End of discussion." It is not how I want the words to come out but they are gone from me. I risk a look at her, unable to hide my disappointment. But it is a disappointment more so in myself.

"Really, Mom, I can stay here, with you."

"Monet? What did I just say?"

"That I was going."

"Right. It's settled."

But she does not move, her eyes, liquid wonders. I raise a hand, shake my head. Insist. "Don't. Don't even start. Not a thing to be crying over." But I eat my own words as tears spring into my own. I wipe them, take a deep breath, try to end them. My daughter and I have shared more than enough tears. We have wallowed in disappointment long enough. I will not allow another pity party.

"I'm okay," I say. "It may not look like it, may not even feel like it, but I am. Your mom's gonna be alright." I risk my eyes her way. "Okay?"

She nods hesitantly. Fumbles for some silver lining. "I was thinking, maybe I can bring you back something, like your cigarettes. I think they're really cheap down there."

"Know what I want you to bring me back?" I said through smiling, too-damp eyes.

"What?"

"You. That's what I want." Mean it.

The echo of slamming doors and the car shifting gears has faded a minute ago, yet I cannot pull myself from my front door. I stand on the nubby rock-cement little stoop, holding my coat around me tight, breathing in the crisp cold dark morning air.

I feel my family drifting from me second by second. Imagine the rented SUV as it winds its way through the still-dark quiet streets heading toward the expressway. I sense the big empty hollow space of my home that awaits me. Refuse to cry.

I stand there until I am near numb. Stand there until the cold forces me inside. I go around turning off lights, look into Monet's bedroom, wondering how I will survive.

My parent's house is full of people and noise, but I can't seem to find a way to enter that realm and by the time the meal is over, I am ready to go home. The tension between my mother and myself about where Philip fits into my present situation has faded. Whatever the cause for the breakup between Emory and myself, she understands it is ours to fix and no one else's.

I stand in my parent's kitchen, wrapping up take-home food I am not certain I want to eat. I think of tomorrow and the job I will go to that I can barely stand. I put my helpings into a shopping bag and head out to say good night, but make my way upstairs.

I open the closed door to my bedroom. See the old album jacket covers that still line the wall. I stare into the image of the sunglassed-face of Stevie Wonder. Study the perfect halo that had been Jermaine Jackson's Afro. I pick up an old stuffed teddy bear and am bringing it to my face before I remember it had been a long-ago gift from Philip. Find myself wondering how it escaped the trash.

I try not to think about where he is, what is he doing on this great family holiday. I try not to put Philip anywhere in my thoughts but he is a part of me, if only in memory. I look around the room that had conceived the beginning of my end and feel not anger but sadness. I can't help but wonder if I had said yes that one last time, how different my life would have been.

But that thought does not last long. Is gone by the time I kiss my parents good night and head to my car. This is my life and it has been played out just the way it was supposed to be. Through all its sorrows, all of its joys. Through all the uncertainties, disruptions and annihilations, this is who I am.

My only hope is that this is not who I remain.

Chapter 26

Fall in and around Metro Atlanta is beautifully deceptive. Often it suggests summer when winter is well on its way.

Trees show off autumn colors above shimmering outdoor swimming pools. Tuesdays can see you in shorts and a cotton tee only to be followed by a Wednesday when a heavy jacket and long pants are needed. Lawns remain stubbornly green and spring flowers stay in bloom. Gas grills are fired up for weekend barbecues as breezes worthy of May fill the air.

These paradoxes don't touch Dorothy as she stands at the window in her formal dining room, the heat of the day gathering at the glass with the intensity of a hot oven. The air conditioning is running on the seventy-eight-degree day, clashing with the smell of roasting turkey, candied yams and bubbling macaroni and cheese.

Behind her the table is set with fine china, an off-white damask tablecloth and hand-polished silverware. She has chosen the perfect wine for the meal and has counted blankets and pillows, making sure she will have enough for her arriving guests.

Everything is perfect and ready, but a part of her is not so refined. For the first time in months, she and Philip will share the same bed. For the first time, their farce will be played out to a live audience—her family—and it is a farce that is feeling less valid with each passing day.

Philip places the grocery bags on the counter, fixes a second cup of coffee and goes out onto his backyard deck. He sits, feet up, mug nestled in his hand, staring at the thick explosion of autumn color that is the forest behind his house.

Above him the sun is bright in the powder blue sky. Closing his eyes, he inhales the fresh soft dew of the late morning. The deck French door opens. Without words, Dorothy settles into the lawn chair next to him. It is the first time she has felt a need to.

Something rustles in the forest. Its approach is careful and quick. In a blink of an eye, it is there, standing on the lush grass. Huge brown eyes turn softly their way; the white spotted back, equestrian flanks, picture still.

Dorothy's breath catches—"A deer?"—releases as she goes to rise.

Philip stops her. Whispers "Shhh."

The doe turns its head toward the forest, looks back at its captive audience forty feet away. One hoof rises, another follows and soon it glides back into the density.

"A deer," Dorothy admonishes, "right here in our backyard."

"Not a deer, a doe. The spots on its back. Female, like Bambi." His voice is soft, but knowledgeable, holding the timbre Dorothy had long ago been drawn to. Philip, wise, mature, full of knowledge. Philip, a man so high above the rest she'd committed the ultimate betrayal to have him.

Dorothy does not fight the feelings that flow through her now. Understands, remembers that this moment, this life, this Philip, the one of quiet want is what she'd longed for. "How rare is that?" she finds herself asking. "All the years we've been here. I've never spotted one back here before."

"That's how they come, when you least expect it," Philip says softly.

Dorothy doesn't comment. Just stares toward the gather of woods. She sips her coffee. Listens to the rustle of leaves in the trees. Inside, the phone burrs softly. She is standing, but Philip waves her off. "I got it."

He leaves, comes back. "They've just left North Carolina. They should be getting here about four."

"Still can't believe it."

"What?"

"My family, here with us for Thanksgiving."

"It's time. Don't you think?"

Dorothy knows the answer. Doesn't speak it.

The onslaught of slamming doors and quick agitated Northern accents is what announces Dorothy's family's arrival. A part of her twinges, the other part of her smiles as she spies her mother helping her father out of the high-up Suburban. Dorothy becomes tenderhearted as she sees the smaller-than-she-can-ever-remember man and recalls the power and fear with which he once drove her life.

Time is the great alternator, the ultimate shifter of how you look at things and how things look back at you. As Dorothy sees her father's face, his first visit to the home she lives in, the life she has carved, there is marvel there, marvel and pleasure, a type she has never seen in his eyes and somehow senses, she never will again.

"Boy, wait!" echoes up around the house, seeping through the walls, the stained glass and wood door. "Damn," comes a lower mutter beneath the rumble of excited weary voices. As her family of eight spills from the SUV, she knows they realize they are as far removed from their South Jamaica, New York, neighborhood as they will ever be.

They know that the quiet, winding street of two-storied homes—some with columns of white, arches of stacked stone, pushed thirty feet back from the curb, offering an oasis of lush green lawns, smartly trimmed hedges, bay windows and shiny chandeliers suspended from two-story foyers—is part of a world they will never live in—but this day, will be a part of.

Dorothy's great nieces and nephews toss slang around like popcorn, expressions exploding in the air. Things like "slamming," "the shi-zit." "Bling bling, bay-bee." She opens her front door to shut down the euphoria. To tone down their uncouth amazement, to greet them, give hugs, kisses. She opens the door to bask in their unfettered adoration at the wondrous life she has created.

She moves to her father first, keeps her smile tight even though his gait is slow, near limp. In his later years he has come down with diabetes, and it has affected the mobility of his feet. "Daddy," she nearly sings, as she moves to him, embraces the man who no longer towers over her but has shrunk into the fold in her arms.

His arms are slow to move around her, tempered as they go around her back. They do not remain long as he steps from her, takes one more look at the expansive ranch and heads toward the front door.

Her sister is the one Dorothy wishes to greet next, but her mother cuts off her destination. "Lord, didn't think I could sit in the thing another minute," she tells Doe as she tugs at her wig with one hand and reaches for her oldest with the other.

Dorothy takes the embrace, allows her mother to linger, eyes finding DeAnna's with need. Of all her family, this is the one she feels the closest to. This is the one she has missed the most. Of all her family, this is the one who knows the new roles of Dorothy and Philip, one she has promised not to share.

She eases out of her mother's embrace, makes quick steps toward her sister.

"How you doing?" DeAnna wants to know.

"Doing okay," Dorothy answers back, meaning it.

"Aunt Doe, Aunt Doe, y'all got a pool?"

"Aunt Doe, dey got a park?"

"Damn your house is big. Shoot, I may have to relocate," offers her brother, Dean, and though it has been some time since she's seen him, she is happy to see he is, at least for now, sober.

Dorothy moves away from her sister. Waves a hand toward her front door. "Come on in everybody. Dinner's ready and I'm sure you guys are starved."

She spies her grandnephew, Keifer, peering into the window of her garage. "Dat yours?" he wants to know.

Dorothy shakes her head. Knows he is referring to Philip's Escalade. "No, your uncle Philip's," the words strangely sweet on her tongue.

"No drinking in the family room," Dorothy calls out from the kitchen. It is the twentieth time she has given that warning, the twentieth time she has seen her family wander into the room of off-white carpet and lush leather with glass tumblers full of Hawaiian punch, apple cider, expensive dry wine.

She had sponge-mopped spilled gravy from the Persian rug under her dining room table and red wine from the white kitchen floor. She has wiped a dozen prints from the pristine refrigerator door and reminded her brother that smoking is only allowed out on the deck.

This has led to bitter words about trying to be something she isn't and it's just a house, not a damn museum. But her father comes to her rescue and though she no longer cowers under his will, the rest of her family does.

"She got nice stuff. She wants to keep it that way. Nobody got a right to come in here and mess a damn thing up, hear?" That was the end of such talk.

By the evening, after the meal is served and more than second helpings are eaten, her brother, her grandnieces and grandnephew go out on the deck in the back to marvel at the somewhat spring weather though it is nearly December. Dorothy, Philip, her parents, her sister and her sister's child gather in the family room to watch TV.

And though they have not shared many words, there is no sense of the great divide between husband and wife. For all accounts, Dorothy and Philip are forever.

It is strange to have him here.

Strange to feel his energy, his presence filling the massive master bedroom though he clings to what used to be his side of the king-size bed.

His back is to her, his breathing even, faint, and Dorothy knows he is not sleeping. That he is waiting in the land of hopelessness, waiting for what, by all accounts, will never be again.

She doesn't want to consider it. Doesn't want the choice to lie between them like a third body full of promise, a third body full of hope. But no matter how often she tosses and turns, adjusts covers, the puff of pillows, it remains there, demanding acknowledgement, demanding a new choice.

She is not supposed to want her husband. She is not supposed to entertain the possibility of a whole new loving life. She is not supposed to make this moment anymore than it is—a farce to fool her family, but her body, her soul betrays her.

Want has found her. Want has claimed her. Need demands supply. Need demands the man not sleeping three feet away. It demands that she lift a hand and touch a shoulder. Demands she scoot over to the inert body. It demands she open her mouth and call his name, letting all the passion now burning in her soul betray her.

But Dorothy will not do it. She sits up, hangs her feet over the edge of the bed. Nestles her head into her hand. Stands. Across the carpeting she walks, the closed bedroom door her destination. But a voice comes to her in the darkness. Comes to her in the soft even silence of the late November night.

"Doe?"

It is not a question as much as a pleading. Not a question as much as a wanting, that needing, stirring up the one in her soul she now struggles to control. She does not answer, cannot answer, but her left foot refuses to follow her right. Dorothy Alexander Butler is stuck, rooted, thick inside of old dreams that were no longer supposed to matter.

"Doe?" the voice a little higher, less certain, fearful but still needy. Still wanting.

She wants to scream *Shut up;* she wants to whisper no. But her mouth is locked and the day is a mosaic of perfection that loops through her mind on an endless reel. Moments, sweet, tender, full of joy, all the day was.

Every second of this day, she has felt him near, felt him as if he had snuck up behind her and nestled her, his chest to her back, arms around her, safe, ethereal. Warm.

Across the dinner table she felt it. As she stood loading the dishwasher and washing pots, she felt it. Philip, ethereally holding her. Making her world perfect, her world safe, his love new and real.

Dorothy finds her footing. Grabs the doorknob. But Philip is there before she can turn it. There before she can open it, step outside, walk away. He is there as she has emotionally felt him this Thanksgiving day, arms about her, his chest to her back, love running from his soul like a sap.

She does not struggle from his embrace but attempts to close off her pores from all that oozes from him. But effort comes too late and she feels herself surrender, as he turns her, looks into her eyes until she is forced to look back. Until she sees what she has never seen before. Knows that this time, there is no need for her mouth, her smarts or the expense of a best friend. This time, without effort, he offers forever.

While Philip, understanding what he feels for Sylvia will always be light years from what he can offer Dorothy, uses his heart, his soul, his arms and his tongue to urge Dorothy toward him. Toward the life he finds most wanting: a life of being loved and loving back.

Chapter 27

What is it about life that makes you surrender? Is it the day-to-day or the hurtful sums that have gathered over the years until they fill your life and steal all of your hope? Is it the battles you wage and the defeats that gather like hard clay up under your feet until you're against a ceiling, unable to move? I'm not certain, only that survival has kicked in.

Spring has come, taking away winter's chill and inside me something struggles for rebirth as I entered my workplace for the one hundred and twenty-first time. I look around the massive office full of ringing phones and suits of blue and I want to scream.

I stare at the desk I'd been chained to for five days a week for all these months and know I cannot sit there another day. That I am quitting with nothing but my abilities and faith to keep me afloat.

I drove to work, window down, music up, breathing deeply of the fresh air of a new spring. Beyond the fumes of fast-moving cars I smelled blades of grass, apple blossom sun, perfumed air.

I thought about what I wanted, who I wanted to be and understood that being an administrative assistant dictated by panty hose and mandatory business suits was not it. That going back into the workforce was Emory's decision.

I go directly to my boss and tell her I am quitting. She sits there, blinking and stunned and I do not care. For months my life had been in the hands of others and I am claiming it back. I have a few dollars saved and have kept up my grant writing. I will be okay and if not, I will find a way.

"Today?" my boss asks.

"Yes, today. Right now. You can mail me my check."

I turn and walk out, saying good-bye to no one. I take the elevator down for the last time and step out into the soft spring weekday morning. I go to my car, get in and light up a cigarette. Heading home, I stop at Blockbuster and rent two movies. I spend the next five hours watching flicks, munching Pop Secret, swigging Coca-Cola and smoking cigarettes, halfway through my healing.

Lisa calls me that night. She has heard I quit and I am ready to apologize for the abruptness. Her words are not what I expect, but all I need to hear.

"It wasn't you anyway, Suvie. I've always known that. It's not where you was suppose to be."

"Thank you, Lisa."

"No need to thank me. Sometimes we just got to do what we have to do." A pause comes. "So what are you going to do?"

"Go back to grant writing."

"Is that going to be enough?"

"I'll have to make it enough."

"You tell Emory?"

"Why should I? So he can tell me I have to go back?"

"Well, if times ever get tight, you know I'm here. I still can't get over how much I have now that I've left Mack." That she has done it, left her husband, still fills me with amazement and utmost respect. When school started and her son refused to come back home, she knew she had to make a choice between her husband and her son.

Her son won.

She told Mack she was going back home to her parents and that she was filing for a divorce. She has done both.

"Do you know he still refuses to move out? My father has to start an eviction proceeding to get him out of the house."

"Does Mack know?"

"My father called him, giving him one more chance to leave willingly. Mack told my father he wasn't going nowhere. He don't think my daddy will do it." Lisa sucks her teeth. "It's obvious that he don't know my daddy."

It's hard to believe my friend's life has come to this. I tell her so.

"Don't feel sorry, Suvie. I should have left a long time ago."

But within her proclamation I hear a thousand lonely nights and I cannot stop myself from asking, "You miss him?"

"Not a day goes by that I don't. But it's not about that anymore."

I hear her words, wonder if they match the timbre of Emory's heart, unable to remember the last time I saw me inside his eyes.

Chapter 28

Monet and I are having a TV night together. We gather on the living room sofa and put our feet up. Since our house has been diminished by two, we have grown closer. Our downtime is often spent together.

Tonight we watch an episode of *Survivor.* We make bets on who will be booted and who will remain. I've told Monet I quit my job and she's glad I did. She's missed me being here. "Felt weird, Mom, leaving in the morning and coming back in the afternoon and you weren't here."

I've told her not to say anything to Emory because it's something I need to do. Tomorrow I will tell him, letting the cards fall where they may. But for tonight, it's about Monet and me.

"He needs to be booted off," Monet decides. "Look at him, trying to make nice with her. Just a few minutes ago he was scheming to have her gone."

"Human nature," I say. "We do what we have to do to survive, just like the name of the show."

"You think he'll be mad?'

"Who?"

"Daddy?"

"About me quitting?"

"Yeah."

I shrug my shoulders, gaze off into my own uncertain future. "I won't be asking him for a penny more, so I don't see how he could be." But in truth I am not sure how Emory will react only that I will tell him.

I call him the next day at work. "There's something I have to talk to you about," I say.

"Everything okay?"

I think about everything and know that it could be better. "Yes, but there is something I have to tell you and I don't want to do it over the phone."

"What's this about, Suvie?"

"I'll tell you when I see you. Later, after work, can you drop by?"

"Sounds serious."

"Serious enough. After work. Today. Can you come by?"

"I'll be there by six."

At quarter after five, I'm in my kitchen trying to decide on cooking two pork chops or four. I don't know if Emory plans on joining us for dinner, but I don't want to make a fool of myself by not having enough just in case.

It is a minute dilemma, an almost stupid one, but I've been viewed as the bad guy for so long that I'm not trying to add any more leverage to the title. I look at the thawed chops and suddenly I'm angry that making dinner has become an issue.

My life now, I think quietly to myself and feel freedom in the thought. I have been nothing but politically correct and I'm tired of holding my thoughts, my emotions, my wants in check.

I take two chops from the pack and put the rest into first a freezer bag and then the freezer, my anxiety fading as resolve moves in. I sprinkle the chops with a bit of seasoned salt and black pepper. Turn the oven to three hundred and seventy-five degrees. I've cut back on fried foods and do more broiling and baking. Not only is it good for Monet, it is good for me, too.

She appears at the kitchen, goes to the refrigerator. "What will it be tonight? Veggies or just salad?' she wants to know. We split the dinner duties now. I do the meats, she the side dishes.

"How about some steamed broccoli and mashed potatoes?"

"Okay." Monet takes out the fresh broccoli and the cutting board. Gets the box of instant mash potatoes, butter and milk. I leave the kitchen, allowing her free reign. Under my direction, she is becoming quite the cook.

Dinner is done and we are eating by the time Emory arrives. "Just having dinner. I'll be finished in a few." I go back to the table and resume my eating. Emory takes a seat, too.

His eyes wander over what is left of my mashed potatoes, the delicately steamed broccoli and half of my baked pork chop. "Looks good," he offers, eyes to my plate. I say nothing, continue eating, happy to see that Monet hasn't offered up any of hers.

"How's school?" he asks her.

"Fine," she responds.

"You ace that science test?"

"Uh-huh," but her eyes are everywhere but on him.

We have weathered some rough storms, and as a result the wide-eyed little girl who once adored her father is becoming someone else.

I finish my meal and take my plate to the sink.

"You have anything to drink?" Emory wants to know.

"We have juice and soda. You can help yourself," I offer. Emory gets up and get a glass.

Monet finishes her meal, scrapes her plate. Puts it in the sink. She goes to her dad, gives him a hug, which catches him off-guard. Her hugs have become far and few lately.

She leaves and we hear the sound of a door closing. It's her bedroom door, not the bathroom. For now, there is no throwing up.

"She's changing," he says a few seconds after she leaves.

"We all are," I answer. I settle back into the chair and wait for his undivided attention even though nothing in me wants to look him in the face. "I asked you over because I quit my job."

"You did what?"

"Before you start jumping to all types of conclusions, you need to understand that being there, doing that five days a week isn't me. That it wasn't my choice, but yours. Since last year, I've been abiding by everybody's decisions but my own. I'm doing the choosing now."

"Not everybody's."

"We're not going there. This is not about then, this is about now. And I am going back to what I love—grant writing."

"What about the money?'

"What about it?"

"Will it be enough?"

"I'll have to make it enough and I won't ask for a penny more from you."

That bit of news surprises him. He looks off, thinking. "You sure about this, Suvie?"

"I never been surer of anything in my life." Even as I say this, the thought scares me. But I am determined to make it—on my own terms. If I have to live away from Emory, I should at least live it my way.

"It's a big risk, you know that?"

Something softens me—wisdom. Its arrival takes me by surprise but calms me. "You take chances in life, Em. You throw the dice and hope for the best. Sometimes you get lucky; sometimes you don't and that's okay, as long as you try."

He looks away, unable to behold my new-found self. "Okay," he utters, but it is a word I have no use for. He can no longer grant my wishes.

Chapter 29

Thirteen is not eleven. Thirteen is not twelve. Thirteen is the magic number all little girls wish for, the marker in life that says they are entering teenagehood.

It is for this reason that my mother and father came by earlier, bearing gifts and reluctantly leaving before the magic hour of six o'clock. It is for this reason that Emory's parents are planning a special dinner tomorrow at their house to celebrate with Monet.

At ten, grandparents are welcomed at birthday gatherings. At thirteen it can be a fate worse than death, especially if you are having your first real party with boys and girls and music. She asked me to explain it to them and I did. And while both sets of grandparents were a little stung by her request, they understood.

I stand at my stove and chicken pieces pop and sizzle inside the cast-iron frying pan. The noise from the exhaust fan whirs loudly. I open the side door letting the spring air in and the smell of frying chicken out. Lisa finger-pops from the living room.

Monet comes into the kitchen, the short knit dress and clunky platform shoes stealing all resemblance of adolescent from her newly arrived teenaged body. "How I look?"

I take in her ringlets of curls falling heavy against her shoulders, the slicked over the side sweep of hair across her forehead, the hint of lip gloss on her lips, the butter-soft skin aglow with a newly discovered self. My eyes fill with tears.

"Mom?"

I cannot stop the flow. I wipe my eyes absently and take in the daughter who has grown beautiful and remained sweet despite the bad times. I swallow, swallow again. Nod my head. "Absolutely beautiful."

Her face screws up, uncertainty dusting the corner of her eyes. "You sure?"

"Absolutely."

She goes out of the kitchen. I go back to frying chicken; my eye fast on the clock. I take in the pile of cooked wings, thighs and legs. I check the spread of potato chips, popcorn and pretzels. It is Monet's milestone, but in many ways it is mine.

That my daughter is now thirteen fills me with awe. That she had discovered enough of herself to ease into the shoes of beauty and the fit of grace is a blessing from God. Today her friends and family will come and help her celebrate the moment. I am buzzing with anticipation.

I finish up the last of the chicken. Wipe counters of grease and do a last-minute check of the house. I take a shower and get dressed, a new-found joy filling me. My life has turned a corner.

The doorbell rings at exactly six. Before I can think to get it, Monet is racing toward it. It swings open and a group of kids are clustered at the door. Monet lets out a squeal as she greets them.

Most faces I recognize; others I do not. Monet takes the time to introduce the whole group to both Lisa and myself. But it is Lamar who holds my attention. He is the one who has captured my daughter's heart.

At thirteen he has yet to grow into his full height and he is barely two inches taller than Monet. Plain and brown, he is an ordinary boy. He takes my hand and says, "Nice to meet you, Mrs. Allen."

"Nice to meet you, too, Lamar," I reply, resisting the urge to say how much I've heard about him. Then Monet is pulling him away and soon they are in the living room, four feet separating them, shyness clinging to them both.

Lisa and I sip punch watching, smiles coating both of our faces.

"Average," I say to her.

"Just the type of boy you want for Monet. Not too fast and not too wise."

I nod in agreement.

"I knew my baby would be alright," Lisa tells me. I don't know if it's a true statement or an afterthought, but I am just glad to hear Lisa say it.

"How's Kelvin?"

"Studying for his SATs. Quite a few colleges want him. I told him the choice was his."

"You raised a good son, Lisa."

She smiles self-consciously. "Yeah, I was able to do that much."

The door opens. Emory steps inside. The sight of twenty-something teenagers crowded up in the house catches him off-guard. I smile at his surprise.

He searches the room, sees me and heads my way. "Hey," he offers, confusion full on his face.

"Hey," I say glad that he made it.

He leans over and kisses my cheek. In the reclaiming of myself, I have changed in Emory's eyes. He has begun to see the old Suvie, not the later version full of betrayal and lies and though he did not like the fact that I quit my job, I have not demanded a penny more from him than he has been giving me and I am managing with the money grant writing brings in.

"Where's Aaron?"

"She's working till seven. I'm going to pick her up later." I nod my head, tuck away the information, glad to see she has managed to hold onto her job.

"How you doing, Emory?" Lisa says.

"Doing alright." Emory replies, searching the crowd. "Where's Monet?"

I laugh, point ten feet away at the happy lip-glossed girl. "Right there, Em."

His eyes grow wide. He stares at her for a minute. I feel his thoughts before they even reach his lips. "What's with the hair?"

"It's her thirteenth birthday party."

"That dress is kinda short."

"She's growing up." The right way I want to add. "That's Lamar she's dancing with."

"That's the kid that's been calling her?"

"Yeah. Seems nice enough." But my comment goes over his head. Emory does not trust my judgment and he searches Lamar from head to toe for perceived flaws. I know he will find none.

"You want some punch?" Lisa asks him.

Emory nods absently, his eyes fast on Lamar.

"Well, come on in the kitchen and we'll get you some," she decides, taking him by the arm. I follow.

His eyes take in the dish full of fried chicken. Without thought he reaches for a leg, pauses and looks at me. "Is it alright?"

"Of course it is," Lisa says, reaching for a plate. She hands it to him. "Knock yourself out."

Surprise fills Emory's eyes, softening to a gratitude I never thought he'd have toward her. Lisa smiles, shrugs, then heads out. It is just us two.

He pulls out a chair. I find myself joining him. "I didn't mean what I said about Monet, just that she looks so—"

"Special? She's always been special to me, Emory."

"I've been thinking," he says as he takes a bite of my chicken, then another. "This is good."

"Nothing but some chicken."

He puts the leg down. Plucks a napkin. Wipes grease from his fingers and lips. "More than chicken, Suvie."

I look away.

I have spent a lot of time alone and I have no desire to be without someone. I cannot get used to the empty space of my bed and having no companion to share a laugh. I want that other half to complete my whole. But for all the sadness I have encountered, I am discovering the old Suvie. The Suvie who will not beg, entice or grovel to gain someone's love.

I'm not sure if this is something Emory knows, but I have no desire to share. I have sat back and analyzed our life for all it's worth and keep returning to the same stubborn point—he should have known me better.

"Remember what you said about coming back to all of us?"

I nod my head absently.

"I want to do that, Suvie."

"But do you know how?"

His eyes find mine. "I love you, Suvie. I never stopped loving you. I'm trying to get on with my life, but it's just not working."

"Trying how?" But I already know. Monet is a pipeline to her father's life and she doesn't hesitate in telling me everything. There have been two women since he left me. There has been no other man in mine.

"You know," he mutters.

"No, Emory, I don't."

Monet comes into the kitchen. "Daddy!" she squeals with delight. He is up out of his chair and she is in his arms before I can take my next breath. I smile a sad smile and rise from the table. I am halfway through the door before Emory is calling me back. "No, don't leave."

"Just going to check on the snacks," I say.

"Monie, baby, can you give me and your mom a few minutes?"

She looks up at him. Studies me. If I indicate it's what I want, she'll concede. If I indicate otherwise, she will not. But I am not sure. Not sure I want to hear all Emory has to say. Not sure I want to know about him lying with other women, about him crossing the line in a way I never did.

I'm not sure if I want to open the door that could let him back. Not sure if it is the right move or the wrong. My life is not perfect, but I look at Monet and see how much better it is. I don't know if I am willing to risk forsaking that milestone.

But Monet takes my indecision and decides for me. "Sure, Daddy." Leaves his embrace. She is through the kitchen door and swallowed in the crowd. I lean against the counter, arms folded.

"Can you sit?" he asks me.

I can sit, walk, spit or cartwheel if I want, I think, but the question still remained if I want to. Emotions are tricky. They warp-drive you in one direction, only to turn around and send you on a whole different course. The trick is to decide on where you want to stop, then dig in. But I can't decide.

"Then I'll stand," Emory says, moving in front of me.

We are so close, I can see the beginnings of his five o'clock shadow. So close I can smell his cologne, see his nose hairs and the formerly cartoon sharp chin that has softened over the years.

We are so close that if I breathe too deeply, it will impact his chest like a ripple on a pond. My head swims. I am scared, afraid and want to run away.

I do not look at him even as his fingers land softly on the slope of my chin. His touch weakens my resistance and I know exactly what I will see when our eyes meet. It will be what I needed those many months before. My heart is greedy for it, but my head is dead-set against it.

Who will win? I am thinking as Lisa comes into the kitchen, disrupting the flow.

"Oops," she says, back tracking. But it is enough for me to regain myself, come back to the Suvie I have become. I move away, rearrange napkins, line up forks. Hear Emory leave the kitchen, taking the beat of my heart with him.

We are sitting outside, Lisa and I, having a smoke. Emory has left and I don't know if he will return. I try not to worry about it, but I do.

"Not like he wasn't a good husband, Suvie," Lisa says after a while.

"Yes, but he couldn't forgive me, Lisa."

"Just because he didn't forgive you on the spot doesn't mean he can't or hasn't."

I turn away from the thought, take a deep drag on my cigarette. "You don't know what he said."

"I don't have to know. All I know is what I saw. And I saw a man who worked hard and treated his family good. I saw a man who made my best friend so damn happy I couldn't stand her ass half the time. I saw a man who was good and kind and loving. And tonight I saw that same man."

"You don't know."

"You keep saying I don't know and I don't need to know. You did something to him that tore up his whole world. Human nature says whatever he did, he was entitled. But that's the past, Suvie, and right now you sitting in your present. You talk about forgiveness, but you ain't willing to forgive him."

"Because he won't forgive me."

"How do you even know that? Have you even tried to let him show you? He wanted to come back home, you told him no. When I busted you in the kitchen, there was so much love stirring up between you two you could have lit the world. But what you do, turn from it." She pauses, catching her breath. "You want to go on being separated and by yourself?

"All those years Philip had you like the walking dead. That's what you want again? Now you can go to your grave refusing Emory or you can take a chance on saving nearly twenty-two years of good love." Finished with me, Lisa stands up and goes back inside.

I sit on the step, the spring night chilly, the stars above me flecks of white in the dark blue sky. I sit there, thinking, smoking, seeking the right answers, knowing them with every breath I take.

The sound of a car door slamming shakes me from my thoughts. I look up, see Emory, see Aaron, a big boxed present in her hand. I am standing, watching, my heart beating too fast for the confinement of my chest.

I wait, still, wide-eyed as they enter the front yard. Aaron is half smiling, Emory is stone-faced as they head toward me.

"I bought Monet a present," Aaron says. I must remind myself she is only sixteen though in the darkness she could pass for twenty easily.

I nod absently, search Emory's face for some sign of tenderness, but it has vanished. Aaron moves past me. Emory attempts to, but I stop him. "Wait."

"For what?"

I don't know. I can't get my mouth to work.

"You want something with me?" he asks. I nod furiously, afraid to speak it, to say it, just want to feel all that we shared in the kitchen an hour ago.

"What?"

I open my mouth. One word comes forward. So tiny, so miniscule, it nearly fades before I can utter it. "You."

He does not believe me. Doubt crawls about his eyes, the furrow of his brow. He stands there, reading me, sensing my confusion, my fear. "Me." It is not a question, it is a challenge.

I nod my head once more, faith filling me as I wait for the same faith to find him, too.

We are in the basement, entwined, up against the wall. How we got here, why we got here has no merit, no reason. All that matters is that we are.

Above us are the sounds of the party, the heavy beats of music, the pounding of dancing feet. The floorboards creak rhythmically as I lose myself in Emory's hot kisses.

We are panting, needy, sweaty and out of breath. We are on fire with our passion, lost to the world, clinging to each other desperately and without concern. I come in an avalanche of pleasure, feel Emory pull out as he ejaculates against my thigh. We pull apart and stare at each other, slowly coming back into the world.

We stare at each other, unsure, uncertain. Breathe hard on the musty basement air. No love, no hate, just a brittle emptiness. We are strangers in our own midst.

I pull back from the wall, go to the laundry room and retrieve a clean towel. I wipe sperm from my leg, the edge of my skirt, the joining between my thighs. I pass the towel to Emory, unable to look in his eyes. *Wrong,* my head chants like a bell towing. *Wrong, wrong, wrong.*

In silence we finish cleaning ourselves. I use the mirror over the sink to fix my hair. I feel dirty and long for a shower. Decide to at least change my clothes.

Emory is heading for the stairs when my voice finds him. "What now?"

He turns and considers me, uncertainty in his eyes.

"What do you mean?"

"Us. What happens?" I manage, mouth full of cotton.

I see it in his eyes. He doesn't know.

I turn away, hurting with a new pain. Emory heads up the basement steps. I wait a few minutes then follow.

Lisa stops me as I head for my bedroom. Considers me with puzzled eyes. Her mouth drops open and I raise my hand to quiet her question, go into my room and close the door.

I smell Emory on me every time I take a breath, even though I have changed my clothes and washed my body with soap, warm water. It is the scent of indecision and backsliding, and it zips through my lungs like acid.

I am in a fog as I bring out the birthday cake. Light years away as I place thirteen candles upon its pretty iced surface. I tremble as I light them, burning the side of my hand, my fingers. I feel Emory in the crowd like a thief among honorable men.

Someone turns off the lights. I stand beside Monet. There is a mild movement of bodies, and I know Emory is coming to stand on the other side. Then people are singing and my mouth barely wants to work. I open my lips but no words come. A camera flashes making me blink.

"Make a wish, Monet! Make a wish!" Monet closes her eyes, lifts her face heaven bound, mouths words and bends down and blows. Shouts of joy and claps erupt as the lights come back on and Lisa hands her a knife.

"Okay, everybody look up," she insists and the three of us smile for the photo. I see Aaron against the wall, far away. I possess no strength to call her into the fold.

Emory holds the large plastic garbage bag while I dump in plates of half-eaten cake, red-stained cups and used napkins. We go around the house doing a thorough job of cleaning without a single word.

Aaron is in the room with Monet and though Lisa offered to stay and clean, I've sent her home. My body feels no less dirty, and my brain is filled to the brim with unanswered questions.

I am waiting for Emory to talk. Waiting for him to share all those words he never got the chance to say earlier. But he is mute and I am not strong enough to cull them from them.

I think about the fast sweaty sex we had and the other women he has slept with. I think about the question I'd posed and how he was incapable of answering. I think about what will happen once he walks out the front door.

All too soon our cleanup is done and he is taking the garbage outside to the trash. I sit at the kitchen table waiting for his return. It is only a minute but it seems forever.

He sees me sitting. Stands there looking at the top of my head. Something bubbles up in me fast and furious, a question that I never thought I would have to ask. But it leaves my tongue like a quickly flung danger, hitting its mark with bull's-eye accuracy. "Was that all you wanted?"

"No, Suvie, you know it wasn't."

"Well, what did you want?"

"I guess I just wanted you." There is so much guilt there, so much heavy culpability that it makes my head spin.

"So you didn't want to come back, try again? Just want to sleep with me?"

"No, that wasn't it."

"Then what was it, Emory?"

"I thought I wanted to come back."

"But?" I say the word and find it a difficult part of the sentence.

"It's different now."

"Different how? Because you got some?"

"All I know is when I got here I wanted to come back . . . but what we did in the basement . . ." He won't finish.

"What, Emory?"

"Just . . ."

"Just what?"

"I got this picture in my mind."

"Of what?"

He swallows, his eyes weepy with sadness. "You . . . Philip."

His words take me from the table. I am standing in front of him in a blink of an eye. "Philip! That's what you think we did?" But I can see it, too. Could see us taking that kiss further if time and place allowed it.

"No, yes, I mean, damn it, Suvie. Yes, alright? All I can see, I all I can think, all I can feel. All I know."

"I thought you forgave me."

His tone grows chilly. "I never said that."

I blink, blink again. "If you haven't, how can you even think about coming back?" I laugh, turn away, spin myself in circles. I want to take it all back. Want to wave my hands and change the night. "You are something, you know that? Here I'm thinking that you forgave me, was willing to make it work and you haven't forgiven me nothing. Just go, Emory."

I turn and walk out the kitchen. Go to my room and slam the door, hating Emory, hating Lisa. Hating myself most. But my solitude is interrupted. There is one knock and the door swings open.

"I don't want to go away like this, Suvie. I don't want to leave here with nothing changed, and everything bad between us."

There are tears in Emory's eyes. I cannot turn away from them though I desperately want to.

"I don't want to be away from you, Suvie. I want to come home, be a family again. But I don't know how."

"I can't do it for you, Emory."

He nods, wipes his eyes. Closes the door. "I know you can't. Don't think that I'm not trying to make things better. If I could just wave my hands and make it better, I would in a heartbeat. I didn't want to think what I thought, but I did. And it hurts, Suvie; it hurts, right here, in my heart. Like a knife that keeps twisting and twisting. And I'm tired of the pain." He sits on the edge of the bed. Holds his head. Cries a little. I reach out, rub his back, sorrowed for him in a way I have not felt in a long time. ". . . so tired," he mutters.

I say nothing as he lies back against the bed. Not a word as he rolls on his side. I remain there as his tears give way to whimpers and whimpers move into soft breathing. I study the darkness of what was once our bedroom. When his snores come I grab my pillow, a blanket, head for the solitude of my living room.

It is the noisy chatter and the smell of frying bacon that draws me to consciousness. It is the sound of my daughters' voices that pulls away the last bit of sleep.

"Just don't be stupid," I hear Aaron instruct her sister. "You make sure you keep those grades up."

"Mom says that if I have an *A* average by the time I'm sixteen she's gonna get me a car."

Aaron sighs. "Yeah, told me the same thing. Can't believe I blew that. Could you see me? In my little Accord? Chrome wheels, stereo pumping?"

They laugh and I can't resist a smile. I play possum, eager to hear the conversations between my two children.

"You miss him?"

"Who?"

"J'Qaun."

Aaron pauses. I feel the sadness before she speaks it. "Yeah. He was my heart. Even though he made me mad telling what I should and shouldn't be doing."

"Think you two will ever hook up again?"

"I don't know. He graduating this year, be going off to school next. Monifa says he got somebody else, too." She pauses. "Mom ain't always wrong."

"She loves you, Aaron."

"Yeah, I guess."

"Think she gonna let Daddy stay?"

"I hope so."

"Do I smell breakfast?" Emory. Awake, joyful. Moving into the kitchen.

"Morning, Daddy," my daughters sing. I lie there, hearing birds tweeting, feeling the sunshine all the way through the roof. I lay there, listening to my family's chatter unwilling to stay out of the mix.

I get up. Take my time in folding the blanket. Put the pillow on top and move into the kitchen. Three pairs of eyes find me. All happy to see me. Aaron sucks her teeth through her smile.

"Daddy, your big mouth woke her."

"Yeah," Monet pipes, "we was gonna surprise her with breakfast."

I shoo their words off. "No, he didn't wake me; you two did with all your talking." I look at the plate of fried bacon, see the coffee machine dripping morning elixir into the glass pot. I inhale, exhale, smile in their direction. "I like my eggs over easy and not too much butter on my toast." With that I go and take a long hot shower. By the time I come back, they are all sitting at the table, waiting. For me.

Chapter 30

If I have learned hard lessons, Emory has learned some, too. There is no such thing as a quick fix. It takes a long time for problems to manifest and just as long for them to go away. It is a new knowledge for my husband and one he is learning to respect.

"Watch it, Monie, watch it!" Emory yells from the sidelines as Monet dribbles the ball down court. We are both surprised by her agility and speed, at how well she handles defense and offense. It is hard to believe that our little Monie is a terror on the courts, but I'm just happy to see she has found that thing that makes her special.

"Their cheerleaders are *ti-yard*," Aaron complains from behind us. But we ignore her as Monet scores two points. Emory and I both jump up, proud parents of number fourteen. "Yes!" we scream as the buzzer sounds.

"Oh, they're so tired," Aaron goes on to say as the Rosedale Ramjets go into their halftime cheer routine.

"They're looking for an assistant coach, maybe you might want the job," Emory tells her.

"What, teaching them tired little girls how to cheer?" But there is something in her eyes, possibility. I hold back my smirk. "They paying?" she asks, capitalism having its roots in her deep.

She has kept her job after school at Dunkin' Donuts and I am making her put half her check into a savings account. She has found a new freedom in having money in her pocket, one of the few joys I have allowed.

Since coming back home to live with me, I have become the enforcer in her life; a role, I am happy to see, she welcomes. She has learned a simple lesson early. While one may desire freedom to do as one pleases, such freedom often leads to out-of-control and self-destructive behavior. At sixteen Aaron has thankfully grown tired of her wild days.

J'Qaun came to see her on his college break. He calls often and the two exchange letters. Aaron says they are just friends, but I see the hope that dances in her eyes every time she mentions him. He is a good sensible young man and I hope something good happens between them.

As for Monet, she is getting better with her bulimia. She is continuing her sessions with Dr. Whitaker, but she only goes every six weeks. We no longer do family sessions. We have found a new niche in which to live our lives and though it is not the way it used to be, it is a thousand times better than the way it was.

The whistle blows; the teams get back on the floor. I check the scoreboard, see that Monet's team is down by three. "Come on, guys, you can do," I say, half whisper, half prayer.

Jump ball. A magical moment. I watch Monet's sneakers leave the court and soar high, high into the air. With a hard pounce, she sends the ball toward her home court, Ayeisha snatches it and drives it down. She takes a shot, misses, but Monet is there to recover. One dribble, a fast spin and suddenly the ball is through the net. I am up on my feet again as the gym erupts with loud whistles and cheers.

Lamar leans into me. "She's the best, Ms. Allen."

I nod my head in full agreement. Emory has never looked prouder.

It is Monet who is lingering, Aaron sullen in the backseat. I light a cigarette and watch them hug good-bye. He gives Monet a final squeeze and comes over to the passenger window.

"Eight o clock," he tells me for the third time that evening.

"Yes, Em, eight."

"Not eight o'one or seven-fifty nine."

I smile, despite myself. "Yes, eight."

He leans down and places a kiss on my forehead. "You be good."
I nod my head okay.

Monet gets in the front seat; Lamar is sitting in the back. Her
door closes and I pull off. See Emory watching me in my rearview
mirror.

Aaron shakes her head. "You guys are too weird, you know that?
Who ever heard of two married people living in separate places
but still seeing each other."

"I think it's nice Daddy's taking Mom on a date," Monet pipes.

"Be nicer if he just comes on home."

I say nothing. Leave Aaron's words to hang in the air. I am not
ready to take Emory back in and he has admitted that he is not
quite ready to return. While my daughter does not see the validity
of this situation, it suits us fine.

We are in the midst of building a new foundation and it is one
that must be laid brick by brick. If there is one thing we have both
learned it is that we can't go back, only forward, and we're doing
that, one day at a time.

The doorbell rings. I go to answer. I open it and see a man who
takes my breath. I know it is Emory but one I have not seen in a
long time. The toffee slacks, matching collarless shirt and shiny
black vest fit him model perfect. He has gotten a haircut, a close
shave and his cologne reaches me before his lips do.

I take in the man I have known for over two decades and see
him a way I have never seen before.

"Hey," he says softly, a gather of flowers coming my way.

"Hey back," I pipe, taking them, bringing them to my nose.

"You look great."

"You too," I answer.

"Kids around?"

"They're in the back." I turn, shout, "Monet, Aaron, Daddy's
here."

They come hurriedly down the hall. Wrap their growing arms
around him. Accept his kisses. Take in the father dressed to a tee.

Aaron frowns. "The vest, Daddy?"

Emory tugs on it. "What's wrong with it?"

"It's so nineties."

"I think it looks nice," Monet decides.

"Me, too," I say.

"Cause y'all don't know, that's why," Aaron says. "But don't worry. Next time I'll take you to this store on the Ave. Hook you up right for the next date."

My brow raises in mock surprise. "Next date?"

Aaron smiles at me. It is genuine, full. "Oh, don't even be trying to front. You and Daddy both know this ain't the final one. Shoot, this is just the beginning and y'all know it."

I look at Emory. He is looking back at me. Our smiles grow like a flower in bloom. We have cleared our past of the cobwebs. We have swept away the anger and hurt. We are on a new road armed with a clean slate. A new beginning, we think, happy for the second chance.

A JOURNEY TO HERE

Margaret Johnson-Hodge

ABOUT THIS GUIDE

The suggested questions are intended to enhance
your group's reading of Margaret Johnson-Hodge's
A JOURNEY TO HERE.

Please feel free to visit her website at *www.mjhodge.net*

DISCUSSION QUESTIONS

1. When the story opens, Sylvia sees her life as a "good thing." After reading the novel, do you think her assumption was correct or was she simply looking through life through "rose-colored" glasses?

2. As a teenager, Sylvia was faced with a difficult decision with regards to Philip, one that changed her life forever. Do you think she made the right choice? What do you think would have happened between herself and Dorothy if she had made a different choice?

3. Dorothy betrayed Sylvia and it affected Sylvia deeply. Do you think Sylvia should have "just moved on" and let it go, or was the betrayal too deep to get over?

4. Do you think what Philip did as a teenager was understandable, or should he have been stronger and not have broken Sylvia's heart the way he did?

5. Initially neither Sylvia nor her husband Emory had any idea about the issues their daughters Aaron and Monet were facing. Do you think it's normal for parents to be so unaware of what their children are and aren't up to? Why or why not?

6. Sylvia's daughter Aaron reveals a detrimental truth to Emory. Do you think Aaron had the right to tell what she did, or should she have stayed out of it? Why or why not?

7. Was there ever a real possibility of Philip getting what he returned to New York for? Did he even have the right to try and gain it? Why or why not?

8. Philip stayed with Dorothy for over thirty years. Beyond what the novel implied, were there other reasons why he stayed?

9. If Philip hadn't married Dorothy, what do you think would have become of Dorothy? Would she be happy? Married? Successful?

10. Lisa, Sylvia's best friend, had a lot going for her. Why do you think she married a man like Mack and tried so hard to make it work?

11. Sylvia's actions deeply affected her husband Emory. Do you think his reaction was justified?

12. In the story, Sylvia makes the assumption that Emory's love for one child is more prominent than his love for the other. Do you think she was correct? Is it possible for a parent to love all their children equally?

13. If the characters had a chance to do life over, do you think they would make the same choices? Do you think their choices, in the end, were good ones or poor ones?

14. When the story ends, Sylvia, Emory, Philip and Dorothy are in different places in their lives. What do you think became of them?